"Are you happy, Millie?"

She stopped rocking but didn't reply.

"Uh, Millie?" Adam sounded foolish, but what else was he supposed to say?

She blushed, and he tried not to notice how pretty it looked on her cheeks.

"Am I happy? I don't understand."

The bewildered tone made Adam's heart ache. She sounded absolutely stunned that her husband would care about her happiness.

Adam leaned farther forward, resting his forearms on the tops of his thighs. He wanted to move closer to her, but made himself stay in the rocking chair. They had been living as strangers for a month. Nicely, too. But he wanted more than that. Not love. No, Adam had learned that lesson well. But friendship. Companionship. A sense of shared purpose surely wasn't too much to ask for, was it? That was the goal, and Adam was ready to do the work.

"Millie, it's been a month. I just want to know how you feel about things here. Are you happy with the house? The children? Y̲ ̲ ̲ ̲ ̲ ̲ ̲ ̲ ̲ ̲ ̲ ̲ ̲ ̲ ̲ *me?* He didn't say the l̲ ̲ ̲ ̲ whispered it.

Victoria W. Austin lives in the American Midwest with her husband, children and dogs. Her kids write notes in the furniture dust and the family watches television with the closed captioning on because the house is, um, loud. She likes chocolate, peace and quiet, chocolate and silence. She gets too much of one and too little of the other. This explains the tight pants and the many, many, many gray hairs.

Books by Victoria W. Austin

Love Inspired Historical

Family of Convenience

VICTORIA W. AUSTIN

Family of Convenience

HARLEQUIN® LOVE INSPIRED® HISTORICAL

Recycling programs for this product may not exist in your area.

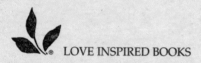

LOVE INSPIRED BOOKS

ISBN-13: 978-0-373-42521-1

Family of Convenience

Copyright © 2017 by Victoria Austin

This edition published by arrangement with Love Inspired Books.

® and TM are trademarks of Love Inspired Books, used under license. Trademarks indicated with ® are registered in the United States Patent and Trademark Office, the Canadian Intellectual Property Office and in other countries.

www.Harlequin.com

Printed in U.S.A.

For God hath not given us the spirit of fear;
but of power, and of love, and of a sound mind.
—*2 Timothy* 1:7

To my family—
I have everything because I have you

Acknowledgments

I have almost too many people to thank,
which is a blessing in and of itself. Thank you to
my family for supporting me no matter what. Thank
you to Harlequin and the Manuscript Matchmaker
contest for this opportunity. Thank you to
Elizabeth Mazer, my incredible editor,
for all the help and guidance. Thank you to my
critique partners and fellow romance-writer friends
for the advice and encouragement.

Chapter One

Kansas
1889

> *To Do:*
> *Get married*
> *Meet my new children*
> *Figure out how to run a ranch*
> *Find a way to make money on the side*
> *Find a safe place to hide money*
> *Start saving an emergency fund without drawing attention*
> *Find the ranch financial books and look at them*

Marrison, Kansas, didn't have a hotel. Just the boardinghouse she'd checked into the day before. Her room had a bed with a clean, worn quilt. A simple chest of drawers. A rocking chair.

But, no mirror.

That was okay. Millie Steele wasn't sure she could

go through with this if she had to look at herself in a mirror. This way was better.

She smoothed her hand over her long brown hair and the front of her dress for the tenth time. Maybe eleventh. When would Mrs. Sinclair knock on the door and say it was time? Had the woman forgotten about her? Could you forget about the bride?

Hysteria rose in Millie's throat as she actually contemplated that question. She and Mr. Beale had exchanged exactly one letter. One. They had seen each other for the first and only time yesterday, for all of ten minutes. Just long enough to confirm the time he would come to marry her today.

Maybe he'd changed his mind. She was past the period when her short thin frame could hide the baby. Pastor Thompson said Mr. Beale knew, but maybe seeing the truth of it yesterday had been too much.

What was she going to do if he changed his mind?

A quick knock, and the door to the room opened. Mrs. Sinclair strode inside. "We're all ready, dear."

Millie sucked in a breath, ignoring the stars that had appeared in her vision. She licked her lips and nodded.

Mrs. Sinclair's eyes were gentle as she surveyed Millie from head to toe. "You look lovely. Absolutely—"

Millie looked at her hand. It was shaking, but that wasn't what had caught Mrs. Sinclair's attention. No. It was the slim circle of gold on the ring finger of her left hand. She flushed at the sight of it. She couldn't very well get married today while wearing another man's ring.

Millie quickly yanked off the ring, ignoring the burn

of metal scraping over her knuckle. It was the first time she had taken it off since Marcus had placed it there two years ago. How different that day had been compared to today. Millie had been certain that her future would be secure. Safe. Orderly.

What a fool she had been.

Mrs. Sinclair cleared her throat, and Millie realized she had been staring at the thin band. Millie couldn't look at the kind woman as she walked over to her suitcase and placed the ring inside.

There. It was done. Looking at the past never got a person anywhere. The way forward was to actually move forward.

She had made her plans. It was time to see them through.

Millie cleared her throat. She forced her spine as straight as possible and took in a deep breath. Then she turned and looked at Mrs. Sinclair. "Okay. I'm ready." She was an adult. She was in charge of her life. She had considered all the options and chosen this path. This was her choice.

Mrs. Sinclair still looked uncomfortable. And nervous. The entire town would probably be talking about Adam Beale's crazy new bride for weeks. Once again, Millie would be the outsider who didn't belong.

Mrs. Sinclair walked up and hugged Millie. She just reached out and pulled Millie into her body. Warm, soft arms wrapped around Millie, who could smell bread on the woman's clothes. It was impossible to stay stiff and remote in such an embrace. Millie couldn't remember her mother ever hugging her, but surely this was what it had felt like. Only a mother's hug could be this comforting.

"It's going to be okay, dear. Adam Beale is a good man. You're going to be okay."

The tears sprang up and welled in Millie's eyes. They obeyed her rule against crying and did not fall down her cheeks, but they were there. Hot and stinging. She knew she wouldn't be able to speak without them spilling over. All she could do was nod.

She hoped Mrs. Sinclair understood.

The older woman let go, and Millie pushed down the yearning for the hug to continue. No more stalling. Time to get on with her new life.

Millie followed Mrs. Sinclair down the hallway of the boardinghouse to the top of the stairs. She looked down and saw Mr. Beale there waiting.

Adam.

Her new husband's name was Adam.

Embarrassed at keeping him waiting, Millie hurried down the stairs. "I'm sorry. I know I'm late. It's not a habit, I promise."

Millie despised the desperation she heard in her voice. She needed this man. She needed a husband and a home and safe place to have this baby. Need. But, she still hated feeling so dependent on anyone. *I don't understand this world, God. I don't understand why things are this way.*

Mr. Beale—Adam—didn't look angry. But, they were in public. He wouldn't be the first man to put on a kind facade outside of his house.

"It's okay, Millie. We're not late at all."

He'd called her by her given name yesterday, too. It shouldn't have surprised her. They were, after all, about to get married.

"Thank you, Mr. Beale. I'm ready now."

"Adam, Millie. Call me Adam."

Millie just nodded.

The church was close to the boardinghouse. Actually, from what Millie could see, *everything* in town was close to the boardinghouse. She certainly wasn't in Saint Louis anymore.

Being small and simple did not inhibit the atmosphere inside the church. Millie looked at the worn wooden pews and the gleaming cross hanging on the wall behind the lectern. There was something indescribable here. Millie breathed in slow and deep, trying to literally take it in and keep it with her.

She did not understand God. She did not agree with how this world was set up. But, she believed. She knew of His love. His peace. And, she felt it here.

She and Adam, along with Mr. and Mrs. Sinclair, stood in front of the pastor. The wedding did not take long. They said their vows. Then, the pastor told Mr. Beale—Adam—that he could kiss his bride. Her.

It was quick and perfunctory, and Adam seemed as glad to have it over with as she was. Though marriages resulting from mail-order brides were not exactly uncommon, theirs probably was more unusual than most. For one thing, she was clearly carrying another man's child. And for another, they had no intention of truly living as man and wife.

Adam had been almost shockingly clear on that point

in his sole letter to her. He needed a mother for his young children. He needed help on his farm, especially with domestic tasks. He was looking for function and practicality, not romance.

Millie had ignored the twinge in her heart as she'd readily agreed with his vision for their future. This world was too unpredictable, too cruel, for dreams of sappy emotions and love. Millie and her child needed shelter. Food.

Adam was providing those things, and it would be enough.

Mr. and Mrs. Sinclair congratulated them and then returned to the boardinghouse, but not before Mrs. Sinclair invited Millie to "come and visit at any time." Millie forced a smile and said she would.

She wouldn't actually do so, though. The notebook in her case contained a very long list of things Millie needed to do, and making friends wasn't anywhere on it.

"Are you ready to go?" Adam touched her arm as he spoke, and Millie flinched. The unexpected contact was made even more startling by the fact that Millie had been so far gone inside her head that she hadn't noticed his approach. That needed to stop. Things would not get done unless she did them, and that left no room for daydreaming and wandering thoughts.

"Yes. My case is all packed. I just need to get it from the boardinghouse."

"Sounds good." Adam placed a hand at the small of her back and almost led her across the street. What was he thinking? For a man who had written in black and white that he was not looking for a romantic relationship with a wife, he sure was touching her an awful lot. Maybe he was concerned with appearances. Didn't want the town to know about the true nature of their relationship.

He followed her up the stairs and down the hallway to the door of the room she had been staying in. Millie had packed before the wedding and had already checked the room for stray belongings. That didn't stop her from checking again, quickly this time since Adam was waiting. But, everything was inside her suitcase.

Including that ring.

Millie watched with almost disbelief as Adam came inside the room and picked up the suitcase. She was more than capable of carrying it herself—and had done so as needed during the trip from Saint Louis. But if he wanted to carry it, she wouldn't complain. He gestured for her to walk ahead of him and then followed her as they retraced their prior steps and headed out the front door of the boardinghouse.

Her new husband was carrying the case that contained the ring given to her by her old husband. The naive girl who had become a bride who had become a widow had become a bride again. And would soon be a mother.

This was going to work out. Millie had a plan. She had a list of steps to accomplish that plan. She could do this. She would do this and it would all work out.

It just had to.

Adam hated this. It was a glorious day. The sky was blue and the grass was green and it should have filled his soul with peace and awe at what the Creator had made for them. Instead, he felt like a bug trapped in a canning jar.

Adam focused on the breeze on his face. The heat of sun coming through his clothes. The feel of the reins in his hand and the sound of Gray's and Ellie's hooves as they pulled the wagon toward home.

He reminded himself that he wasn't a bug trapped in a glass. He was a man in control of his life. Adam had not come to the decision to seek a mail-order bride lightly. And, he'd made a good choice. This awkward phase would pass and things would settle just as he'd pictured. Eugene and Catherine would have a mother. A home full of the comforts that had been missing since Sarah had died two years ago.

And Adam would be helping Millie, too. That was what he had liked the most about her. When he had mentioned the idea of a mail-order bride, word had spread through town. He wasn't the first man to find a wife that way, but people seemed to enjoy talking about it nonetheless.

Based on some of the other local men's experiences, Adam had anticipated months of corresponding with different women, trying to decide from words on paper whether the woman would be the help his children needed or a mistake. Another mistake.

Then, Mr. Carter had come all the way out to the farm to talk to Adam. Mr. Carter's sister was married to a pastor outside of Saint Louis. She had just written about a young woman who needed a husband. This woman—Millie—was recently widowed and pregnant.

Her husband had been deep in debt at the time of his death, and Millie had found herself completely destitute. Alone. Homeless. Though she was staying with friends from church, Millie was looking for a husband. Somewhere to go.

And Adam had an empty room and the need for a wife.

Of course Adam's heart had hurt for the woman who had been through so much already. His heart also hurt for his children who were similarly suffering through no fault of their own. They could help each other and maybe ease some of the pain all around.

Please, God, let that be true. I need my children to be happy. Well cared for. I want them to grow up in the kind of home I had.

"How far is it? To your home, I mean."

Adam couldn't tell from her tone of voice whether she was genuinely curious or just trying to fill the silence between him. Either one was fine. They needed to work from where they were and go up. Build something.

"It's your home now, too, you know. And it's not too far, about forty-five minutes from town."

"Forty-five minutes is not too far?"

Adam turned to look at her. "I always thought forty-five minutes was close to town, at least for this part of the country. How close to Saint Louis was your farm?"

"My farm? The farm I was staying at after my husband died?"

Millie's voice was slow and hesitant, and Adam felt his stomach harden with dread.

"I was asking about the farm you and your husband had before he died."

Millie's eyes widened in something that looked an awful lot like panic. She sat very still, her body not moving despite the jostling of the buggy. "I didn't live on a farm before my husband died."

Adam felt his own body freeze. "Where did you live?"

"In the city. In Saint Louis. My husband owned a store there, and I helped him."

"How about before that? You were raised on a farm, right?" Yes. The answer had to be yes. One of the things that had made Sarah try to leave was the isolation of life on the farm. Adam had tried marrying a city woman unfamiliar with farm life, and it had been a disaster. Surely he hadn't made the same mistake with his second marriage. But he hadn't actually asked, had he? He'd just seen the ranch address of the home where she was staying and he'd assumed.

Millie's eyes stayed wide this time, large and frightened in her pale face. "I was born in the city. In Saint Louis. I lived there every day of my life until the debt collectors took the house after my husband died. I only lived at the Keller ranch for the last month."

Adam clenched his jaw and forced himself to keep his eyes on the road ahead. The path that they were going to have to go down. They were married. This was their road to travel together. And suddenly every bump in it felt more like hitting a boulder. His fingers were white and numb around the reins, and he forced himself to relax his grip. The last thing they needed was for the horses to react to his anger.

He went through the events that had led to his second marriage to a second city woman. He had been a fool yet again. And he was trapped, yet again. But, just because Millie was not familiar with farm life did not mean she would hate it like Sarah had. He just needed to show Millie all the farm had to offer. He could still have a full partner in the day-to-day activities of farm life.

"Did you like where you were staying at before you came here?"

Millie's smile was small but it was there. "I did. I mean, I didn't really get out much. I spent a lot of the time alone in my room, thinking. But I liked what I did see. It was so different at first from what I was used to, but it was really nice. Almost soothing."

Adam could work with that. "Then I think you'll like our home, too."

"I'm sure I will. I've been looking forward to the peace and quiet, to be honest."

Millie sounded sincere. Almost eager to prove that statement correct. She was trying. Millie had come into this marriage with the same goals as Adam. A good future for their children. And Millie was obviously trying to hold up her end of the bargain. That was all Adam could hope for.

Surely this could work if they both tried. "There's plenty of quiet. But, there's also a whole lot of not quiet. Between the children and the animals, sometimes I think the country is noisier than the city."

"You've lived in a city before?"

"Yes. But, not for too long. It never felt like home."

That was an understatement. Adam had been miserable in the city. He had hated the way it felt. The way it smelled. The way it seemed to settle on his skin like a coating he could never completely wash off. Having gone through that feeling of not fitting and not belonging, having fled that, how had he not understood what Sarah was going through?

"So you came back here?"

Adam nodded. "I wanted to settle down. Have children. And I wanted my children to grow up in the country, with fresh air and room to be."

"Children." This time, Adam didn't have a bit of trouble picking out the fear in Millie's voice. "Will you tell me about them? Please? I remember everything you told me in the letter. What Mrs. Thompson told me. But, I'd like to hear more. I need to be as prepared as possible before meeting them in person."

This was safe territory. His marriage to Sarah might have ended in disaster, but his children were nothing but joy. "They're great kids. I know I told you that in the letter, and I'm definitely biased, but they are. Catherine, the five-year-old, has such a kind heart. She always wants to be helpful."

Adam's throat tightened, but he continued. He wanted Millie to give his children what they needed. "Caty just wants to be loved. She spends a lot of time doing things to please people so they will like her. Love her."

Adam looked at Millie, to see if he could tell what she was thinking. She was staring at her hands, and her profile wasn't giving him any hints. "Genie—Eugene—is three. He's happy so long as he has two things to bang together. It doesn't matter at all what they are. Two forks. Two blocks. Two of anything so long as he can crash them into one another and make noise."

Millie's hands moved from her lap to her mouth. She turned and looked at him. There was definitely a smile under there. Adam couldn't stop his own grin. He wasn't exaggerating his little boy's love of crashing and making noise. Though it could become aggravating, it was mainly adorable.

"They sound wonderful."

"They are. Don't misunderstand me, they are children. They can be cross and demanding and ungrateful. And, don't ever try to reason with them because I promise you you'll lose your mind before they understand your point. Even if it is eminently logical."

Millie laughed out loud at that. Hearing the sound made the embarrassment of admitting his parenting failure completely worth it.

"What did you try to reason with them about?"

"Oh, too many things to count. You'd think I would learn, but I just keep hoping that they'll see my point. Eventually."

"I think you might have a long wait. I'm not an expert when it comes to children, but I have a feeling that logic is one of the last things to develop."

Adam told her more about the kids, enjoying both reliving the memories and sharing them with someone else. It was such a shame that the happiness Caty and

Genie brought to the world was shared only with him. But, that would change now that Millie was here.

"Will you tell me about the routine?" Millie's question was almost abrupt.

"Routine?"

"Yes. How does the day go where you live? I want to know what to expect. Make sure I do the right thing in the right order."

Adam looked at Millie, trying yet again to read her face.

There was nothing he could decipher, though her face was lovely, as it had been from the moment he first saw her. Framed by dark brown hair with a slight wave. Brown eyes. Fair complexion with a trail of freckles across her nose and cheeks. Her cheeks had been slightly pink since yesterday. Adam didn't know if that was from nerves or excitement or if her cheeks usually had that tint. Regardless, she was a beautiful woman.

But not exactly readable. She might come in a pretty package, but it didn't take a genius to see that a beautiful, collected facade was exactly what Millie Steele— now Beale—presented to the world. She sure kept everything else locked down tight.

Except when Adam moved his gaze from her face down to her hands, he saw that they were clenched tight. Her fingers were white around the edges from the pressure. That was not a casual question.

Lord, I feel like I'm trying to walk through mud here. I can't find solid ground. I just want to cross this passage and get to the good land on the other side. Help me say the right things, be the right thing. Please.

"There's not too much of right and wrong out on the farm. A lot of what gets done is determined by the weather and current status of crops and livestock."

"Farm? I thought you lived on a ranch?"

"Well, it's a bit of both. I grew up on a ranch, so I consider myself a born-and-raised rancher. And, we have quite a bit of livestock. Cattle and horses. But, it's also a nice little farm. I have a variety of crops planted. Plus, we have chickens, hogs and a couple of dairy cattle."

Adam knew he had failed as a husband the first time around. Sometimes, he questioned whether he was a good enough father to his children. But, he was proud of what he had accomplished with his land. It had taken years, but he finally felt like he was established. His cattle and horses had a growing reputation and provided enough income to live on. The amount of land planted in crops was also expanding.

"I barely know anything about living on a ranch. Or a farm."

Millie's mask was good, but her hands were still clenched. He had not managed to put her at ease at all. Adam fought the urge to touch her. Reassure her.

Then he stopped fighting. He was determined that this was going to be a good marriage. He might not want the intimate aspects of having a wife, but he did want a friendship. He wanted his children to be surrounded by love. Companionship. Adam transferred the reins to one hand and used the other to reach out and touch Millie's arm. He tried to make his touch safe and comforting.

"I can teach you anything you need to know. I told

you I lived in the city for a bit. I have a good understanding of what you're used to. The farm won't be that different. Day-to-day life inside a home is pretty much the same everywhere."

Millie nodded her head and smiled. But, her hands were still clenched like she was clinging on to something for dear life.

Adam drew his hand back, unsure yet again whether he had helped at all. He sure didn't feel like he had lessened her fears.

Chapter Two

To Do:
Breathe
Get to know the children
Learn about farms—Livestock? Crops?
Is it better to live on a farm or a ranch?

Millie needed her notebook. Her pencil. And fifteen minutes alone to lose her composure without an audience. But, she was not going to get any of those things, so she concentrated on the scenery. It was, well, beautiful. Absolutely breathtaking in fact.

Funny, when she made her long list of pros and cons for marrying a total stranger, the place where he lived did not ever cross her mind. She was looking for security. Safety. To feel like she could breathe again. She'd have been willing to take up residence at the bottom of a coal mine as long as she could have those things. Millie would never, ever forget what it felt like when she realized that she was, indeed, pregnant and homeless. And without the skills to find a job. Dependent on the kindness of strangers in a world that had never been very full of kind strangers to Millie's eye.

She tried to suppress a shiver, tightening her muscles viciously. She didn't want Adam to see and ask if she was okay. And he would. She had already learned some things about her new husband.

Millie slowly relaxed her muscles, and refocused her eyes on the scene in front of her. *Beautiful* was still the primary word she could find to describe it. Yes, it was the same blue sky that had been above her in Saint Louis. But, the rest was revelation.

Gold-and-green grass, at least four feet tall, swayed in the wind. She was looking at a never-ending golden-green sea, in fact. There were waves. Honest-to-goodness waves. In grass. The ground was so straight here that the dark spots on the horizon could well be hundreds of miles away.

Her first impression off the train was that Marrison was small and remote and quaint. A little settling trying to be a town. And now she was going to live almost an hour away from even that small civilization. It didn't seem possible, but the landscape just got more and more remote the farther they went.

Millie was used to being on her own. However, she wasn't used to being in a place that felt so foreign. The Keller ranch had been right outside Saint Louis. Knowing she was near the city had made the location feel close. Familiar.

Not now, though. Millie was far from the rivers and bluffs and the buzz of the city that she'd known all her life. A whole new start in a whole new land. It was both one of the scariest and one of the most comforting things Millie had ever seen.

Her plan for how she would act in this new marriage had not accounted for all the details of her new reality. How could it, though? She'd never been to Kansas. Never lived on a farm.

But, she would figure it out. She always figured it out. Millie just needed to gather as much information as possible. She would ask questions. Pay attention to what everyone else was doing. Take notes. And then, she could make her plan.

Millie sat up straighter as Adam turned the wagon off the worn trail of dirt that she assumed counted as a main road out here. The new path they had turned onto barely looked like a path at all. Instead of a solid width of light brown dirt, the way was designated by yet more grass. The grass was just shorter than the golden-green ocean surrounding them.

There was also a parting of the waves, so to speak. The moving grass gave way to rectangles of what had to be crops. Millie didn't know what was growing, but she saw the neat rows of dark earth and the green plants seemingly shooting up out of the ground. She also saw cattle and horses.

Millie couldn't contain her excitement. Though the large animals frightened her, they also thrilled her. She had never seen such creatures up close before. Sure, there were horses in the city, not to mention plenty of them at the Keller ranch, but these horses looked bigger. Rougher. More fitting to the wild frontier she'd been told existed once a person traveled past Saint Louis. She could hear them. And, though it was strange and perhaps unpleasant, she could smell them—a stronger odor than she'd noted at the Kellers' home, where she'd rarely been outside. Instead of being a picture through a frame, they were very much real.

"This is our land. We're only about ten minutes from the house."

Our land. He'd done that earlier today, too. Millie wondered at how Adam seemed to have no problem moving from being a widower to being completely married. He acted as though he was pleased to share everything he had worked for with her.

Or else, he was very good at pretending. Millie had known more than one man who could put on a grand show of being generous and kind in public while being secretly stingy or cruel behind closed doors.

You're too cynical, Millie. There are good people in this world, who genuinely want to help others without any strings attached. You need to have a little faith.

Mrs. Thompson's words echoed through Millie's head. It wasn't the first time they had made an appearance. It seemed as though they had done nothing but ricochet around since the pastor's wife had said them.

"Well, what do you think?"

Millie realized that she could see buildings now. A small house. A barn. A couple of other structures whose function she couldn't place. The house looked sturdy. There was a porch and couple of windows out front. Millie saw two rocking chairs, and the whole scene reminded her of a picture she had seen in a book about life on the prairie. Seeing essentially the same picture now, in living color, with sunshine and a breeze on her face, and the ambient noise of animals was nicer.

She had a place to live. Food. Her baby would not be born fatherless and on the streets. No. He or she would have a home and a family and would never know the experiences that plagued Millie's own youth. That was what she had wanted. What she had planned for. And what she had accomplished. For uneducated street trash, Millie had done just fine for herself.

"Millie?"

Again, Adam touched her arm. Again, it struck her as shockingly gentle and overly familiar. Again, Millie found that she really liked it. A lot. That touch was dangerously appealing, making her head spin when she needed to be calm and rational.

"It looks nice. Really nice."

"It's bigger than it looks."

Did he think she found his home to be too small?

"It looks like the perfect size. I don't know what some of those buildings are." Millie hated her ignorance. It seemed she had spent the entirety of her life in situations where she did not know what she needed to know. What she should have been taught as a child.

"That's okay. I know it's a change from the city." Adam did not sound concerned that he had married a woman unfit to survive out here.

"I mean, I recognize the house. And the barn. But what are the others?"

"The long one behind the barn is the bunkhouse. It's where the hired hands live. I only have a couple right now, but I built it big enough to house ten or so. I'll need them someday."

He sounded so confident. It soothed the edge of the fear Millie had been shoving down into her belly for the past few months. If he planned on hiring several hands, then he planned on paying them. And, if he planned on paying them, that meant he had money. And if he had money, then he had security.

"What about the others? The smaller ones?"

"One is a root cellar, for storing food. The other is a meat house."

"I do know what those are, so don't be too scared. I've been told I'm an excellent cook." She had tried to play up her assets in her letter to him, but it never hurt to reiterate them. Besides, that part was the absolute truth.

"I'll give you a tour once we say hello to the children."

"Where are they?"

"Probably inside. Napping I'd guess, based on the time. Edith, a neighbor, is watching them for me. You'll be a bit of a change, so we wanted to leave everything else as familiar as possible."

"Are they going to be upset?" Millie had not really worried too much about that. They were so young, and she had every intention of being a good change. Millie might not know about men like Adam Beale, but she knew about children. She had never met a child that she couldn't eventually win over. In fact, more than one matron in The Home had put her in charge of the younger kids because of her way with them.

"I told them where I was going, so they know that

I am getting married and bringing home a wife. A mother."

"A mother." Millie's voice was soft as reverence washed across her heart. She knew she would be a mother, but it had always felt like some future event. Even with the life growing in her womb, the reality of actually being a mother had always been in the category of someday.

Someday had come. She was a mother now. Right now.

Help me, Lord. Help.

She still felt silly talking in her head to God, but it was becoming increasingly instinctual. Millie's faith was getting stronger every single day, no matter how much she tried to reason herself out of it. It had already saved her. Literally.

Millie had walked into a church a year ago out of some kind of curiosity she couldn't contain. After making her list and determining it couldn't do any harm to just see what the church looked like on the inside, she'd forced her legs to go up those steps and walk through the doorway. Mrs. Thompson had been inside. That action had put into motion a chain of events that had led to Millie being in Kansas about to face her new children for the first time. The Lord sure had a way of doing things.

"This is still what you want, isn't it? It will be much harder to change your mind once you meet the children. I—"

"No, Adam. Don't." It was hard to speak past the panic that put spots in her vision. He thought she had changed her mind? He was going to take her back. But, back to what? She was so close to having a steady, stable home, and now it was all going to disappear. Like the mirages she had read about.

This time it was Millie who reached out and initiated touch. "I'm sorry, Adam. I don't know what I said wrong, but I haven't changed my mind. Please, don't make me go back. Please."

She was begging. Millie had gone from awe at the thought of being a mother to sheer, humiliating desperation in the span of a heartbeat. She had to fix this.

Adam immediately pulled on the reins and stopped the wagon. Was he getting ready to turn around and take her back?

How had this gone wrong so fast? He had been enjoying the day, enjoying watching Millie take in her new home. Then, he opened his mouth and ruined it all. Like always. Apparently, he hadn't learned a single thing from his first wife leaving him.

Adam dropped the reins and turned to Millie. What would he have done with Sarah? He would have tried to hold her. Comfort her. Yeah. He needed to do the opposite of that. His instincts had proven to be disastrously wrong. He needed to change his course or he'd end up in the same place.

"Millie. Calm down." Adam infused his voice with as much authority as he could manage. It seemed to work, because she stopped begging him to let her stay. She seemed to stop everything. The new Mrs. Beale seemed to have frozen. Her eyes were still wide with panic, but she was no longer gasping for breath. Instead, her breathing had become too shallow. Too still.

"Millie, breathe. Please. Just calm down. I have not changed my mind at all. Not even a little bit. I did not marry you on some whim. I knew what I was doing, and I'm standing by that decision."

Statue Millie did not so much as blink. His instincts were wrong and apparently the opposite of his instincts were not much better. Maybe Adam was never meant to be in a successful relationship with a woman. Lots of men went through life single. It seemed as though Adam should have taken that path.

But, he hadn't. And he had two incredible children as a result. Children he needed to provide for. Meant to be a family man or not, Adam had a family. He had a responsibility to those children to give them a real home—including a loving mother. And he would. If he could just figure out how.

"I'm sorry. It was a stupid thing to say. Of course you're sure. I know you're sure. If I thought you might change your mind, I never would have married you. I don't know why I said that. I'm sorry."

She started breathing again. Finally. Finally, finally.

"Please. I didn't mean to upset you."

"I'm okay." She didn't sound okay, but she was moving and talking and that was more than statue Millie had been doing.

"It's my fault, too. I overreacted. It was just a misunderstanding."

Adam ran a hand down his face, feeling his body tremble slightly. This had spun out of control so fast.

Too fast. Adam hated this feeling. He just wanted to move on.

"It doesn't matter whose fault it was."

Millie just looked at him with her dark brown eyes. Adam tried to give her as much time as possible, to be as patient as possible. Patience had never been his strong suit.

"Are we okay? Edith probably heard us coming. I'm sure she's waiting for us."

Millie breathed a small breath and looked at the house. Then she looked at him and nodded. "Yes. We're okay. Let's go meet the children."

Adam picked the reins back up and flicked them. The horses were well trained and did not need any more encouragement to finish the trip. They were probably looking forward to the familiar barn just as much as Adam was yearning to be back home. Even though he'd only been gone since early this morning, Adam had missed this place terribly.

They came up to the area between the house and barn, and the front door opened. Adam saw Edith standing there, smiling. Her husband was a good friend of Adam's, and they were good neighbors. She had been excited for Adam to go and fetch his new bride.

Edith was holding Genie in her arms. Caty was standing next to her, one little fist buried in Edith's apron. Adam jumped down from the wagon and hurried to help Millie down. He should probably face the children with Millie by his side, present them as a united front, but he could not help himself. Adam bounded up the stairs and knelt down in front of his little girl.

"Hi there, Caty-girl. Did you miss me? I missed you a whole lot."

Caty let go of Edith's apron and stepped into Adam's arms. Adam stood, relishing as always the slight weight of his sweet girl in his arms. She wrapped her arms around his neck and buried her face in his neck. Adam let her hide for a moment.

He looked at Genie and smiled. "Hey there, bud. Did you miss me?"

Genie nodded, still looking a bit uncertain. Adam reached out with his free hand and brushed it affectionately over the top of his son's head.

Adam turned and walked down the stairs, murmuring to Caty as he went. "Are you ready to meet Millie, Caty-girl? Remember I told you that I was going to come back with a woman. A new mother?"

Caty nodded slightly, but still did not lift her face from Adam's neck. He came to a stop in front of Millie.

"Caty, sit up and say hi to Millie. She really wants to meet you."

Caty lifted her head, but she still looked down at Adam's chest instead of in Millie's direction.

"Hi, Caty. I'm so happy to meet you. Your daddy told me all about you, and I am so excited to be here." Millie's tone was just right. Genuine and friendly without being too condescending.

Caty looked at Millie, and Millie smiled gently. The smile made dimples appear in her cheeks. How had Adam not noticed the dimples earlier? He found he really liked them.

Caty bit her lip, but her face lost some of its wariness. Her death grip on Adam lessened. His girlie was definitely curious about Millie, but not scared.

That was good. Adam turned to look at Edith.

"Do you and Genie want to come and meet Millie, Edith?"

Edith came down the stairs at once, a huge smile splitting her face. "I thought you'd never ask. Standing back quietly is not something I'm skilled at, Adam Beale, and I think I've exercised a lifetime's amount of restraint in the last five minutes."

That was Edith. Cheerful and exuberant. But, also a good friend. Willing to help anyone she encountered. He had been beyond blessed to have the Potters as neighbors.

Still holding Genie, Edith came up to Millie, leaned in and hugged her. Millie looked surprised, but she returned the brief embrace. Edith then turned and stood so that Genie was angled toward Millie.

"I'm so glad you're here, Millie. We've been excited all day, waiting for your arrival. My husband and I are your closest neighbors here, and I can't wait to get to know you. I just know we'll be friends."

Millie's eyes were wide, and Adam almost laughed. She had no idea what was in store for her now that Edith Potter had decided they would be friends. Though Edith was probably a year or two younger than Millie, she had the kind of personality that charged in and took control of things. Edith's husband, Mike, had said more than once that his wife was a tornado.

Adam set Caty on the ground, not surprised at all when he felt her move as close as possible to his legs. He stepped up and took Genie out of Edith's arms. "Genie, this is Millie."

Millie stepped closer to Adam and smiled at Genie. Given Genie's place in Adam's arms, the boy and Millie were almost eye level with one another. "Hi, Genie. Your daddy told me all about you, too. I'm very happy that I finally get to meet you."

"Well, I've got my things all gathered together and loaded in the wagon. I think I'll be on my way." Edith was still grinning like a fool.

"I appreciate all your help, Edith. You don't have to rush off right away, you know."

"It wasn't any trouble at all." Edith looked over at Millie and smiled an encouraging smile. "Millie needs time to settle. Both into the house and with the children. Don't get too excited about me being gone, though. I'll come back in a few days. Just to see if I can help."

Adam had no doubt that Edith would be back. Neighbors were scarce enough out here and opportunities for socializing were few. A woman near her own age for a neighbor? That had to feel like treasure to someone as outgoing as Edith.

"I'll get your horses and hitch them." Adam set Genie down by the women and walked into the barn, pausing in the cool shadows inside. He turned to watch the group.

Edith was talking to Millie, her lips never seeming to stop and her hands moving in motions that probably corresponded to her words. Millie was watching, but was not talking in response. Caty and Genie were just standing there. The awkwardness seemed to reach out and blanket the entire front yard.

Well, it was done. He had a wife. His children had a mother.

Please, God. Don't let this have been another mistake.

Chapter Three

To Do:
Wake up early
Gather eggs
Get water
Bring in wood for the day
Milk cow—well, try to milk the cow
Wash clothes
Hang clothes to dry
Churn butter
Make beds
Make stew for supper
Make bread
Beat dust out of rugs
Tackle mending pile
Weed garden
Work on knitting things to sell for extra money
Milk cow again?

Millie looked at her to-do list and frowned. She was hopelessly behind today. No, that wasn't the full extent of it. She was hopelessly behind this month. Making her plans and lists was one thing. Actually doing them was a completely different thing. An increasingly frustrating thing, it turned out.

Between the two children outside her womb and the one inside, Millie was not getting anything done. At all.

Millie looked at her plans for the day and then scratched them out with a giant X. She hated that proof of her failure, right there for all to see. If she could, Millie would erase the always-uncompleted lists and pretend they never existed. But, she had used up all of her eraser doing that already. And, it hadn't helped. She was still looking at a book of archived failures instead of a book of accomplishment.

"Miyi."

Gene was awake. Millie closed her book and walked to the bedroom where the children were napping. She opened the door and was not surprised at all to see the little boy sitting up and grinning at her from the bed. Caty was still sleeping soundly next to him.

This had been their pattern for the past month. Both children would go down for their nap without a fuss, and both would quickly fall asleep. But, Genie woke up early. Every. Single. Time. Then, he grinned and charmed his way out of the rest of his nap. Millie supposed she should be firmer with him, but she just couldn't. Not with that smile.

Millie came in and picked Gene up out of the bed. Holding him on one hip, she leaned down and adjusted the covers so they fully covered Caty. The girl would sleep for another hour or so, yet. Millie wasn't too concerned about the difference in their nap time each day. Both children went to bed easily and on time. Both woke easily enough, too. Millie felt sure that each child was getting enough rest.

Millie left the door cracked as she went back out into the main room. She sat down in the rocking chair, adjusting Gene so he sat in her lap facing her.

"Well, Mr. Beale, did you have a good nap?"

"Yes!"

"Shh, you'll wake your sister."

"Blocks!"

Millie gave him her best mock-stern look. "May you please play with blocks?"

"Blocks, please?"

Good enough. Millie leaned forward and kissed his forehead before standing up and carrying him to the small area rug in the center of the room. She set him down and went to get the basket full of blocks from the corner. Genie would happily sit there, banging and making noises as he played, for hours.

He was a good boy. Actually, they were both good children. Millie had settled into life with them fairly easily. Compared to most of the children in The Home, Caty and Genie were amazingly well behaved.

Millie walked over to the kitchen table and eyed her notebook with disgust. No, it wasn't the children's fault that she was not getting things done. They took up some of her time, of course. But, they were not demanding children. And the time she spent with them was a joy.

She was the problem. Millie had been around women who were expecting before. She knew about the sickness that could plague the first few months of pregnancy. Or, she thought she knew.

It seemed that knowing and seeing were nothing like actually experiencing. Millie was past the first few months of her pregnancy. This feeling of illness should be over, but it wasn't. Millie was tired. Really, really tired. And she was still getting physically sick every day.

The result was that notebook full of failed plans and more than one night spent obsessing about her failure. Just seeing it on the table made Millie want to go back to bed, pull the covers up over her head and hide from the world.

But, that wasn't going to help anything.

Instead, Millie went into the kitchen and began cutting vegetables for the stew she planned for supper. She listened to Genie's noises, pictured a sleeping Caty and looked at the main room of the house. Despite all her shortcomings, she had made her way to a nice place. A safe one.

The house was as charming as those two rocking chairs on the front porch had promised. The kitchen and family room were combined in one large room. At first, Millie had been surprised by the lack of privacy in the kitchen. She'd never worked in one that wasn't enclosed in its own separate space.

But, she'd come to think the design was pure genius after only a few days with the children. Millie was able to work in the kitchen or sit at the table and still see exactly where Caty and Gene were and what they were doing.

Beyond the main room, the house had three bed-
rooms. Three seemed like a lot for this part of the
country, and Millie felt almost spoiled. Adam had a
bedroom, the children shared a room, and the third
one was Millie's.

Millie had never had her own bedroom before. She
still felt a sense of wonder at the thought. Adam's letter had made clear that he was seeking a mother for his
children and someone to help with his home. Not for
more intimate companionship. Even so, Millie never
considered she would have a room of her own. At best,
she'd hoped for a separate bed in with the children.

Even now, weeks later, Millie sometimes found herself standing in the doorway and staring at it. Making sure it was real. The room had a bed and a chest
of drawers and too many small, comforting details to
count.

The bed was covered in a gorgeous quilt. The care
and love with which it was made was only enhanced
by the softness that came from many washings. A vase
of flowers sat on top of the chest. They had been there
that first day, and Millie had kept fresh ones there ever
since. The current assortment had been picked by the
children. Especially for her. Curtains hung at the windows, sheer lace that let the light dance across the room
early in the morning. A hooked rug lay on the floor next
to the bed. And there was a rocking chair.

Millie had her own rocking chair in her own room.

When she'd commented on how beautiful it was,
Adam had blushed. The man's cheeks actually turned
pink. He'd said that Edith was responsible, that it was

all her doing. But, when Millie thanked Edith the next time she came out to visit, Edith had said it was all Adam's doing. That he had requested a room for Millie that was both feminine and comforting.

Regardless of who did it, Millie loved her room.

She also loved this house. And these children. Really, it would be hard not to love Catherine and Eugene after spending more than five minutes with them.

Yes, things were going well. By anyone's standards—with the exception of her failure to follow through on her carefully wrought plans for each day. Somehow, she could never seem to catch up…or escape the feeling of being on the edge of some sort of precipice.

Part of the problem was Millie's sense of unfamiliarity with what was outside her front door. Inside the house, life was not too different from life in Saint Louis. Once she figured out where to find water, wood and food that was. But, outside was very different from anything Millie had ever encountered. And it intimidated her beyond belief.

Adam had tried to teach her what she needed to know. But he was busy every day. Between the fields from the farm aspect of the land and the livestock from the ranch aspect, he worked fifteen hours each day, coming home only for supper and an hour with the kids before bedtime. Edith said that was normal for this time of year. That things would slow down in late fall and winter and then they would have plenty of time together.

Millie didn't know how she felt about that.

But, that was a worry for another day.

Despite his busy schedule, Adam had made sure Millie was comfortable gathering eggs and milking the cow. So far, those bare necessities and laundry had been the only reasons Millie had left the house. Until today.

Feeling like she had things inside the house under her control, today's plan had included tackling the vegetable garden out back. It was in deplorable shape, largely due to inattention. Now that she was here, though, she wanted to get it back to its full glory. It wasn't just aesthetic—they needed that garden for food.

Millie had some experience with small gardens, but had never tended anything as large as the monster out back. Of course, gardens in the city were meant to supplement food purchased from merchants. Here, though, the garden was supposed to be one of their primary sources of food. That made it a priority.

Millie glared at her notebook again. The one with the plan for her to work peacefully in that wreck of a garden while the children were napping. Too late for that now.

Well, it seemed that Millie was going to learn how to tend a garden and keep an eye on two small children at the same time. There was simply no other choice. Besides, the fresh air would probably do the children some good.

Two hours later, Millie found herself on her knees in the dirt. The plants here were definitely struggling, but they were not dead. Adam's attempts at keeping the garden going around all his other duties had been enough to sustain life. Millie felt certain—okay, she really, really hoped—that the plants would flourish now that she was here to tend them regularly.

Oddly, the prospect excited her. Much like her room, this was a piece of earth that Adam had said was all hers. And, she wanted to do something with it. Make these dying plants and dark earth turn into a bounty of food that could feed them all year long.

"Am I doing it right, Millie?"

Caty and Gene had not hesitated to get down in the dirt with her. Genie's chubby little fists were almost a blur in the beginning as he had just started pulling anything growing and tossing it in a pile. Vegetable or weed, if it was in his path it was yanked and thrown, all with an accompanying grin and nonstop chatter.

But, he was where Millie could see him, and was trying. Good enough. Besides, it took less than five minutes for Genie to decide playing in the dirt was more fun than dealing with pesky plants anyway.

Unlike her brother, Caty was taking her job very seriously. She spent long minutes considering the plants in front of her, fingering the leaves with solemn eyes and an intensity that almost made Millie sad. The girl looked so terribly fearful of getting anything wrong.

"You're doing a great job, Caty. In fact, I'm watching what you do to make sure I get it right."

Caty didn't smile. "Really? I don't think I am doing it the way I'm supposed to."

Oh, Millie wanted to gather this child in her arms and just create a space where all Caty felt was love and acceptance. She didn't. Instead she sat back and brushed the dirt off her hands. "I know what you mean."

Caty looked at her. "You do?"

Millie nodded and smiled, heart still feeling almost

too tender. "I've never had a large farm garden before, Caty. And certainly not a garden with weeds as big as the plants, all of them looking a little worse for wear. I am kind of guessing what to do here."

Caty twisted her fingers in her lap. "Daddy tried to make a good garden. He tried really hard."

There was no stopping Millie's hand from reaching out and brushing down Caty's hair. Then stroking her fingers over the child's cheek. Millie's muscles twitched with the urge to pull the child onto her lap, but she held back. She'd resolved to wait until Caty was ready to come to her, not wanting to push the girl. "I know he did, honey. And you know what? He did a good job."

Caty's eyes were still far too serious. Doubting.

"He did. I mean, look at all the vegetables that are growing here. I can't wait to see what else comes up."

Caty looked at the garden and nodded.

"And now all we have to do is clean it up a little. Then, we'll have the best garden I've ever seen in my whole entire life."

"Really? I mean, Daddy tried. But, it's—" Caty was clearly trying to balance honesty and her loyalty to her father.

"A mess. Yep. But, it's our mess, Caty-girl. And it will be our wonderful garden when we're done." This was the first time Millie had used Adam's nickname for Caty. She watched, trying to decide if it made the girl uncomfortable. Really hoping it didn't.

Caty went back to leaning over the area of garden where they were working, this time pulling a weed quickly and surely. "Yeah. It's our mess."

Millie smiled and took up a similar position. They were going to weed their garden in the sunshine. Life was good.

Millie's enthusiasm had dampened somewhat an hour later. She was hot and sticky and absolutely filthy. She and Caty had also only made progress in about one fourth of the garden. Growing vegetables was harder than it looked. But, Millie pictured the end result and pulled at the next weed she saw.

She stopped when she heard a horse ride into the yard. The children ran to greet Adam as he dismounted. He gave them hugs and set them back down, telling them to go play as though nothing was amiss.

But something must be. Why else would Adam be home at this hour?

"Good afternoon, Millie. I see you've decided to deal with the disaster I made of the vegetable garden."

His voice was courteous, as always. Adam's treatment of her had not wavered since the first day. He was kind. Gentle. And distant. In other words, he was everything he had promised Millie he would be. And that was another thing that unsettled her to no end.

"I'm trying. I've never had a garden this big before, so I'm not sure I'm doing it right. Caty has been a huge help."

Adam walked over and looked at her work. "You're doing a good job. The part you two worked on looks perfect. You got all the weeds out, so the vegetables won't be fighting them for space or water. All we'll need is a couple of good rains and lots of sunshine."

Millie had thought so, but it still felt really good to hear someone else say it.

"You're home early. Is everything okay?" His praise had given her enough courage to ask the question.

"For us, yes. We're just fine."

She liked that, too. Whether he thought it was easier or because he had picked up on her need for it, Adam often reassured her that everything was okay. His words did not make it so, obviously, but they still helped give her a sense of security.

Adam took off his hat, and wiped his hand across his brow. "I'm home because Jonas Miller came out to see me. He found me in the fields."

"Jonas Miller? I haven't met him yet, have I?"

"No. He's another neighbor. A couple of farms out from the Potters."

"Oh. Why did he come see you today? Isn't he as busy as you are?" Sorrow crossed over Adam's face, and Millie's sense of unease grew. Adam did not come home in the middle of the day to have a simple conversation.

"No, he's not. Not anymore at least."

"What does that mean?"

"He's giving up. Selling his farm and moving to Kansas City. Going to try to find some work there."

"I don't understand. He waited until the growing season, until he had paid for seeds and done the work to plant them, to decide he didn't want to be a farmer?" Her tone gave away her bewilderment, but she was struggling to understand. Millie loathed being in situations she didn't understand.

Adam looked at the kids, smiling at their antics as

Gene pretended to be a chicken and chased a shrieking Caty. "This has been coming on for some time now," he explained. "With the drought last year, Jonas used up all his savings to have a go at putting in the crops this year."

"So, why is he quitting?"

Adam huffed out a small breath. He looked almost apologetic. "He's thinking that this year will be a repeat of last year. He found a seller who wants the farm right away, crops and all, and he took the offer. Hopes to find better work in the city."

Spots danced in Millie's vision, and she sat down on the steps. "Why does Mr. Miller think that this year is going to be a repeat of last year?"

Adam sat down next to her on the step. "Because it's looking like it might. We haven't had a good soaker in months. Spring is usually a rainy, muddy time."

"It *has* been raining," Millie argued.

Adam shrugged. "More like drizzling. We've been getting damp, not drenched."

"So, you're going to lose all the crops? Again? Everything is just going to die?" How could that be? He went out and worked every single day. Why would Adam do that if all of his hard work was going to dry up and die? And why hadn't she known that there was a drought in Kansas last year? That it had been too dry already this spring?

Adam moved to kneel on the step below her, his body slightly in front of hers. Facing her. "It's okay."

The man kept saying that. Adam had a very different definition of okay than Millie did, that was for sure.

"That's why I have the cattle and horses. They will sustain us if we have another bad harvest of crops. Plus, the weather is unpredictable. Just because it's been dry so far doesn't mean there will be another drought."

"Why?"

"Why?" Adam sounded confused now. Good.

"Why do you do it? Farm? Why not just have the ranch? I don't understand why you would spend so much time and energy on such a risky endeavor."

Understanding flashed across his face. "I do it because I'm a farmer. I enjoy the cattle and horses, but I'm meant to be a farmer. I've always known it. Planting. Tending. Harvesting. It all feels so right, Millie. I'm a farmer." Adam took his hat off his head and brushed it against his thigh. He was looking in the distance, but his voice was still steady. Almost imploring. "You're a farmer's wife."

Millie had no response to that. She certainly wasn't in a position to order him around. To change anything about their circumstances.

Adam stood up. "I'm sorry I upset you. I didn't mean to. And we can talk about this in more detail, if you want. But, later. Jonas came to ask for my help with fixing and loading some things as he packs up his belongings. That's why I came home. I need to get my tools and head out to his place. He's waiting for me."

Millie stood up, too. "It's fine, Adam. We're fine. Will you be home for supper?"

"For that stew I smell? Absolutely."

Millie nodded and straightened her apron. No way out but forward.

Adam said goodbye to the children, gathered his tools and left.

Millie decided to finish the section of her garden that she'd started. That was the next task. That was all she needed to focus on right now. But, this time when Millie looked at her vegetable patch, she didn't see the promise of a bounty to come. No. She saw her future. So fragile and capable of being destroyed by a single whim of man or nature.

Not just her future. Her child's future. And that of the two children she was quickly growing to love and claim as her own.

It was dark by the time Adam returned home that evening. Jonas had needed more help than he'd expected, but Adam hadn't wanted to leave the man to finish on his own. Adam opened the front door and walked inside, uncertain of what his reception might be.

In the month since he had been married, life had been quite good. They had fallen into an easy routine, and his children were thriving. Today's discussion was the first bump since their conversation about her meeting the children.

His new wife was very reserved and Adam did not understand everything that Millie kept hidden from him, but he knew she was afraid of the future. That was immensely logical to Adam's mind. What little he knew about Millie's past combined with the nature of being a woman in this world spoke volumes about her fear. She had been homeless. Penniless. Alone. She was afraid of being that again.

Adam looked around the room, hoping to see Millie and the kids waiting for him. But it was empty. Disappointment warred with frustration. Adam didn't want tension anywhere in his home or marriage.

A glance in the kitchen showed the stew still being kept warm. That was something. He checked in on the kids, satisfied to see them tucked in and sleeping. Then, he walked to Millie's closed bedroom door. Should he knock, see if she wanted to continue their conversation from earlier? She had been upset. Worried about drought and the future. And he had had to leave before he could soothe her fears. Adam felt bad for that, but she needed to learn that these things were part of life on a farm. And, she had married a farmer.

Adam moved his ear closer to the door when he heard a noise from inside. He didn't want to intrude on Millie's privacy or force a conversation if she wasn't ready, but something about that sound set his nerves on edge. He heard the noise again.

Millie was getting sick.

Adam rapped on the door. "Millie, it's Adam. I'm coming inside." He probably should have waited until she gave him permission. But, Adam heard the sound of Millie retching again and refused to stand by and simply listen.

He opened the door and strode inside. Millie was sitting in the rocking chair, still wearing her dress and apron from earlier. Her hair was coming out of its bun as she bent over a chamber pot held on her lap. He walked over and crouched down beside her.

"Adam, you should go. You don't—" Millie stopped speaking as she got sick again.

Adam couldn't be here and not touch her. Not try to comfort her. He reached out and rested a hand on her back, rubbing up and down in what he hoped was a soothing manner. "Shh. It's okay. I'm not going anywhere, and you don't need to worry about anything. Just let it pass."

They stayed like that for a few more minutes. Millie hunched over her bowl and Adam just being there, with a hand on her back. Had she been ill all day? Or for longer? Adam hadn't noticed anything earlier, but they also hadn't exactly been spending a lot of time together.

Adam moved his hand from her back to stroke her hair away from her face. He incorporated wiping a palm across her forehead into the motion. She didn't feel feverish.

"I don't have a fever." Millie's voice was hoarse, and she wasn't looking up at him.

"Did you eat something spoiled?" He and the children were just fine, so that was unlikely.

"I'm fine. Please, just leave me alone."

Adam winced at the hoarseness in her voice. She was not fine.

"It will take me a while to go get the doctor. I'll leave just as soon as I think you'll be okay alone."

"I'm all right alone. I'm always alone and always all right."

Adam flinched back at the force of her words. He put his hand back, trying to figure out how to get her to calm down. So far, he was only riling her up more.

"Okay. It's okay. Just try to calm down."

"Don't tell me to calm down. I told you I'm not sick." Millie had moved from despair to flat-out grumpy. Her mood swings were giving Adam a headache. He decided the best course of action was to keep quiet and just be here.

A few minutes later, Millie sat up all the way. She set the bowl down on the floor on the opposite side of where Adam was crouching. Then, she hunched back over and rested her face in her hands.

Adam saw a pitcher of water and a toweling cloth on top of the chest. He stood up and walked over to it. After wetting the cloth, he came back down to her side. When she looked up, Adam took the cloth and wiped her face, trying to both refresh and comfort her. She reached up and put her hands over his. Took the towel out of his hands.

"I'm sorry. I was rude to you."

"It's okay."

"You say that a lot."

"Say what?"

"That it's okay. You're always telling me that it's okay."

She had a point, but he wasn't sorry. "That's because I think everything will be okay."

Millie just gave him a look he couldn't decipher. Then, she took the cloth and wiped her face again, much rougher than Adam had. She started to stand, and Adam reached out and placed his hands over hers.

"You should rest a few minutes longer."

"Well, to use your favorite words, I'm okay, Adam."

"Millie. People who are okay do not get sick like that."

"They do if they're pregnant."

Oh. Of course. Adam had been through this before. Twice. He should have known.

"You look surprised. Didn't Sarah ever get sick while carrying?"

"She did. Just never this late into her pregnancy."

"Yeah, well, I didn't expect it to last this long either."

Adam clenched his jaw to stop his smile. Millie sounded decidedly put out. It was kind of cute. "How long have you been getting sick?"

"Oh, about every day for forever."

Yep. She was definitely not feeling any kind of glow. "Why didn't you say anything? I could have helped out more if I had known."

Millie stood up, brushed her hands down her apron. "It wasn't worth mentioning. It's just part of life. I am perfectly capable of handling anything this baby throws my way." She moved over and picked up the chamber pot. "If you'll excuse me, I want to clean this up and then go to bed. I'm tired."

Millie started to hurry out of the room. She stopped, turned and looked at him. "Thank you for being concerned. I left the stew on for you."

"Thanks. I'm famished."

Left alone in her room, Adam breathed out a long

sigh. He opened her window, hoping she would appreciate the fresh air when she returned. Feeling foolish standing there and waiting for some unknown something, he headed to the kitchen and dished up a bowl of Millie's stew. Millie came back in the front door with a cleaned-out chamber pot. She gave Adam a small smile and went inside her room, closing her door behind her.

Adam ate the delicious stew with a slice of thick bread Millie must have made earlier in the day. He found himself thinking about that life inside Millie's womb with a smile. His regrets about his first wife seemed to be endless, but his children were nowhere on the list. He cherished every moment his children had been in his life, including his wife's pregnancies.

And now, he was going to be a father again. He'd been so focused on keeping his distance from Millie and being a good father to his children that he'd missed something so very obvious. He couldn't do both. He could not be distant from Millie and love his children because one of his children was currently inside of Millie. And, Millie was the mother of his children.

He had sought out a mother for them, had brought her here. She was not an unrelated person he could keep on the sidelines. She was integral to his family.

He needed her.

He thought of Millie as being a person who needed safety and reassurance, but Adam was the exact same. He wanted more than a mother for his children. He wanted a partner. Out there. On his farm. But he was afraid Millie would see his need and refuse to stay by his side. That she would feel stifled or trapped. That she would be Sarah. Again.

Yes, Adam needed Millie to have the life he wanted. The companionship he was craving. That meant he needed to start doing his part. But how could he connect with his wife and build the foundation for a strong partnership without risking his heart again?

Chapter Four

To Do:
Learn about drought
Find time to knit more—figure out how to sell
the items
Come up with a way to hide part of my knitting
proceeds without Adam noticing
Check crops—see if they look dry
Check cattle—see if they look thirsty
Learn what not dry crops look like
Learn what not thirsty cattle look like
Talk to Edith? Is she worried?
Find out if Adam has savings

"What are you working on?"

Millie quickly put down her pencil and closed her notebook. Too late she realized that was acting like someone guilty of, well, something. Great. Adam was going to think she was plotting his demise if she didn't figure out how to be less secretive.

But, she couldn't help it. Her notebook was hers. Her lists were hers. They had always been the one thing that had belonged entirely to her. The matron and other kids at The Home had often taken her belongings. One of the first rules of surviving in that place was to not get too closely attached to things. Various items were there for her to use, but they were temporary. They were not hers.

Except for her notebook and lists. No one had ever been interested in taking them away from her. Honestly, most children tried to avoid things related to writing. To school. So, her notebook had been safe.

And now Adam was asking her about it and she was acting like a lunatic.

"It's just a notebook." Despite her best effort, the note of defensiveness was obvious in her tone.

"What do you write in it?"

If Adam was accusing her of something, he was hiding it well. He sounded curious. Just curious. Millie didn't know what to make of that. They had been married for a month, and had seemed to settle into a nice routine where he left her alone as much as possible and she did the same. They spoke as needed to ensure the smooth running of the household. And they put on a good show of friendliness for the children.

Except, it wasn't really a show. Their companionship was real. It was just distant. A kind of separated friendship that suited Millie perfectly.

So, why was Adam suddenly asking her about her notebook?

It was early evening. Supper had been eaten. The kitchen cleaned. Caty with her dolls and Genie with his blocks were happily playing in front of the fire. Adam was sitting in a rocking chair, watching the children and joining in with their chatter.

And Millie was at the table with her notebook. Looking at what she had accomplished today and planning for tomorrow.

"It's okay if you don't want to tell me. I was just wondering. You spend every night sitting over there writing, and it made me curious."

Adam's voice was not accusatory, but the way he said "over there" caught Millie's attention. It was like she was in the next county. She wasn't even in the next room, for pity's sake. She was right there. In the same room.

Was he unhappy with her behavior? Did he want something else?

"It's not a secret. I just make lists in here."

"Lists?"

"Yes. Lists. You know. I write down things I want to do so I don't forget."

Adam was looking at her like she was a crazy person. Great.

"I know it's weird, but I like to write down my to-do list and then cross the things off."

Adam looked at the kids. Genie was still banging his blocks, making growly noises and giggling at his own antics. Caty had a doll and brush in her hands, but she wasn't playing anymore. Instead, she was watching them with worried eyes. She had probably picked up on the same undercurrent that Millie noticed.

"I don't think it's weird at all. I can't tell you how

many times I wish I had written something down."
Adam began rocking again and the tension left the
room. Caty started brushing her doll's hair again.

Millie looked down at her closed notebook. Every
part of her body wanted to open it back up and start
writing again. Review what she had already written. But
she forced her hands to stay where they were.

Millie couldn't stay at the table with her notebook
and not review what was inside. That was just asking
too much. She stood and walked to where Genie was
playing on the ground with his blocks. He grinned at
her, all teeth and mischief. He held a block up to her,
and Millie took it and sat down next to him.

She ran her thumb over the smooth wood, wondering how something so simple could be so absolutely en-
tertaining to a little boy. Genie reached out and stilled
her hand, positioning it so she was holding the block in
just the right position. Then he picked up a block with
his own hand and proceeded to bang his block into her
block. He giggled like this was the most fun he had
ever had in his life.

Millie held her block still and played along, resisting
the urge to hug this child with every bit of her strength.
Wherever he was, whatever he had, this little boy found a
way to be happy. Millie had never been like that, not even
as a child. She swallowed hard, trying to ease the tension
in her throat and the regrets in her mind. Then, she just
played with the little boy God had brought into her life.

The rest of the evening passed quickly. Children
were put in nightclothes. Prayers were said. Covers
were tucked, and lamps were blown out.

Millie followed Adam out of the children's room, fully intending to head to her own bedroom. That had been the routine for the past month, and it was one Millie enjoyed. She would have some time alone before heading to bed. Time where she could open her notebook back up and finish planning for the days ahead.

"Millie?"

She stopped about a foot outside her doorway and freedom. Millie turned her eyes back to where Adam was waiting behind her in the family room. "Yes?"

"Would you stay out here tonight? For a little bit?"

Millie wanted to hide in her room. She wanted a closed door and time to think. She was still processing her thoughts about a drought, and needed to work on her list of questions to get answered. Once she had answers, she could work on a plan for if they lost all the crops.

But, Millie could not tell Adam no. He was her husband. And his request was not unreasonable. Presumably, he had some reason for wanting her to stay and talk with him.

Millie nodded her consent and walked toward the kitchen, intending to take her familiar place at the table.

"Maybe we could sit in front of the fire?"

Millie froze. Sit in front of the fire? While there were two rocking chairs positioned there, they had never sat together in them. Millie had used her chair to knit during the day. Sometimes in the evening if Adam was still out working. But, never while he was home and sitting in his chair.

The two of them. Rocking together in front of a fire while children were soundly sleeping. That was too much. It seemed too much like…something she couldn't really name.

"Please? I just want to talk to you."

Adam's tone was one he used with a scared animal. Was that how he saw her? Did he think she was weak? Helpless? Millie felt anger surge up. It was a ridiculous reaction to his obvious kindness, but the anger was there nonetheless.

Millie managed to not stomp as she headed for the rocking chair. She did not, however, manage to sit down calmly or gracefully. Instead, she almost huffed down into the chair.

Then the chair rocked.

Then she felt the world spin.

Then that spinning landed in her stomach, which lurched with nausea.

Millie planted her feet to stop the chair from its incessant motion. She closed her eyes and counted the ways she could manage to further embarrass herself this evening. Nope. There weren't any more. That was reassuring at least.

Millie kept her eyes closed when she felt Adam crouch down in front of her. His warm hands picked hers up from her lap. She could smell him. Dirt shouldn't be an appealing smell, but it was somehow on this man. He loved the earth and often carried its scent with him through his day.

"Is it passing?"

Millie smiled. She simply couldn't help herself. She'd gone from fury to amusement in seconds. Alternating between strong emotions had been a constant pattern in her life for months now. Whether it was the baby or the man, Millie had no clue. But, she really hoped it was the baby. Her pregnancy would eventually end, and she prayed the turbulent emotions currently ruling her behavior would end with it.

Millie opened her eyes and saw exactly what she expected. Adam kneeling in front of her, looking both amused and concerned. But, mainly amused. At least he wasn't upset by her not-so-subtle tantrum.

Adam squeezed her hands and smiled back at her. That smile moved Millie's attention from her stomach to the ping in her heart. She had not married Adam for his looks. In fact, she had no clue what he looked like until the day before their wedding.

But, there was no denying that she had married a handsome man. His black hair and dark eyes were hard to ignore. Those striking looks were only magnified by his grin with the hint of mischief that Genie had clearly inherited. Both Beale men were easy on the eyes and trouble through and through. And, Millie found that she had as hard a time resisting Adam as she did Genie when he wanted something.

"Do you feel better? I wanted to talk to you, but I understand if you need to go to bed."

Oh, that option was beyond tempting. But, hiding from problems had never made them disappear. "I'm fine now, Adam. I just sat down too fast."

His lips twitched, but Adam didn't point out that she had done a bit more than sit too fast. He stood and headed for his own chair. He positioned it across from her, moving it slightly closer than it had been before.

Adam sat, looking at the floor for several never-ending seconds. One of the things Millie liked the most about Adam was his predictability and tendency to do things in a routine manner. But this felt anything but predictable or routine.

Adam breathed out a long, audible breath. Her own breath caught in her throat when he lifted his head and looked at her.

Knowing what he wanted and making it happen had never been a problem for Adam. He wasn't afraid of hard work. He wasn't even intimidated by the prospect of waiting for results. No. He could work and be patient. Deal with setbacks. Adam's life had been one big exercise in following those principles and getting results.

Until now.

Adam wasn't dealing with uncultivated land, a struggling seedling or a wild animal.

This was a relationship with a woman. His wife. And he had no idea how to build the relationship he wanted with her. Adam usually trusted his instincts, but they had led him wrong down this very same road. Not that long ago, either.

So here he was. Sitting in front of a fire with the woman he had married. Two people rocking because it was the polite thing to do, both wanting to get up and run far away.

Millie was turning out to be an excellent mother for his children. Truly, he could not imagine a woman caring for Caty and Genie any better than she did. More than caring for them, she was nurturing them. Loving them even. But, Adam wanted more.

He wanted a partner. He wanted to be part of the cozy little family Millie was creating inside the house he'd built. Adam wasn't looking for romantic love, but the fields that used to bring him joy were starting to feel like banishment.

He actually found himself wishing Millie was with him throughout the day, or that he could go to her without feeling like he was intruding. He wanted another adult to share his life with. *Their* life. Once he realized what he wanted, he was willing to do what it took to make more happen. If only he knew what to do.

"Are you happy, Millie?"

She stopped rocking, and seemed to almost freeze. Apparently, he had a talent for catching this woman so off guard that she turned into a statue. That wasn't a talent Adam relished, but it seemed about right given his relationship with women in general.

"Uh, Millie?" He sounded foolish, but what else was he supposed to say?

Millie closed her mouth and blinked, and Adam felt the pressure in his chest lessen as she came back to life. She blushed, and Adam tried not to notice how pretty it looked on her cheeks.

"Am I happy? I don't understand."

The bewildered tone made Adam's heart ache. She sounded absolutely stunned that her husband would care about her happiness. Had nothing in her life led her to expect that her happiness would be a concern? Of importance?

Adam leaned farther forward, resting his forearms on the tops of his thighs. They had been living as strangers for a month. It had gone nicely, too. But, he wanted more than that for his children, including the one currently growing in Millie's womb. Not love. No, Adam had learned that lesson well. But, friendship. Companionship. A sense of shared purpose surely wasn't too much to ask for, was it? That was the goal, and Adam was ready to do the work.

"It's been a month. I just want to know how you feel about things here. Are you happy with the house? The children? Your day-to-day life?" *With me?* He didn't say the last part, but Adam's heart whispered it.

"I'm happy here?"

"That sounded more like a question than a reply. There isn't a right answer. I know things have been overwhelming. You left the city and came to a new state. You came to a new house. You're living with three strangers, two of whom are children."

Millie's eyes were wide and fearful. She had scooted forward in her rocking chair and was perched on the edge, almost as though she was preparing to flee. If Adam's goal was to put Millie at ease around him, he was failing.

"I'm messing this up." No need to hide it, his inability to have a simple conversation with his wife was completely and utterly obvious. "It's not a test. I'm not angry or upset with you—and I won't be, no matter what you tell me. If you're not happy, I want to know so that I can try to fix it. We're married, and I want us both to work together to build a good life. For Caty and Genie. And the baby. That child you're carrying is mine. In every way that counts, that child will be mine to love and care for and provide for. And, I'm excited. I want to share in every moment."

Statue Millie was back. Well, at least statues couldn't run away.

"But, it's not just about the children. It's also for us. We count, too. I want both of us to be happy. I believe we still agree that we don't want a romantic relationship. But, I feel like we are still strangers. We've lived together as a family for a month, and you and I don't know each other." Adam swallowed and looked at his hands. Might as well say it all. It certainly couldn't make things more awkward. "I get lonely sometimes. I'd like to know you as a friend. Not as the nice woman living in my house and caring for my children who is practically a stranger."

"Um, okay."

Yeah, her mouth might have agreed with his proposal, but her tone certainly didn't. And neither did the way she was still perched on the edge of that chair like she was ready to bolt at any moment. But, Adam would take what he could get. Go slow. Easy.

The Adam of years ago would never have put himself in such a position. No. That Adam had assumed that such work was unnecessary to sustain a strong marriage. Once married, a husband and a wife were one until death they did part. Why put energy into such a relationship? It was a foregone conclusion that the other person would be there.

Until it wasn't. His first wife had proven with tragic

competency that Adam couldn't just assume Millie would stay and keep up her end of the bargain if she was unhappy.

Adam felt like this conversation was a foot deep in the thickest mud the prairie had to offer. But, he'd wanted to go down this road, so now was the time to follow through. "Great."

They sat and stared at each other for several long seconds. Not great.

"Did your friend get all moved out?"

Adam blinked at the abrupt question. He knew their prior conversation about drought had made Millie uneasy, so he was surprised that she chose that topic. But she was trying, and Adam wasn't about to cut her off.

"Yes, he and his wife should arrive in Kansas City by the end of next week. I hope they'll get settled quickly. And be happy."

"I've been praying for them."

Adam stopped rocking at her words. Then, he made himself resume. That was probably the most personal thing Millie had ever said to him, but he didn't want to make a big deal out of it. More than anything, he wanted things to feel natural between them. Normal.

Adam hadn't felt at ease and normal in this house for years. Not since the day he'd come home to find Sarah's note that she was leaving him. But, he remembered his parents, who had always had a solid, stable marriage. They'd spent hours talking in the evenings. It had just been a part of his childhood. A good one.

"That's nice. I'm also praying for them. Starting over

won't be easy, and I hope they find everything they're looking for."

"You pray, too?" She sounded surprised. "I mean, I know you pray for us before meals, obviously, and in church on Sundays, but you pray other times, too?"

Adam felt the ground steady beneath him. "Yes. I pray a lot. My relationship with the Lord has deepened significantly since my wife died." Well, that came out wrong. "My first wife, I mean."

"I know what you meant. I'm kind of the same. I found the church before my first husband died, but my faith has really grown since he passed."

Adam knew the bones of her story. She hadn't told him any of it herself, though, either in the letter she had sent him or in the brief conversations they'd had since her arrival. No, the people who had facilitated their marriage had filled Adam in on those details.

Was Millie aware that Adam knew those details? Maybe. But, it still felt too intimate to bring them up. Those weeks after her husband had died must have been terrifying.

"I'm glad. My faith has helped me through a number of hard times. I'm glad yours has done the same for you."

"It has." Millie was rocking steadily, looking into the fire. This silence still felt charged, but not so much as before. Progress.

Millie kept rocking, but her hands were fidgeting in her lap, fingers twisting and intertwining. "Will you tell me about drought?"

He managed to stop his head halfway through its

rapid jerk in her direction. Her body was screaming that asking the question had been hard and awkward for her and that she feared his reaction—but he could tell that she feared drought more, and wanted answers. It didn't take a genius to pick up on the fact that Millie worried about the future. A lot. That seemed fairly rational given what she had been through.

Adam had done his best to reassure her that he would take care of her and their family. But, Millie was still visibly concerned about being secure long-term. He understood that, given that she had recently found herself pregnant and homeless. But, it still kind of rankled. Even if he died tomorrow, he wasn't the type of man to leave his family alone and unprotected. There were provisions in place.

"I'm not sure what you want to know, Millie. I mean, we haven't been getting enough rain. Without rain, the crops aren't getting any water. And they need water to grow."

"So all those crops are going to die? I mean, there's nothing you can do?"

Adam considered her question. Tried to give it respect and treat it seriously. "I don't know. I don't think all the crops will die. I sure hope not. But, when it comes to life in general and farming in particular, nothing is certain."

"When will you know?"

Adam breathed out long and slow. He'd wanted a conversation and now he was getting one. "There's not a clear answer to that. We've had some rain, so the situation isn't dire. Just not as much rain as I'd like. The crops are okay for now, but there's not a lot of margin if that little bit of rain dries up. So, we just have to wait and see."

Millie looked down at her hands in her lap. She was still rocking. Still twisting her fingers as though she could pull answers or solace or whatever she was looking for there. "What about the cattle? They need water, too. Is this drought bad for them?"

"It's not ideal, but the cattle can handle the lack of water better than the crops. The ponds haven't dried up, yet, so that's good. And, if it comes down to it, like last year, I can sell the nonessential cattle and take the rest to where there is water."

"That's what you did last year?"

"Yes. And we were okay."

"Did you have to use all your savings last year? Like that family that moved away? Do you have any left?"

His savings? Was she that concerned about his ability to provide? Did she really doubt him that much? Adam clenched his jaw so hard it began to ache. What would it take for his wife to simply trust that he could be a good husband and father? He'd been trying so hard, but it still wasn't enough.

This conversation was a bad idea.

Chapter Five

Option 1: All the crops die. We still have the cattle. Things are lean, but we are fine. We still have shelter and food. But what about next year?

Option 2: The crops die. The cattle die. We use all of Adam's savings. Things are lean, but we are fine. We still have shelter and food. But what about next year?

Option 3: The crops die. The cattle die. Adam's savings are not enough and we lose the land. Adam can get a job in the city to support us?

Option 4: The crops die. The cattle die. Adam's savings are not enough and we lose the land. Adam refuses to move to the city?

Millie usually used the time right after she woke up to map out the day. Today, though, she'd felt compelled to list possible scenarios. That was a mistake. Millie should have stuck to her to-do lists. At least then, she was in charge. She did things and she crossed them off and she went to bed at night knowing she had accomplished something. But, no. She'd had to work through the worst that could happen—and terrify herself in the process.

How did she expect it was going to end? If life had taught Millie one thing, it was that the worst could indeed happen. Their crops were going to die. Millie was going to end up homeless again. Homeless and pregnant and alone. Millie pushed away from the table where she had been writing in her notebook. Moving to her bedroom, she pulled out her suitcase. Placed it on the bed. Opened her chest drawer and grabbed a handful of clothes.

Froze.

What was she doing? Packing? Running away?

Where would she go?

And, what would she end up leaving behind?

Still clutching the clothes in her hand, Millie sank down into her rocking chair. Buried her face into the cloth she was gripping for dear life. Sucked in a shaky breath and pressed against her eyes that suddenly felt like they were on fire.

She could feel the beat of her heart, pounding in her chest. She felt the sting of tears. The tightness of her throat.

Millie felt the distinct swell of her stomach. The movement of life inside, apparently unwilling to sit idly by as Millie panicked.

Hunched almost into a ball as she was, Millie also felt a hardness in her bundle of clothes. She felt through the balled-up material until she found the pouch of beads. She opened the pouch and poured several out onto her hand. Large. Wooden. Painted bright colors. Each one had a hole in the center, perfect for a small child to thread string or yarn through. When the family she'd been staying with after her husband died had learned that Millie was marrying into a family with a little girl, they'd given the beads to Millie. Something she could use as a game with her new daughter.

Caty. Could she really leave that sweet girl? And Genie? Would she be that woman? The one who hurt those children by abandoning them after working so hard to earn their affection and trust? And, what about her own heart? She, well, she loved those children. All of her fears that they would not accept her had been completely unfounded.

They were good children. Ones who craved a mother's love and attention. They'd soaked every bit of affection that Millie offered. Took it. Were grateful. Reciprocated.

Millie wasn't mothering them out of a sense of duty. Not anymore. It wasn't about some kind of mutual agreement with Adam where they each got something out of the deal. No, she enjoyed every minute of being their mother.

She couldn't leave them. She could not leave at all.

How ironic that Millie had spent hours working out ways to get the children to like her. Had worried. Obsessed. Thought of ways to win them over. Then she met the children and things had gone better than any scenario she'd been able to imagine. And now, the thing she had wanted, a good relationship with the children, was the thing keeping her here with certain failure.

Millie forced her hands to put the beads back inside the pouch. She got up to put the clothes back in the drawer. Running away wasn't going to solve the problem. Whatever the answer turned out to be, she needed to find it here.

Though, running away seemed like it would be easier in the short term. Adam had not been happy at the end of their conversation last night. In fact, Millie thought last night had been their first fight. She'd known she was treading on shaky ground when she asked about his savings, but she was his wife. Wasn't she entitled to know? Millie had blindly trusted a man before. Had assumed that getting married would end her lifelong quest for security.

But, it wasn't the end. In a very real way, it led to Millie being in the most unsecure situation she'd ever had. The only thing worse than being alone on the streets was being alone on the streets while pregnant with a defenseless child. Millie repressed a shudder.

But, leaving now wasn't the answer. Millie closed the drawer and went to put the suitcase away. There. Like the last five minutes had never happened. Caty and Genie were still sleeping, so no one would ever know that she had almost done the unthinkable.

Millie paused in front of the mirror, but couldn't quite make eye contact with herself. Sometimes Millie didn't understand all the bad things that happened to her. Sometimes she thought she maybe deserved them.

No.

That was not God talking. She used to think that, back when she thought she was alone. But, Millie wasn't alone. Not now and not when she'd realized she was about to be homeless and pregnant. God was with her always. And He loved her.

Not just God, but His people, too. The only place Millie had been homeless and pregnant was in the scenarios in her notebook. In reality, her new friends from the church had not hesitated to help after her first husband's death, and she had been comfortably settled with the Kellers by the time her home was repossessed. They even went out of their way to make Millie feel like a welcome guest instead of a charitable obligation.

Millie walked over to her Bible and picked it up. Sat back down in her rocking chair and opened the book. She wished for a minute that she was back in the city, back with those church friends. The women had been surprisingly easy to talk to. And safe. Millie knew that whatever she told them wouldn't be used for gossip.

She'd had so many conversations with those women about faith. About not trying to be in control. About putting her time into prayer instead of worrying.

Millie had never been good at that, but she knew she'd only gotten worse since coming out to Kansas. Her time with the Lord had decreased each morning as her time with her notebook had increased. And as a result, her sense that everything was going to go wrong was spiraling out of control.

Something needed to change. She needed to change.

Millie closed her eyes and held her Bible to her chest. She prayed for the strength to trust the Lord. She prayed for the ability to look around and see the blessings in her life. To see the joy.

Millie opened her eyes and tried to see the world with new eyes. But, it looked the same. This was the hardest part of her new faith. She was truly blind. But, Millie still believed.

Millie set her Bible down and quickly washed her face using the pitcher and bowl on her dresser. She smoothed a hand over her apron. Walking out to the notebook, Millie turned the page and took a second to relish the clean white paper.

Fresh starts abounded in this world. Truly, they did. Millie focused on today and today only. She needed to go through her normal routine of chores and house-work. Work in the garden. Play with the children. She could knit during their nap and that would be enough planning for her future for today.

Looking at her to-do list with extreme satisfaction, Millie stood up, ready to begin the day again. She took her Bible to the table and sat back down. Opened it and spent long minutes reading God's word. As her eyes took in the words, her heart began to take in the peace those words provided. Millie closed the Bible, ready to face whatever might come next.

She got the fire going and made breakfast. Leaving the oatmeal to cook, Millie gathered eggs and milked the cow. She set her bounty down on the kitchen table and took a minute to admire the fruits of her work. She might not be any good at being Adam's wife, but she had learned to excel at being a farm woman. Adam hadn't had to help her with the household chores in weeks, and the cow and squawking chickens no longer intimidated her.

"Miyi!" Genie stood in the doorway in his nightshirt, hair sticking up all over the place and grinning like he had just found the most wonderful thing in the world. He came over to Millie and held up his hands. "Up!"

Millie's pregnancy was advancing, and the bump that had been only slightly noticeable on her wedding day was clearly visible now. It was getting harder to bend down and pick up the little boy, but Millie did it anyway. And, she'd keep doing it until it became physically impossible. Holding this cheerful little boy as he chattered about horsies and blocks was one of the best parts of Millie's day. A consistent, sure reminder that joy and innocence still existed.

Millie got Genie settled with a bowl of oatmeal and went to wake up Caty. The little girl had both hands tucked up under her head. She was breathing softly and her eyelashes stood out against her pale cheeks. She looked so peaceful. And very much like Adam.

Millie leaned down and brushed a hand down Caty's back. "Good morning, sweet girl. Are you ready to get up? We're having oatmeal for breakfast."

Caty opened her eyes and smiled at Millie. "Good morning, Millie."

She rolled onto her back and stretched, pushing her arms above her head and reaching out with her hands and feet. Millie smiled as how much she looked like the barn cats that lazed in the sun. She got Caty settled at the table with her own bowl of oatmeal and then opened her notebook to cross off the things she'd done so far.

See? The day was back on track, exactly where it belonged.

Breakfast over, Millie was supposed to move on to the rest of her chores. Her list said so. Her routine said so. Instead, Millie closed her notebook and sat back down at the now cleared-off table. Genie was busy with another epic war between his blocks and wooden animals. Caty had a doll, but she was just watching Millie with those quiet eyes of hers. Lingering off to the side, waiting to be helpful.

Millie pulled the pouch of beads out of her apron pocket. "Can you get my knitting basket and come here, please, Caty-girl?" Once Caty walked over, Millie pulled out the chair right next to her, scooting it to almost touch her chair. Millie poured the beads into a pile on the table, watching Caty climb up and eye them with interest.

"Beads." Caty said the word quietly, but her interest was clearly turning to excitement.

"Aren't they pretty? A friend gave them to me, and I've been saving them for the perfect project. I think we should make a necklace for you, what do you think?"

Caty grinned and nodded her head fast and hard.

"What color yarn should we use for the string?" Millie pulled several balls of yarn out of the basket and set the various colors on the table next to the beads.

Caty turned the question back on her. "What color do *you* think we should use?" Caty's hands were still clasped together in front of her, but Millie could tell she wanted to reach out and touch.

"Oh, I think they're all pretty. Here. Look at them and tell me which one you want for a necklace."

Millie pushed the balls of yarn to sit right in front

of Caty. The little girl reached out, skimming a finger on top of the rainbow of choices, pausing on the light blue. "I like this one."

Millie nodded and pulled her scissors out of the basket. "Me, too. I saw that in the store and could not resist the pretty color. Like the sky on a summer day."

She cut a length of yarn and handed it to Caty. Then they spent the next hour making a beaded necklace, starting over several times until Caty declared the necklace both perfect and done. Millie tied it around her neck and watched the girl stroke the beads as though she'd been given a treasure.

Millie did open her notebook then.

Buy Caty more beads.

Adam shut the barn door behind him and looked at the house. It looked so homey, with light shining out through the windows. The curtains were blowing in the breeze and Adam could smell something delicious cooking inside. Maybe Millie's biscuits, which were quickly becoming Adam's favorite food.

It looked like a scene from a book Adam had read as a child. One about a happy family and a perfect life. The book had entertained him. It was probably what his own childhood home had looked like from the outside. The reality of this current house, though, made him want to go back in the barn and brush down his horse another time—anything to delay going inside. He and Millie definitely got along better when they were not in the same room. Last night's fight had echoed through his mind all day.

But, his children were inside that house. He spent so much time in the fields this time of year that each minute with Caty and Genie was precious. And, he was starving. He'd snuck out of the house earlier than normal, and the cold meat and bread he'd eaten for both breakfast and lunch couldn't compare to Millie's biscuits with butter slathered all over them dipped into one of her stews or roasts.

As Adam approached the door, he heard feminine laughter inside. He also heard the familiar sounds of Genie playing, yelling and making animal noises. He paused, relishing the sounds. They would probably stop once he opened the door and walked inside.

Adam walked inside the house and saw Millie and Caty on the floor, both playing with her dolls. Genie was next to them, sitting in the middle of a pile of blocks and wooden horses and cows. They all turned and looked at him, and as predicted, the sounds of a happy family ceased.

"Daddy!" Caty and Genie both stood up and ran to him. Millie used a rocking chair to help her get to her feet. Adam wanted to go and help her, but he had an armful of children. And, he didn't want to give her the opportunity to say she didn't need his help. Or to question his ability to help her at all.

He helped his children sit at the table, listening to their rambling accounts about their day. He dished up the thick stew from the pot Millie had set on the table. They passed around the basket of biscuits and the butter, and Adam found himself looking at the meal he'd been dreaming about just ten minutes prior.

Once the food was distributed, they bowed their heads and Adam prayed. He had barely said *Amen* when Genie yelled, "Eat!" Adam smiled at the exclamation, looking at Millie. She was smiling, too. Their eyes met, and both smiles disappeared. The tension exploded.

They were still looking at one another across the table when Caty spoke. "Daddy? Is it okay to eat?"

"What?" Adam realized she and Genie were watching them, waiting for them to start eating before they did the same. Guilt festered in Adam's gut. If the awkwardness between him and Millie was noticeable enough for Genie to not start immediately eating, then it was bad. Really bad.

"I'm sorry, kids. That was my fault. I got a little sad for a second, but I'm better now." Millie broke off a piece of biscuit and began to eat, and the children followed without hesitation. "Caty, did you tell your dad how you helped make the biscuits today? I bet he'd like to hear that."

Adam began eating his own biscuit. "Yes, I would, Caty-girl. Did you get all of Millie's secrets about how she makes them so yummy?"

Caty smiled and nodded. "I'm going to make them with her again and again until I can do it by myself."

"Then you can make biscuits and Millie can make biscuits and we'll get to eat biscuits all day long." Adam teased his daughter, feeling his frustration melt away as it always did in Caty and Genie's presence. He loved ranching and loved farming, but his children were the real source of joy in his life.

He looked at his daughter, blushing and proud of

what she had learned. Looked at his son, with his toothy grin and mouth full of food, bursting to tell his daddy all about his day. He had wanted Millie to come into this structure and make it a home. He'd wanted his children loved and cared for. Not just physically cared for, but emotionally nourished. He'd wanted this. This very moment.

And Millie had given it to him. To them. She'd done everything he had told her he wanted in his letter. Not only done it, but done it with a cheerful heart. Instead of making his children feel like some sort of obligation, she'd made them feel special and loved.

No, Millie wasn't the one trying to change the bargain. That had been him. He'd sprung one-on-one night-time conversations on her. Had insisted on talking about feelings. Adam was the one who had made things too personal. He'd been hoping for a deeper friendship, but now saw that maybe he'd taken it too far. By pushing for more, he was jeopardizing the good thing they'd managed to create in the last month.

They needed to talk. Again. Not to become closer friends, but to clear up the argument they'd had. Then, things could go back to how they were before.

Adam felt a dread building in his gut as this night replayed the exact same way as the night before. They spent time together, tucked the children into bed, said prayers. Adam once again found himself waiting for Millie to come out of the kids' room.

She seemed to stay in there longer than normal, and Adam wondered if she was avoiding him. Maybe she would find a way to spend all night with the kids and never have to face him. Adam hoped she would be braver than that.

Adam sat in his rocking chair and pulled out the Bible, trying to find some guidance. His parents had loved one another deeply. They'd made being married look easy. Fun. They had even died together, when Adam was nineteen.

His mom had come down with what they had believed was the flu, and his dad had tended her devotedly. He would never balk at playing nurse for the woman he adored. It quickly became obvious that his mother's illness was more severe than they'd first expected. By the time the doctor made it out to their place, the scarlet fever had infected both of his parents. They died within a week of one another. In a way, that made sense. Adam couldn't conceive of a world with one of his parents in it without the other one.

Seeing that kind of love had been a gift. And then it had been a curse. Even before she became tired of being a farmer's wife, his marriage to his first wife had fallen far short of the great love he'd expected. The one he'd grown up seeing.

But that was a past mistake. A lesson Adam had learned. He had entered this marriage with Millie with very different expectations. Love, in Adam's experience, faded fast. It was much more important to have common goals.

Adam looked up when he heard Millie come out of the children's bedroom. She gently shut the door, one hand guiding it to close without making a sound. When she turned, she did not look the least bit surprised to see him there waiting for her. Instead, she looked resigned. Like Adam was some kind of unpleasant task to be endured. He tried to focus on the book in his hand and not the defensiveness coating his skin like some kind of armor.

"Adam."

"Millie."

They just watched each other, him in the rocking chair and her standing, hands pulling her shawl tight around her shoulders.

This was ridiculous. Adam sighed and set the Bible down on the table. He held both hands out, palms up, as though trying to prove that he meant her no harm. "Let's talk. Please."

She nodded and sat down in the other rocking chair, moving it to face him more directly rather than sit beside him. She did not speak.

"I want to talk about last night," Adam continued. "We were having a nice conversation, at least I thought we were, and then it went bad. I got upset and you got upset and we both left upset. But, I don't want to live that way, with tension between us. I don't want the kids exposed to that kind of discord. So, we need to talk it out."

Millie sighed, but it sounded much more weary than exasperated. She leaned back into the rocking chair and shut her eyes, squeezing them so tight that the skin around them went white.

"I got offended when you asked about my savings. It felt like you don't trust me to take care of you. That insults me." There. He'd said it as bluntly as possible.

That, at its core, was the hurdle they needed to get over. He couldn't do this if she was constantly doubting him.

Not just because it made him feel like less of a man, though that was a large part to be sure. But also because this was the exact road he'd stumbled down with his first wife. Sarah had doubted him. Sarah had tried to change him. Sarah had left him. Them.

"I grew up in an orphanage." Millie was still sitting back in her rocking chair, as withdrawn as she could be without getting up and walking away. Her eyes were still pressed shut. But, she was talking, her voice low. Steady. Adam couldn't hear any emotion in her tone, and that made his skin prickle.

"Orphans learn real quick not to trust people. That people simply can't be trusted. Even the good people. Workers who were kind to you left. Workers who were mean to you were mean, though they pretended to be nice in front of other adults, so anything you said against them was never believed. And even the mean ones left—you couldn't count on them either way."

She was still rocking. Still using that flat tone. She didn't even sound sad about her wretched childhood, just resigned in a way that hurt to hear. Adam wanted to stop her, to tell her never mind. He also found that, despite all his earlier protestations to the contrary, he very much wanted to hear what was on Millie's mind. And how this story ended.

"Us kids just looked out for ourselves. I mean, we tried to stick together. To be a team. But, at the end of the day, the only person who cared about me was me.

And every sad story began with one of us being naive fools and trusting someone."

Adam held his breath when Millie stopped rocking and sat up. Looked right at him with the most direct gaze Adam could remember having focused on him.

"But I didn't learn that lesson well enough. I trusted my first husband. Trusted that he would always be there and that he would take care of me. I thought we had a good marriage." Millie's voice turned hard, the first emotion Adam had heard since she started talking. It wasn't a pleasant emotion. "Then he died. And I found out about his secret life. The debt. And that I was in a worse position than I had ever been before. And that was saying something."

Adam felt the vise that had been around his chest lessen as Millie took her gaze off him. She leaned back again. Began rocking again. But her eyes were open this time, looking up at the ceiling.

"I know that part, Millie. I knew it before I married you." Adam tried to gentle his voice as much as possible. It was a hard story, had been hard to hear it when considering marrying her. He had worried that a woman who had faced that difficult experience might be bitter or harsh in a way that would make her an unsuitable mother for his sweet, impressionable children. Millie's church friends had assured him that she was gentle and kind and would be wonderful with the children—all of which turned out to be true. But, that did not change her not trusting him, her possibly leaving him. And that was a problem.

"You don't. Not really. You might know the facts as

they appear written down on a piece of paper but there is no way you know the experience as I lived it. You couldn't." Millie's voice held the second emotion of the night, a despair that made the vise reappear, only this time on his throat instead of his chest.

"Adam, I thought I was going to be alone. Pregnant. Homeless and penniless. And all I knew how to do was keep house, straighten things on store shelves, read and make to-do lists. That was it." Her voice broke. "I thought I was going to have to give my baby away to an orphanage. That my baby would grow up the exact same way I did because there was no way I could take care of myself and a baby."

Millie said more, but the words were just the inhalations and exhalations of her sobs. Every logical, reasonable, implacable reason Adam had to be mad at Millie crumbled, and he rushed over to somehow hug her in that rocking chair. She was right. He knew the words that described her past, but he didn't know the fear. Even this small glimpse of it was almost too much to bear.

The floor was punishing against Adam's knees and the armrests of the rocking chair were digging into his ribs, but Adam pressed forward, keeping his arms tight around her. It didn't help. Millie just continued to sob, arms wrapped around the womb where her child grew.

Chapter Six

To Do:
Daily chores
Die of mortification
Weed garden, collect vegetables
Sew my big mouth shut
Put on a roast for supper
Pretend that the last two nights never happened
Go into town for supplies and see if the store
will sell my knitting
Find a way to go to bed early

Millie wasn't sure how she had made it through the morning, but she had. And she would keep doing so. Keep going forward, performing the daily tasks of life. So she had broken down last night. So she had cried like a baby and told Adam her most shameful secret—that she had almost given up her child. So what?

Millie felt paralyzed, but forced her arms to keep moving as she chopped potatoes to put in with the roast.

Then, she would force herself to smile when Edith came to pick her up. Force her way through life.

Millie could do that. She could.

Edith had suggested the shopping trip to town last week. In truth, she had ridden into the yard and all but announced that they were going. At the time, Millie had been nervous about spending hours alone in a wagon with the woman. Today, though, Millie's relief at getting off the farm, if only for a few hours, made her dizzy.

Caty and Genie were playing together on the rug in front of the fireplace. They were having a party, blocks and horses and dolls all dancing and making noises. Millie was thankful that they had not picked up on her current mood. She wasn't exactly sure what her current mood was, but she knew that at some point, she needed to figure it out and make it better. Just, not today. Today was for getting through. That was all.

She'd run to her room last night just as soon as her faltering legs would carry her. And then this morning, Millie came out of her room later than normal. It had taken all her courage to come out at all. She usually made Adam breakfast, something hot and substantial to see him though a morning of hard work. But, like yesterday, he was already gone. She'd had no chance to remind him that she was going to town today, though he'd been supportive of the idea last week when Edith came over. But, given how early he'd left to avoid her, Millie doubted he would be home before well past sunset. And she should be back in time for supper.

Caty and Genie stopped playing when they heard

the sound of a wagon approaching the house. Caty ran to the window and peeked out. "Edith!"

Millie smiled as she watched them open the door and rush out on the porch. Millie followed, feeling like a rescue party had arrived. She hadn't been back to town since the day she'd married Adam. He kept the farm pretty well supplied, so she didn't exactly have to go right now. But, Edith had declared the need for people and civilization, and today, being able to think about something other than this farm or her marriage sounded like a vacation to Millie.

Edith smiled and waved from the wagon. "Good morning! Are you ready to leave cows and chickens behind for a few hours? Go look at pretty fabric? Eat cake?"

"Cake! Cake! Cake!" Genie clapped each time he shouted the world, stomping his way around in a little circle. This little boy was such a gift. Such a bundle of joy, ready to share his glee with anyone he met.

Caty wasn't yelling about cake like her brother, but her smile took up most of her face, and Millie saw she was rocking back and forth on her feet as though just waiting for the word *go*. This sweet girl was also a gift. Millie's life was not entirely composed of mortification and fear and resentment. There was also a whole lot of love.

Millie made sure she had the money she'd brought with her from Saint Louis. The last bit of currency that she had to her name. She stowed her basket of knitting in the back of the wagon with both kids, and then she climbed up to sit by Edith.

"I have to tell you, Millie, I've been looking forward to this for months. Absolutely months."

"Months? I've only been here a little over a month, and you just told me about the trip last week."

"That may be, but I've still been looking forward to this. Going to town with another woman. Having a chance to talk and just be silly for a day. When Adam told me he was getting remarried, I was happy for him. But, I was even happier for myself, if you want to know the selfish truth."

"Well, I guess I'm glad I could help you out." Millie was smiling, but she was a bit in awe of this woman. She seemed so happy and in charge. So secure.

Millie needed to figure out how to get her questions about drought answered in between the small talk without drawing attention to her concerns. Millie needed answers, but Edith would likely wonder why Millie wasn't directing those questions at Adam. She'd have to be careful not to reveal that these weren't issues she felt she could discuss with her husband. She wasn't in a good place with Adam, but she didn't want to talk badly about him.

"So, Millie, what do you think about living on a farm? Adam told me you had lived in a city for most of your life."

"I actually lived in a city for *all* of my life before moving here. I like the farm. Once I got the hang of the chores, it's been a nice experience."

"I went to Saint Louis once, when I was a little girl. All I remember is the noise. And people being everywhere."

Millie felt an unexpected wave of homesickness rise up. She had not had a good life in the city, but it had been the only home she'd ever known, and there had also been good things that she still missed. Sometimes Millie really wished she could drown out her own thoughts and get lost in a crowd. "Yes, it was loud and crazy. Always."

"But it was home, too, wasn't it?" Edith's voice was incredibly sympathetic.

"Yes. It was."

"If you ever get lonely, you can come visit me. I'm not that far from you, and Adam can show you the way. I could come visit you, too. We can even just do chores and things together." There was a note of yearning in Edith's voice that made Millie realize the woman was lonely herself. That made a lot of sense. She didn't have children, so she was completely by herself during the day.

"I think I would like that, Edith. I do miss talking to another woman. And, I bet you know all kinds of secrets when it comes to being a farm wife. I'd like to steal them."

Edith laughed. "I don't know about that. But the work does go so much faster when you're not alone. That is probably the one thing I miss the most now that Mike and I are on our own. When we first married, he helped my dad farm his land. Mike would go to the fields, and I would spend the day working with my mom and sisters."

"Are they far from here?"

"A few hours. I'm relieved that Mike was able to find land so close, really. He thought we might have to go much farther to find property of our own. I just don't get to see them that often this time of year. Mike doesn't like me making the trip by myself, and he's busy from sunup to sundown."

"Adam, too. It seems like all he does is work in the fields."

"That's typical for this time of year, unfortunately. It'll get better, though. In the winter, you'll probably wish he would get out of the house more." Edith's tone suggested she'd experienced that feeling more than once in prior winters.

Millie intentionally kept her voice as casual as possible, hoping Edith would think she was still just making conversation. "I thought maybe he was working longer hours because of the drought."

"Not really. At least, Mike isn't. I mean, compared to last year, this year hasn't been dry at all."

"I hadn't heard about the drought last year until Adam told me. It was really bad?"

"Oh, it was horrible. All that work and those plants just shriveled up and died. The harvest was the worst one farmers had seen around here in several years."

"I know I have no idea what I'm looking at, but these plants don't look like they're drying up. They look green and healthy. To me, at least."

"Yep. That's how last year was, too, at this point. It's amazing how fast they can turn from that to dead twigs."

Adam would never say he was particularly good with women. To the contrary, his first marriage strongly suggested that he was downright useless with them. But last night was the first time, to his knowledge, that he'd ever made one cry for hours and then run and lock herself in her room to get away from him. It wasn't an experience he ever wanted to repeat.

He needed to figure out what to do and actually do it. No. Adam just needed to do *something*. Last night, he had let her go without protest. This morning, he had left an hour earlier than normal just to avoid her. It needed to end.

And yet, Adam was not at home talking to his wife. He had gone to the fields, worked for several hours and eaten his lunch. Now he was sitting beside the creek, watching the water go by. Trickle by, actually. As summer progressed, the ground became drier and the water level went lower. Adam felt like he was reliving last summer. He closed his eyes and leaned back. *Oh, Lord, we need water. Two years of drought in a row is almost too much to ask us to bear.*

Adam had faith, though. He couldn't explain it, but he felt called to farming. The ranching was practical Adam. The Adam who understood that his family needed a reliable source of income. The Adam who saved for rainy days. Or, not rainy in this situation.

But, the Adam who farmed wasn't practical Adam. The Adam who farmed was a man who didn't care if farming was easy or profitable or even logical. No, that Adam was a man who walked out into the fields and felt as though he was pleasing his Creator. Who felt like God had created him, specifically him, to work this specific piece of land.

Even when it was hard. Even when he failed.

Adam moved his hat to shade his face as he remembered last year. That had been the first time his high hopes for his crops had been unfulfilled. He had been hurt. Upset. Confused. But, he had never considered quitting. Adam's belief that he was a farmer in the being of his soul had not wavered for a second. So, he was a farmer. Then. Today. Tomorrow.

Not all farmers felt the same. He'd met more than one who had quit. Urged him to do the same. Told him he was being foolish.

Thank You for Mike. Thank You so much, Lord. I cannot imagine how lonely I would be right now if you had not sent him to buy the farm next to ours. Mike and Adam had spent hours talking about their calling to work the land. It was one of the great blessings in his life that Adam had a friend who understood.

Mike also had a wife who understood. A wife who trusted him. Who had faith that Mike could both honor his calling and provide for his family.

Adam did not.

Lord, tell me what to do. Please.

"Well now, I was going to see if you wanted to go goof off with me, but I see you're already there."

Adam's hat fell to the ground as he sat up. Mike was sitting atop his horse, openly laughing at him in a way that made Adam actually blush. He hadn't even heard Mike approach, though that horse had surely made some noise.

Adam picked up his hat and put it back on his head. He leaned forward and rested his forearms on his bent knees, trying to look like he was not currently flushed with embarrassment. From the way Mike smirked as he got off his horse and joined him on the ground, Adam knew he wasn't doing a very good job.

"How many hours a day do you spend lounging around daydreaming?" Oh yes, he was smug.

"I wasn't daydreaming." Adam sounded like Caty when she was pouting about getting caught doing something naughty.

"Uh-huh." Mike clearly didn't believe him.

"I wasn't." Adam winced after the words came out of his mouth. Now he sounded angry, and Mike was just teasing him. He sighed, long and deep. "I'm sorry, Mike. I'm just having a rough week."

All the teasing left Mike's voice. "I'm sorry, Adam. Can I help?"

That was Mike. He cared. He showed it. And, he always offered to help.

"No, I'm the one who's sorry. I was just embarrassed. I didn't mean to snap at you."

And like that, they sat in peace there on the bank, watching what was left of the creek. Why was it so hard with Millie and so easy with Mike?

"I'm messing it up, Mike."

Mike just sat there, silent. Supportive. Looking off in the horizon and putting absolutely no pressure on Adam to talk.

"Or maybe I already messed it up when I married Millie. I don't know. It doesn't really matter, because I did marry her."

"Yes. You did." There wasn't any judgment in his

tone, but Mike would never soften the truth. Not even to make a friend feel better. "So, I guess you have a couple of choices. You can either do what it takes to make it work. Or not."

"That's easy for you to say, Mike."

"Maybe. Maybe not. You can't judge another man's marriage."

"Yeah, well, Edith trusts you to take care of her, and you're not afraid that your wife is going to leave you." Again. Adam wanted to say *again*. But, Mike didn't know about his first wife. Everything had happened so quickly after Sarah left, and he'd never told the other man. It certainly wouldn't have changed the outcome.

Mike just sat there, picking long blades of grass and twirling them between his fingers. His body language was hard to read, which was unusual because Mike was about the most open and straightforward man Adam had ever met. Finally Mike dropped the grass and brushed his hands off on the legs of his pants.

"I'm not going to go into specifics, because they are between me and my wife. But you know you're family to us. And I get that things have been really hard. You never talked about it, but I know you and Sarah were not in a good place for a long time before she died. And then she was gone. After that happened, I felt so guilty that I had not done more to help you. That I had let you suffer without ever reaching out to you. I kept quiet because it would have been hard to talk about. And I regret it. So, I'm not doing that again."

Adam couldn't look at Mike. He wasn't saying anything mean or untrue, but it stung to hear that he had not hidden his disastrous first marriage as well as he had thought.

"What I am willing to say is that Edith and I have problems. Real problems." His voice got thicker. "We can't have children. Or, at least, we haven't been able to yet. And I worry about the toll that is taking on her. You were wrong. I do have to worry about my wife leaving. About her just quitting. But that worry doesn't help either one of us."

Adam breathed out hard, not able to come up with any words.

"And sometimes our frustration with the things we can't control bleeds out all over our marriage. We fight. We don't know why things are happening to us. But here is what I do know, Adam. I love my wife. The fear we have is not from God, but our love *is*. And it doesn't make me less of a man to talk about my feelings or say sorry to her. If it helps her, then it helps my marriage." Adam heard Mike swallow. "That's all I know. The manly thing is supporting my wife and giving her what she needs."

There was no way to brush off those words lightly. No way to murmur platitudes. The only thing Adam could do to truly honor what Mike had done by sharing this with him was to honestly think about it. Consider it.

So, he did. And he suspected he would for a good long while.

They sat there for another hour, talking about nothing important. It was a nice break. Adam loved his daily life, but he admitted it felt good to just relax and talk with a friend. Especially a good friend.

When they both stood, Adam groaned as he stretched, his body cramped from sitting on the hard ground.

"You okay there, old man?" Mike's voice was distorted by his own stretching.

"I'm not the one who had to go see a neighbor and take a break from work."

"Ha. Well, I didn't exactly find you hard at work, now did I? Besides, I thought we deserved a break. Both of our wives are in town, probably eating cake if I know Edith at all. And shopping."

Adam had forgotten about that. Millie wasn't at home. She was in town. Or, she had been. Adam looked at the sky and guessed that they were probably on their way home by now. When she got home, he needed to be there, too. He needed to talk to his wife.

Mike headed home, and Adam finished up his work for the day. It wasn't his hardest day, but Adam felt as though he had labored for five days straight. His body was suddenly very, very tired. The past days had taken more than his physical energy. Mentally and emotionally, he was exhausted.

When he got to the house, Adam could smell something delicious coming from inside the cabin. He listened for a second. Silence. No giggling or screaming or the ever-present sound of things being crashed together. Millie and the kids were not back from town yet.

Adam put away his tools and horse. He walked inside the house, missing the sight of Millie at the table with her notebook. His kids running and greeting him.

Adam checked on the roast and was debating trying to sneak some of the delicious-smelling food when he heard Edith's wagon return. He went out to meet them, helped Millie unload her purchases, helped get the children washed up. They ate and went through their normal routine. The interactions between him and Millie weren't earmarked by easy companionship, but they also weren't horrible. It seemed that both of them had decided to pretend that this entire week had never happened. That was good enough to get through the evening with the children. It wasn't going to be enough to get through a lifetime.

For the third night in a row, Adam waited in the family room for Millie to come out of the children's room. For the third night in a row, Adam debated just going to his room. And, for the third night in a row, Adam decided that staying and trying to talk to Millie was what he needed to do. For all of them.

Millie came out and shut the children's door behind her. She stood there, looking at him, and Adam could tell she was as tired of this new nightly routine of drama as he was. Time to break that pattern.

"Will you please sit at the table with me?" Adam wasn't about to ask her to sit in the rocking chair. Not again. Besides, he needed a flat surface for what he was about to do.

"I don't know that I can do all of this again tonight. I don't want to." Her voice was soft, but Adam heard the determination in it.

"Please." He almost broke into a long explanation about how he didn't want to fight with her. But, Adam did not think another emotionally charged conversation would lead to the kind of peaceful evening he was craving. And while he was going to try, truly, there was a limit to the degree to which Adam was going to cut himself open and invite Millie inside.

Millie blew out a breath, an audible long and slow puff that sounded tired and reluctant. But, she came and sat at her usual seat at the table. Instead of sitting in his standard position across from her, Adam moved a chair and sat right next to her. She became very still, but did not get up and leave.

Adam had prepared while Millie was still in with the children. He reached for the paper and pencil he had set on the table, pulling it between the two of them. A blank sheet of paper. Clean. Fresh. New.

He wasn't a big writer, did not do it on a daily basis. And, he was self-conscious writing in front of Millie who obviously read and wrote better than he did. Adam pushed that feeling aside, and concentrated on what he wanted to do.

He wrote *The Beale Family Savings* on the top of the paper. Millie sucked in a quick breath as she read his words, but he kept writing, narrating as he did so.

"So, we have a savings account at the bank in town. Your name is on it, and you have full rights to go in and withdraw as much money as you want." Adam thought about his first wife and almost told Millie not to take money without getting his permission first. But he didn't. They were married as one. She would never trust him if he did not trust her. Trust wasn't something that could be forced, but Adam could act like he trusted Millie and hopefully she would do the same and then one day those actions might be followed by genuine feeling.

He hoped.

Adam made himself keep going. "Here is the amount of money we have in there." He moved the pencil down to the next line. "I also have some cash here in the house. It is in my bedroom, in a box under a loose floorboard under my bed. Here is how much is in the box."

Millie was sitting so still. Was she listening or was she so shocked that none of his words were registering? Adam risked a quick glance at her face. She was staring at the numbers and words he had written. Her voice was a whisper. "Adam. Thank you."

So she *was* listening. He went on to a third row. "We also have things of value that we could sell if we needed to. Here is how many head of cattle we have." He made a list of the last five years. "Here is how much we have made each year when we sold them." He made another column. "Here is how much profit we made each year, after paying for ranch hands and other supplies."

The paper was only half full. The fruit of all of Adam's labor, there in a few roughly scratched letters and numbers. He kept going.

"Here is how much money we lost last year farming." He then made another list of years. "And here is how much we made farming for the years before. This is the profit after deducting the cost of seeds and other supplies."

Almost done. Adam wasn't a write-it-down kind of man, but that didn't mean he was ignorant of his finances. He farmed because he loved it, but he also understood the financial and business realities. These numbers were always in his head, were always there for him to reference.

That was something he had understood this afternoon. He'd been sitting on the hard ground, looking at the trickle of water that was not going to be near enough for the crops, and he'd thought about these figures. Worked it through.

And that was what Millie had been asking for. She wanted to do the same thing he did to reassure himself that all was well. Only, she didn't have the numbers in her head to do that with. So, Adam had realized he needed to give them to her.

He drew a line under the last numbers, big and bold to separate the numbers and figures from what he was going to write next.

"Here is a list of people who would help you if you ever needed it. Not out of obligation. Not because they want something in return. Just because we are a community out here, and we all help each other." He then filled the paper with names, some of them people she had met, like the Potters. Some of the names were currently strangers to her. It didn't matter. They would still help.

There. He was done. He set down the pencil and slid the piece of paper over to sit on the table in front of Millie. Adam's heart was racing as though he'd just run the length of his land. He didn't even know what he hoped Millie's reaction would be. He just knew that he wanted her to believe he was a man who could and would take care of his family. But, he also wanted her to feel safe. To not live in that fear she had shown him last night. Adam never wanted Millie to think she was going to have to give her baby away just so they could both survive.

Millie stared at the paper, and Adam stared at her. She reached out and stroked the paper with her hand. Stroked it. Like it was some kind of precious, amazing thing. Her hands were shaking.

She didn't make a sound.

Chapter Seven

To Do:
Morning routine
Make butter
Knit more things to sell—maybe shawls?
Read farming book
Try to understand my husband

Millie left her notebook on the table and walked back
to her bedroom. It was barely daylight, and both children were still sleeping. This morning had felt more
like the first weeks of her marriage. Unfamiliar. Uncertain. But infinitely better than the last couple of days
when things had been so tense and awkward between
her and Adam.

She'd made Adam breakfast and lunch. Wished him
a good day as he went out the door. Opened her Bible
and spent time trying to find peace and understanding.
Closed her Bible with her questions still unanswered.
Opened her Bible again and read about others who did

not understand, but believed anyway. Closed her Bible and resolved to try.

Then, Millie sat down with her notebook. Usually, she liked to list out every small task she needed to do during the day. Liked to cross them off one by one. Liked to have written proof that she was doing what she had planned. That she was productive.

Today, though, she simply wrote down *morning routine*. She'd been doing that more and more as she became comfortable with all the tasks that made up the first part of her day. She could look at those two words and know what they meant, all the many small tasks that comprised the phrase. The mere fact that Millie had a routine was proof that she was here and trying and succeeding.

Millie's morning sickness had finally ceased. She was spending consistent time with the Lord. She was crossing off more and more items each day. She loved the children, and Millie was certain they loved her, too. Edith was proving to be a good friend and a valuable resource. And she was married to a man who was kind. Who worked hard. Who was trying.

Things were going great. Amazing. Beyond what Millie had ever imagined or plotted out when she'd traveled to marry Adam and begin this life.

So why did she feel as though everything was a disaster? Like she was a failure? Millie didn't know. All she knew was that her stomach had been protesting for days. It had churned when Adam's savings were unknown, and it continued to churn when the savings were known. Nothing felt okay.

Millie went into her room and pulled out the sheet of paper from last night. It was sitting on top of her dresser, propped up where she could see it from her rocking chair and from her bed. She'd woken up more than once last night and looked in its direction. Even though it was dark and she hadn't been able to actually see it, she knew it was there.

Millie brought the paper out to the table and placed it next to her notebook. She ran her fingers over the words, again amazed at their existence. She kept forcing her fingers to pull back, to not smudge Adam's writing. Then, she would look down and realize her fingers were at it again. Touching the lead on paper. Making sure it was real.

Millie opened her notebook and turned to the next clean page. She began to copy Adam's paper. She transferred the numbers and words, placing them in her notebook exactly as they appeared on the page. She copied them once. Then a second time. By the third time, they began to feel real.

Millie was awed that Adam had given her this gift. And, she was absolutely aware that it was a gift. Millie was more mindful than most that women had very little power in this world. Her first husband had refused to discuss his financial situation with her. The one and only time she had asked to look at the store's books, he had been outraged. Had told her it was not her concern. Had strongly implied that she would not understand what she was reading anyway. Millie never asked again. And lived to regret that decision.

But Adam had written the numbers down and given

them to her. And not just numbers. Millie looked at the bottom third of the paper. She couldn't process that list of names right now, so she was going to ignore it.

There would be time enough to deal with it later. Instead, Millie rewrote the numbers a fourth time. Then, she began to do some math.

Adam had not lied when he'd told Millie he had sufficient savings to see them through another drought this year. He had also been spot-on when he'd assured her the ranching and cattle were a reliable source of income, though Millie had learned from Edith that drought could threaten the cattle also. As could a myriad of other things.

To use Adam's words, they would be okay this year. But, Adam was not a rich man. He was obviously frugal. He thought ahead. He believed in saving for the future. But he could not afford to farm year after year if he continued to sustain the kind of losses he'd seen last year. His savings would be dangerously low if this year was as bad as last year. And the savings would be wiped out next year if they had a third drought.

This piece of paper looked like security. But as Millie worked it out, she realized even this tangible safety that she could touch was fleeting. The situation could change in an instant. And after talking to Edith about how this year looked so much like last year, Millie was pretty sure that it would change. Evaporate. Gone up in the literal dust of dry fields and dead plants.

Millie forced herself to take a couple of deep breaths. She had time. This was nothing like when she'd found out her husband was in debt and she was effectively homeless. Millie could handle this, she just needed to stay calm and plan it all out. She turned to the next clean page in her notebook.

Progress Check:
#1: Mr· Robinson agreed to sell my knitting in the store in town· I bought more yarn to make more things· Hopefully, next time I go into town, all my things will have sold and I will be able to sell more·
#2: Adam shared his financial information with me· I know what I'm dealing with now·
#3: Edith answered a lot of my questions about farming and drought· And she helped me find a book in town with more information·

It seemed like she wasn't doing enough, but Millie knew she was not just sitting around waiting for her future to happen. She looked at Caty who was playing with some of Millie's extra yarn. The child had somehow unwound the fiber and was holding in her hand a pile that looked like a giant knot. Genie was having yet another epic battle between blocks and livestock. From the number of wooden cattle and horses that had fallen on their sides, it looked like the blocks were going to win this one.

She was doing what she needed to do to protect her family. All of them. Millie closed her notebook and went to kneel next to Caty.

"What do you have there, Caty-girl?"

Caty looked upset. "It's all stuck together."

Millie used her fingers to gently loosen the strands in the knot. "Oh, this isn't bad. You should see some of the messes I've made with my yarn." She finished unknotting the yarn and handed it back. Millie reached over and picked up another ball of extra yarn, unwinding a good length from it. She started looping the fabric over her fingers, slowly making a chain.

Caty watched her, and Millie slowed down. "This is called finger crocheting. I've always thought it was kind of fun."

Caty began to copy Millie's movements, but frowned in frustration after a minute. "It doesn't look as good as yours."

Millie set her yarn to the side, using her fingers to investigate the chain Caty was creating. "It's just a little loose. I had to practice for a long time before I could get mine to look good. And I was a lot older than you are."

"Really?"

"It's true. I was nearly a teenager when I learned. And I almost quit because it seemed too hard. But, it wasn't."

Caty nodded. "I'm not going to quit. I'm going to practice and practice and practice until I get as good as you are."

"Oh, I know you are. I'm sure you'll get it in no time at all." Millie started working on her own strand again, careful to move slow and with exaggerated movements so Caty could use her as a reference.

"Why did your mama wait so long to teach you?"

Millie forced her fingers to keep going. Caty had no idea that this question was hard for Millie, but the girl certainly knew about the reality of not having a mother. "My mother died when I was little. I learned to knit and crochet from a woman who helped take care of me."

Her teacher had been one of the workers in The Home. The elderly woman was only there for a couple of years, but they were the best years of Millie's time there. Ruth had said that knitting and crocheting could cure almost everything. No matter how bad things got, Ruth believed the situation would be helped by taking sticks and a piece of string and making something beautiful. And she'd been right more often than not.

"My mama died when I was little, too." Caty was looking at the yarn looped over her fingers.

Millie forced her fingers to keep going. Loop over loop. "I know, honey. That's really sad, isn't it?"

Caty nodded, still looking at her hands even though her fingers were no longer looping the strand of yarn.

"Did your daddy marry a new mama?"

This time Millie's hands did still. She wouldn't lie to Caty, but she had to speak carefully to avoid upsetting this sweet girl. At least as much as possible. "My daddy died when I was little, too."

Caty looked at her then, eyes wide. "Your daddy died?"

"He did."

Caty licked her lips. "Where did you live?"

One day Millie would tell Caty her entire story. But not today. There was no way Millie was dragging this precious child into that nightmare. "I lived in a place for kids with no parents. I had lots of people to take care of me."

"Were you sad?"

God, guide my words. Help me to speak truth but not do harm. "I was sometimes. I missed living in a house with a family. But now I get to live in a house with a family again. I get to live with you and Genie. That makes me very happy."

"And Daddy?"

"And Daddy."

Caty scooted closer to Millie, leaning against her as she resumed making her chain. "Okay." Caty reached out and picked up another ball of yarn. "Can we do two colors?"

Millie felt the tightness around her heart start to relax when she realized Caty was done with the hard, emotional conversation. At least for now. "Yes, we can do as many colors as you want."

By the time they were sitting in front of the fire in their usual after-supper routine, Millie was feeling better about things. All the knitting and crocheting she had been doing lately was good for her feeling of control over her future. It was also good for her nerves.

"Are you making baby clothes?"

Millie looked up, trying to stop the flush she felt heating up her cheeks. She wasn't doing anything wrong, but someone needed to tell her body that. "Um, no. I'm making a shawl." She held it up as though Adam actually cared. He was probably just making small talk. Hopefully.

"Oh, that's pretty. What are you going to wear it with?"

Millie stopped breathing. She could just say that she

didn't know yet. Try to brush it off. Figure out a way to answer without lying, but, also without telling the truth.

She didn't want to do that. Millie had done many things to survive in this world that she was not proud of. But she wasn't a liar. Caty, as always, was watching her parents talk. This adorable little girl who loved Millie and for some reason wanted to be just like her.

No. Millie wasn't going to lie.

"I'm not making it for me. I'm going to sell it."

"Sell it? To who?"

Adam did not sound angry. Just curious. He was probably wondering how she could have found someone to sell a shawl to when she didn't really know anyone around here. If the situation had been reversed, she would have been wondering the exact same thing.

"I took some of my knitting into town when I went with Edith. Mr. Robinson liked the pieces I'd brought and agreed to sell them in his store. He is going to keep a percentage of the profit, and I'll get the rest."

"You will?" Adam's voice was still neutral, but his emphasis on the word *you* made chills race up Millie's back. He was always so intentional in referring to his property as *theirs*. His words, and perhaps his mind, firmly held that nothing belonged to just him.

But she had just said the proceeds from her knitting would be *hers*. And they would be. That was the whole point of this knitting endeavor in the first place.

Adam apparently got tired of waiting for Millie to respond. "Okay."

That was a word Adam used all the time, but Millie had never heard him say it like that. This *okay* almost sounded like a challenge. Maybe a resignation? All Millie knew was that she had hurt him. Again.

She was knitting things to sell. To make money. For herself. Of course she was, because why would anything be different today? *I'm tired, God. I know I'm not perfect, but it feels like I'm the only one trying here. That might not be true, but it feels like it.*

"Adam? Can we talk about this later? Please?"

She sounded sorry. She rarely asked him for anything, let alone a chance to talk. And, she was his wife. "Okay. We'll talk later."

She smiled and nodded her thanks.

"Do you want to see what I learned today, Daddy?" Caty's voice was excited, like she'd been waiting for years to ask him that question.

"Absolutely, Caty-girl. What did you learn to do today?"

She spent the next hour showing him how to finger crochet in great detail. Even made him practice on his own fingers, and laughed when he messed it up the first couple of times.

"That's okay, Daddy. I messed it up lots of times, but Millie said that everyone messes up at first. You have to keep on trying and trying and never ever give up until you get it right. That's how you learn things." She sounded like a teacher as she repeated Millie's words. The implication of them beyond finger crocheting was not lost on him.

"Okay, it's time for two children to go to bed. Pick up your toys, please." Millie and Genie had been on the ground building with his blocks. They'd managed to create several towers, many as tall as Genie was.

"Did you get more blocks, Genie-bug?"

"Mama buyed!" He pointed to Millie with a huge smile on his face.

Everyone else in the room froze. Adam had been used to Millie going still as a statue on him, but now he was living the experience himself. Genie's smile faded as he became worried that he'd done something wrong, and he almost joined his family of statues. Almost, because it was probably impossible for Genie to be completely still.

"Daddy?" Caty's voice was a soft vibration where she was sitting in his lap and leaning against his chest. "Are you mad?"

Adam came back to life. "No, baby. No. I was just surprised." He looked to where Millie still sat on the floor. Her eyes were wide, and she was biting her lip. "Come here, Genie-bug." He shifted Caty and gathered both of his children on his lap.

"When I married Millie, she became my wife. And your mama. Do you understand that?"

They both nodded, but Caty was looking at the yarn in her hands instead of at him.

"And she loves you both."

"I do. Very, very much. I love you both so much." Millie's voice wasn't the least bit hesitant, and Adam appreciated her speaking up.

"So, she is your mama. And if you want to call her that, you can. And if you don't want to, you don't have to."

"I love you both, either way. I promise."

Genie was watching them, but it was Caty they were both speaking to. She needed to know that she didn't have to call Millie Mama just because Genie was apparently going to. She also needed to know that she could if she wanted. Caty barely remembered her mom, but some memories still lingered. This was a lot for a child to navigate. Adam was overwhelmingly grateful that he and Millie were united on this issue.

There wasn't much more to say, and Adam didn't want to make a big deal out of it. Well, more than had already been made.

He put Genie back on his feet and moved Caty to where he could cuddle her. "All right, Genie-bug. Why don't you show me some of the new blocks Mama bought you." Bedtime could wait for a few more minutes.

Genie looked at his towers and grinned, pulling out a block from the bottom of the largest tower. It collapsed and fell into the others, which in turn all collapsed. Millie pretended to gasp and flinch as all the towers crashed to piles of rubble on the floor. Adam smiled down as he felt Caty also laughing at her brother's antics.

They looked at the blocks for a few minutes, both Adam and Millie exclaiming over them in exaggerated admiration. Genie beamed. Then, to Adam's relief, Caty wanted to show him the beads and string that Millie had bought her in town to make more necklaces. Adam made sure to be suitably impressed with those also.

Genie yawned and rubbed his eyes, and Adam decided bedtime had been postponed long enough. He sent the kids to get ready, giving Caty an extra squeeze before putting her on her feet. Millie sat on the floor after the kids went to their room.

"Are you stuck down there?" Adam's mood was undeniably good. It felt good to tease her. Even though they had to have yet another hard conversation, this moment was fun. Lighthearted. Adam decided to keep it going for as long as possible.

"I'm almost afraid to find out, to be honest. I lost feeling in my legs after the fourth tower we built, but he was having so much fun I didn't want to stop."

Adam bent down and helped her up, keeping his hands on her arms to make sure she was steady before letting go. They stood there looking at each other, the sounds of children giggling instead of getting ready for bed audible through their open doorway.

"I'm sorry. That came out wrong, earlier. I should have told you about the knitting. And I want to talk to you about the proceeds, but I'm afraid of making you angry."

"Millie—"

"No, I misspoke. Not angry. I'm afraid of disappointing you. Of hurting you. I feel like you're trying and trying and giving and giving while all I am doing is taking. I don't know what's wrong with me. I don't know how to make it better."

The giggling turned to shrieking as Caty ran out of the room chased by Genie. She squeezed in between Millie and Adam, using their bodies as a shelter. Genie ran around and around in circles, sticking his little arms in between them to touch Caty and make her squeal even louder.

Finally, the children were calmed down, changed and tucked into bed after saying prayers. Genie was back to yawning. Most of the time the only secret to getting him to fall asleep was making him actually stay still. Tonight was no exception. Caty didn't look that far behind him, lying on her side with both hands under her face in her usual sleeping position.

Millie kissed them each on the cheek and followed Adam out of the room. It was a welcome break in the pattern that he wasn't out in the family room waiting for her tonight. She shut the door, and they stood there. Neither one seemed to be in such a rush to talk. That sense of urgency was completely gone. Adam loved his children, so much, but right now he really wished they had never come out and interrupted Millie. Getting her to talk was hard enough. Getting her to talk twice in one night would probably be impossible.

Millie sighed, but it didn't sound exasperated. It sounded weary. Maybe frightened, like she was trying to gather up her courage. She had mentioned being afraid of disappointing him. That was a fear Adam wanted to ease.

"Millie, please, let's sit down. I promise I will let you talk without interrupting. And, that's all I want. For you to talk to me. If you can do that, I will do my best to make sure it is all okay."

Millie smiled, shook her head slightly. "You and the word *okay*. It's kind of aggravating." A slight pause as she looked at her empty chair. "It's also very nice to hear sometimes." Millie went and sat down in the chair.

Adam followed, sitting and trying his best to not look at all judgmental or intimidating. He didn't know if he was succeeding. It probably didn't matter, anyway, because Millie wasn't looking at him. She was looking at the table as though the grain of the wood was the most fascinating thing she'd ever seen. But finally she started to talk.

"First, thank you for what you did yesterday. It was an unbelievable gift. I know that. But, I also want to save money. I want to contribute." Millie's voice fell off as she continued to stare at the wood surface.

Adam clenched his jaw and his fists. He wanted to talk. Ask questions. Tell her a few things about how a marriage between a man and a woman out on a farm was supposed to work. But he had told Millie he would listen. So he did so. He would do so. Even if it cracked all of his teeth and made all ten fingers cramp up.

"I said that I wanted to sell my knitting so I could make money. So I could have extra savings. Something to fall back on in case I need it." Another pause. "And that was wrong. I was wrong because there isn't an 'I' anymore. There used to be. But, I married you and became a wife. A mother." Millie's voice cracked. "So, I don't want to sell my knitting so I can have extra emergency money. I want to do it so *we* can. So Caty and Genie can. And, I really hope you don't have a problem with that."

All of the tension left Adam's body. "I don't have a problem with that."

Chapter Eight

To Do:
Morning Routine
Laundry
Go through food in root cellar—how are we doing
with supplies?
Make baby stuff—clothes and blankets
Ask Adam again if the crops are dying?
Learn what dying crops look like

Millie looked at the clock, surprised by how late it already was in the morning. It wasn't intentional, but she had been spending longer and longer with her Bible. When she had first started reading the Bible, back in Saint Louis, Millie had felt like a fraud. Worried that someone would walk in and see her and know that she did not know what she was doing. That she did not feel close to God.

It had been over a year, and Millie was just starting to know what she was doing. Well, at least with the reading part. She had read through the book several times and was beginning to know where to find the passages that would speak to her current mood. It was becoming familiar. Comforting.

Millie looked at her list, and turned her notebook to the next blank page. She didn't pick her pencil back up, though. Her heart began to beat faster as she contemplated the clean white paper. Millie began to see spots, and she forced herself to breathe out a long, slow breath.

Edith had told her all about the hard parts of farming. The fear. Being at the mercy of nature and the commodities market. All the ways it could destroy a man's body and mind. They had covered all of that during the trip into town.

The trip home had been different. Edith said, bluntly, that Millie always focused on how things could go wrong. Looked for the worst possible outcome, expected it to happen, and then assumed she was the only one who could fix it. She suggested Millie try finding the good in her life. Try expecting the best and working at making that happen.

Millie had just stared at Edith at the time, too dumbfounded to even be insulted. How in the world had Edith known that?

Millie had learned over and over that some people were destined for the happily-ever-after and some people were not. And she was not. The first rule of living in The Home was to keep the good things well hidden. Any time Millie had celebrated something good in her life, another person had taken it. Or destroyed it. Or simply left.

But Edith was right. Millie could start to look around and see her blessings instead of her risks. And there were many, large and small. Instead of planning for failure, Millie could plan all the ways things would go right.

She had a little boy who called her Mama. The sweetest little girl who followed and copied her all day long. A baby getting really, really ready to enter this world. And a desire, for the first time in her life, to create some kind of happy home life.

Millie looked at the blank page again. She could list the good things in her life. But not yet. Her hand was not ready to pick up the pencil for that reason today. Maybe tomorrow.

Millie closed the notebook and went to prepare breakfast. The eggs she had gathered this morning were in a bowl, waiting to be cooked for little tummies. She put her skillet on the stove. Picked up an egg. Stopped.

Millie put the egg back in the bowl and set her skillet to the side again. She strode back to the table, plopped down, opened her notebook to that blank page as fast as possible.

Don't think. Don't think. Don't think.

So many of Millie's problems only existed in her mind. And it seemed like the rest of her problems came from using her mind to try to fix them. So now the time had come to use her mind to give herself some peace, and perhaps even a little joy.

Millie made her hand write.

Today I am thankful for:

Her handwriting was not neat. Her words were not centered. This was not going to be a pretty page.

Don't think, she reminded herself. *Just write.*

—The chickens laid eggs for me to gather
—Fresh milk
—Time reading my Bible

Millie looked at the list. It was ridiculous to be so scared of those words. They were not going to hurt her. Writing down the good things in her life would not put those things at risk.

That didn't stop Millie's hands from shaking, though. Or the sweat from rolling down her brow. Millie turned the page, ashamed at the irrational relief that flooded her body once the gratitude list was hidden.

She picked up her glass of water and drank until it was empty. Her mouth still felt as dry as the drought that plagued her nightmares. The drought that Millie still felt compelled to try to plan a way around.

The planning helped with her anxiety. It did. And Millie needed that help right now. But, Edith's point was still valid. Still ringing in Millie's ears.

Okay. Focus on positive things that could happen. Millie wiped her palms off on her skirt and picked the pencil back up.

Things Adam could do other than farming:

Banker—he is good with numbers and money
Sell seeds—he has lots of experience
Make furniture/work in a mill—he is good with
wood and tools
Learn a specialized trade—other people learn
Become a full-time rancher—but still risky

"Mama!" Millie closed her notebook and looked at the little boy standing in the doorway—her little boy—with a smile. It was time to move on from planning to actual doing. For now, anyway.

"Good morning, Genie-bug." Millie held out her arms, relishing the way Genie ran into them. The way he snuggled up to her, close and warm. "How did you sleep?"

"Good." Genie's breath was hot against her neck where he had nestled his head. He always hopped out of bed as soon as possible, but that didn't mean he was ready to be awake and start his day. More often than not he got out of bed to come doze against Millie for an extra half hour or so. Millie leaned back in the chair, trying to accommodate both the child in her womb and the one treating her like the most comfortable bed ever made. Any discomfort in her back was more than off-set by the absolute pleasure these early morning moments gave her.

"Good morning, Millie." Caty's voice was quiet as she stood in the doorway in her white cotton nightgown.

This was new. Caty usually had to be coaxed out of bed in the mornings. "Hi there, Caty-girl. Why are you out of bed so early?"

"I'm hungry." Caty's face was flushed, and Millie laughed.

"I'm starving, too. Do eggs sound good?"

Caty nodded. "Can I help?"

Millie usually woke Caty after she made breakfast, so Caty had never helped with breakfast before. "Absolutely. Let me get Genie settled and then I'll teach you the secret to perfect scrambled eggs."

Millie set Genie on his feet and kissed his warm cheek. "Why don't you go play with your blocks, baby."

He nodded and made his way over to the basket holding his toys.

Millie put the bowl of eggs she'd gathered that morning on the table. She got a second bowl and moved the chair so Caty could reach a little easier. "All right, Caty-girl. We need to crack some eggs." Caty almost scrambled to kneel in the chair and reach for the first egg. "Whoa there, honey. Let me get you an apron first." Millie tied one of the smaller aprons over the front of Caty's nightgown, doing her best to shield the child's clothes from the mess that was sure to follow.

It only took one crack of an egg against a bowl for Genie to abandon his toys and come over to help. Millie resigned herself to having to clean this area after they were done and pulled over a second chair. How could she possibly deny the boy who loved to crash things together more than anything else in the world the chance to crack eggs against a bowl? She couldn't.

Once they'd eaten and cleaned up the raw egg that had splattered an astonishing distance from the table, Millie and the kids made their way through the day.

Millie was almost irritated with all the words of gratitude that leapt into her head. Millie noticed all the food
still in the root cellar and realized they could make that
food last for probably a year. She appreciated the cool-
ness of the water as she did laundry. The feel of sunshine on her back as she hung the clothes to dry. Millie
catalogued the laugher of her children.

So much. Too much. Her blessings were too many
to hide and too many to protect.

The morning passed quickly and the heat became
intense. Even then, Millie found herself appreciating
that they got all the chores done in the morning. The
satisfaction in a simple lunch. The size of the family
room that allowed the children to play while she knitted.

The words would not leave her mind, and Millie
would glance occasionally at her notebook sitting at
her place at the table. The pencil right next to it. But
she shook her head and used that restlessness to rock
her chair.

Genie was asleep on the floor, a block in one hand
and a wooden cow in another. One arm stretched out
over his head, the other splayed to the side. The child
seemed to either be terrorizing his imaginary worlds
or tired out. Millie had yet to see any kind of modera-
tion from him in that respect. Caty was still holding
on to wakefulness, but Millie noticed her movements
brushing her doll's hair were getting slower and slower.

Millie was just about to get up and put the kids down
for their nap, or in Genie's case to finish his nap in
an actual bed, when the front door opened, and Adam
walked in. Millie stopped midrock. The only time he

had come home early had been to help their neighbor move. Was something wrong?

Adam stopped with the door still open, smiling at the sight of Genie asleep on the floor. He looked at Caty and held a finger up to his lips. Adam winked at Millie, walked over and picked up Caty, and took her into the children's bedroom.

Millie felt something move inside at that wink. Probably the baby. Certainly not a reaction to that ridiculous man who winked at her. Really.

Millie heard murmuring coming from the bedroom, and then Adam came out a few minutes later. He bent down and picked up Genie, carefully gathering his arms and making it look a lot easier than it felt whenever Millie tried to do the same.

Millie resumed her rocking, though this time it was a slow and deliberate motion, perhaps, a way to soothe the worry that was trying to rise up and take over. Just why had Adam returned home in the middle of the day?

Adam came out of the children's room, shutting the door. Millie stopped rocking. The two of them were back to staring at one another. They really needed to find a different way to pass the time.

"Is everything okay?" It was weakness to ask. But she wanted to know, and she wanted to fill the space between them with something.

"Everything is very okay." Adam's voice was almost consoling. "I just thought I might come work here for a bit. Do you care if I do that? It'll probably be a little noisy and make a mess. I don't think it will wake the kids."

Adam was asking her for permission to do some-

YOUR PARTICIPATION IS REQUESTED!

Dear Reader,

Since you are a lover of our books – we would like to get to know you!

Inside you will find a short Reader's Survey. Sharing your answers with us will help our editorial staff understand who you are and what activities you enjoy.

To thank you for your participation, we would like to send you 2 books and 2 gifts – **ABSOLUTELY FREE!**

Enjoy your gifts with our appreciation,

Pam Powers

SEE INSIDE FOR READER'S SURVEY

For Your Reading Pleasure...

We'll send you 2 books and 2 gifts
ABSOLUTELY FREE
just for completing our Reader's Survey!

YOUR READER'S SURVEY "THANK YOU" FREE GIFTS INCLUDE:

▶ 2 FREE books

▶ 2 lovely surprise gifts

PLEASE FILL IN THE CIRCLES COMPLETELY TO RESPOND

1) What type of fiction books do you enjoy reading? (Check all that apply)
- ○ Suspense/Thrillers
- ○ Action/Adventure
- ○ Modern-day Romances
- ○ Historical Romance
- ○ Humor
- ○ Paranormal Romance

2) What attracted you most to the last fiction book you purchased on impulse?
- ○ The Title
- ○ The Cover
- ○ The Author
- ○ The Story

3) What is usually the greatest influencer when you plan to buy a book?
- ○ Advertising
- ○ Referral
- ○ Book Review

4) How often do you access the internet?
- ○ Daily
- ○ Weekly
- ○ Monthly
- ○ Rarely or never

5) How many NEW paperback fiction novels have you purchased in the past 3 months?
- ○ 0 - 2
- ○ 3 - 6
- ○ 7 or more

YES! I have completed the Reader's Survey. Please send me the 2 FREE books and 2 FREE gifts (gifts are worth about $10 retail) for which I qualify. I understand that I am under no obligation to purchase any books, as explained on the back of this card.

102/302 IDL GLPD

FIRST NAME	LAST NAME

ADDRESS

APT.#	CITY

STATE/PROV.	ZIP/POSTAL CODE

thing in his house? "Of course you can do whatever you want in here." She glanced at the closed door to the kids' room, trying to express the irony that washed over her. "I have some experience with messes and noise inside the house."

She'd said yes. He could feel his shoulders slump in relief.

It was his house, and Adam knew many men would never have asked their wives for permission to stay inside their own homes. Adam didn't care. He had built this house to keep his family safe, and that family included Millie. During the day, without him being there, this house was one of her safe places. He had not come home and disturbed that without a great deal of thought.

"I'm just going out to the barn. I'll be right back."

It did not take him long to gather what he wanted. Adam had spent all morning going over his marriage with Millie in his head. Their conversations. The way they seemed to make huge leaps forward and then run backward so fast that it made his head hurt. What was possible with respect to his marriage and what he wanted.

Friendship seemed like such a mild word. Tame. But Adam knew it could be rich and fulfilling. He wanted that with Millie. That meant they needed to spend time together. Actually talk to one another without the conversation being so emotional it bordered on traumatic.

There was work to be done in the fields, but there was also work to be done at home. And, today, Adam had not felt called to be in the fields. He'd felt called to be in his home.

Adam came back inside with his supplies and set up at the kitchen table. Millie's notebook was there, as always. His tools made a clunking noise when he set them down, and Adam saw Millie watching him with curious eyes. Sitting down, Adam looked at the wood he had selected for this project. It had a lovely grain that Adam knew would be deep and warm when he was finished with it.

He picked up a piece and began to work with his knife, slowly shaving away the outer layers. Seeing what was inside and what he would reveal. This was a familiar movement for his hands. Adam was thankful this did not require all of his concentration, because he needed to be able to think. Adam wanted to have a nice, normal conversation with Millie. He just couldn't think of anything nice or normal to talk about. Not yet, anyway.

Adam's shoulders lowered, relaxed as he began to whittle. His breathing slowed. He saw from the corner of his eye as Millie began to rock. The sound of his knife gently shaping the wood was joined by her knitting needles clacking against each other. The room felt incredibly calm. Nice.

Millie reached down and changed out yarn. She had been working with a deep blue, but this new color was yellow.

"What are you making?"

"It's a blanket for the baby."

Adam stopped whittling for a minute and looked as she held up the project. He saw the pattern she'd made with the blue, some kind of braiding. "What is the yellow going to be?"

"It's the trim."

"Trim? You're almost done?"

Millie spread the blanket out on her lap and looked at it. "I thought I was. Does it not look okay?"

"Oh, it looks nice. I like the braid thing you did. It just looks…small." And it did. That little square of knitted material looked incredibly small.

Millie laughed. Adam tried not to stare, but the sound was carefree joy such as he'd rarely heard from her before. He liked it.

"Babies are small. They don't need huge blankets." She was teasing him.

"You would think I'd remember that, but I forget. It just seems impossible that Caty and Genie were once that small."

"Well, they were. And this baby will be that small, too. He or she had better be at least, especially if I'm giving birth to him or her."

Now Adam laughed. He knew Millie was smart. Knew she was kind. But, he was relishing this wit of hers.

"No feelings about whether you're giving us a son or a daughter?"

Millie moved one hand to rub her stomach, a gentle mother's touch. "I wish, though if I did have a feeling it would probably be wrong. For the first few months I was pretty sure I was carrying a tornado. I still wonder some days. This child is definitely an attention seeker. He or she spends the days, and nights, reminding me that it exists. And boy, does it exist."

Adam laughed. "So, you're saying we're in trouble here."

"Oh, we're in so much trouble. I suspect that this baby will make Genie look like a calm child."

"Okay, now I'm scared." He wasn't serious. Well, he wasn't completely serious.

Millie laughed again, that glorious sound. "Me, too."

They both went back to their tasks, but it felt easier. The rhythm of repetitive sounds and repetitive motion made the room feel peaceful. His soul was serene.

"I've never seen anyone whittle before."

Adam looked at Millie and smiled. "Not a lot of whittling going on in the city, huh?"

"If there was, I sure never saw it. It doesn't even look like you're touching the wood with the knife, but I see the shavings on the floor so I know you are."

"It's funny like that. Sometimes I feel like whittling is an act of pure faith. I can see what I want the wood to look like in my head, but I never see it actually turn into that. It's like I work and work and nothing happens and then suddenly it's done."

"What are you making?"

Adam paused, looking at the wood in his hand and what he wanted it to be. "It's going to be a cradle for our baby."

Millie stopped knitting and just stared at the wood in Adam's hands. He couldn't read her facial expression. "A cradle?"

Adam went back to whittling, trying to make this a normal conversation. Wanting this to be a normal moment in their lives. "Yes. The baby will need a place to sleep, and I figured I better get started before I run out of time."

Millie still wasn't knitting. "Isn't that a lot of work?"

"Not too much, not really."

Millie set the knitting down altogether in her lap. "The baby could just sleep in a drawer. Maybe a basket? The mothers I knew in Saint Louis did that a lot."

Her words made it sound like she didn't want the cradle, but Adam would have had to be blind to miss the yearning in her eyes. Why the contradiction? He wasn't surprised to be confused by this woman yet again. "I want to do this."

Millie abruptly moved her head, looking at his face instead of the piece of wood he was holding. "Did you make one for Caty and Genie?"

Adam smiled, remembering. "I did."

"You made them each a cradle or one cradle that both of them used?"

Adam had no idea where she was going with this, but he was glad she was talking. "I made the cradle before Caty was born and then we used it again for Genie."

"We could use that one for this baby."

Adam set the wood down, still thinking about the past. This time, the memories were not ones he wanted to savor. "We can't. We don't have it anymore."

"You don't? What happened to it?"

Adam wanted to lie, say that it had gotten damaged accidentally or that they'd given it away to a neighbor. But he couldn't let himself do that, even if it did feel like the easy solution for right now. He was in this for the rest of his life. Hopefully for several decades. Eventually, the children would grow up. Move out. Start their own lives. And he and Millie would still be married. They needed honesty to build a strong marriage. Adam looked at the floor. He would tell Millie as much as he could.

"After my first wife died, I was upset. I destroyed a lot of things that made me think of her. Including the cradle. Actually, all of the baby things." He kept his gaze on the floor, looking at the marks on his work boots. "It was a rash thing to do. But I did."

He breathed in deeply and sat up in his chair. Picked back up the wood and considered what it would become. Not to the baby, but to him. It would become a lot. "Even if it hadn't, though, I would want to make a new cradle. It's important to me, Millie."

"Why?"

"I am going to be this baby's father from the moment he or she is born. I am. I want to be. But the truth is that I am not the father who created this child. That is not going to be a secret. So, I will have a child that I love, a child who will probably one day wonder if I love him or her the same as I love Caty and Genie. I want to make sure this new child knows that the answer is yes." Adam looked at the wood and saw the spindles he would create. Imagined the base that would rock his child. Soothe his child. Protect his child. "Please let me do this. It's important to me."

Millie picked up her knitting. The clicking of needle against needle started back up. "Okay. Thank you, Adam. A cradle would be lovely."

Chapter Nine

To Do:
Plan another trip to town with Edith
Start canning fruits and vegetables
Make Caty a new dress
Make Genie new pants
Make something for Adam?

Millie unrolled the cradle spindles that Adam had wrapped up in a heavy cloth. Set them out on the table. Picked one up and stared at it with almost wonder. Adam had taken blocks of rough wood and made them into gleaming vines. Had spent hours and hours and hours using his knife to make tiny little cuts. Small actions that somehow transformed ordinary wood into something so beautiful it took Millie's breath away.

In the last month, Adam had completed twenty spindles, ten for each side. He'd started the headboard piece a couple of days ago. It still mainly looked like an ordinary piece of wood to Millie but she knew that Adam saw something special underneath. He'd told Millie that he did not create so much as uncover what was already there.

Even if he wanted to make a cradle for their baby, he didn't have to do this. He could have made a basic cradle. Something simple. It would have still been something that he made, but it wouldn't have taken all of this time or all of this effort.

This cradle wasn't just a place for their baby to sleep. This cradle was pure love, and not just for the baby. It was for her, too. There was no way for Millie to look at these pieces of wood and not feel like she was important. Like she was worth something.

She'd written this cradle down in her gratitude list every single day since Adam had first walked in the door with his tools. It was more than the structure. It was the time. Millie counted the time when Adam worked on the cradle as the best part of the day.

Some days he came home right after lunch, and other days he didn't get home until suppertime. It didn't matter. He walked in the door, usually covered in dirt. Usually drenched with sweat. But after he came in and spent time with his children, he then sat down and worked on the cradle.

If he wasn't home when she put the children down for their nap, she spent the time knitting. And listening for the sound of Adam's horse coming in from the fields.

Once he was there, once she wasn't trying to listen to every sound in anticipation for his arrival, then she did any number of chores from her list while he worked. Sometimes she cooked supper. Mended clothes.

Churned butter. It didn't matter what she did, really. Millie just liked being in the same room as Adam. Liked talking with him about his day. Liked it even when they didn't talk at all.

Millie ran her fingers over the spindles one last time and then put them back. She'd just put the kids down for their nap, and Adam could be home at any time. She sat down in her chair, pulled out her knitting and waited. This piece was a scarf for Caty. Millie planned to give it to her for Christmas. The yarn was bright red and soft.

It had been hard to get the yarn home and work it up without Caty finding it, but she had. Millie just knew that Caty was going to love it. She could wear it when winter came in with its snow and wind. It would be something to keep her warm, and remind her that she was loved.

In a way, Millie understood perfectly what Adam was doing with this cradle. She was doing the same thing with yarn. She wanted Genie and Caty to know that she loved them. That she would be with them always. She could have made Caty ten scarves in the time it took to make this one. But, she didn't want Caty to just have any scarf. She wanted her to have *this* scarf.

Millie was working the hardest part of the cable pattern when she paused to listen. That was definitely the horse. Adam was home. She continued knitting until she got to a good stopping point. Millie had just marked her place when Adam came inside.

"Hi, Millie. I'm sure glad to come in the shade."

"I'm sure you are. The sun dried my laundry in about an hour yesterday."

"It's a cooker, that's for sure. I'm going to go wash my face real quick, and then I plan to steal a slice of that pie you made yesterday. I've been dreaming about it since I went to bed last night but I thought you'd frown at me if I ate pie instead of your eggs this morning."

"I'm not sure eating pie for breakfast is the example we want to set for the kids. Genie will know. Even if he never hears or sees you, he will know you ate pie for breakfast. Then, he will demand the same."

Adam chuckled as he walked into his bedroom. "Little terror."

Adam came back out, still wiping his face off with toweling cloth. He pulled out the rough headboard and put it on the table. Adam was looking at it when he almost absently took a bite of the slice of pie and groaned in delight.

Pleasure rose up Millie's throat, coming out of her mouth as a laugh. "If I had known you like pie this much, I would have made it before." Her garden was doing well, and this week's bounty had included strawberries. Lots and lots of strawberries. That, combined with the blackberries and raspberries Adam brought home from the bushes lining one of the fields, left Millie with more berries than she knew what to do with.

So, she'd decided to make pie. She'd been married for three months at this point, but had somehow never made pie. She'd made cake the first week she was here and everyone ate it. Millie was afraid to make something Adam or the children would dislike, so she had stuck to cake.

But berries had been covering every surface of Millie's counters and all she could think about was pie. She had made jelly. Jams. And if only to get her mouth to stop watering, she had made pie.

The pie was an overwhelming success. Millie was pleased as punch and a bit chagrined with herself. Would she have spent the next 50 years never making pie because she did not know for sure that her family would like it?

She might have. But the berries had pushed her in a different direction. Adam had remarked more than once that he had never seen so many berries come in at the same time, especially with the dry soil. Millie's current theory was that God had forced her into making pie. *And thank You, Lord, for that. And the lesson. I'm paying attention, even if I am a slow learner.*

Adam groaned again. "I don't care how far I have to go or how much they cost, I'm buying you more berries when these run out. And we're planting more next year. In fact, I am only planting berries. I'll be the worst farmer but the happiest pie-eating man in the world. You watch and see."

"You're good for my ego, Adam Beale. But I bet you'll be sick of pie by the end of the week."

"I won't. I'm going to sit down and cry like a baby when this pie is gone. I might even throw myself on the ground and kick my feet. I need to watch Genie the next time he's in a temper tantrum mood and take notes. Gotta make sure I get it right."

Millie just shook her head and put away her knitting. Christmas was months away but Caty and Genie were growing right now. They both needed new clothes, sooner rather than later. Millie got the pants she had already cut out and went back to the rocking chair with her sewing box to stitch the seams together. "I can't believe these pants are for Genie. The legs look so long in them."

Adam looked, shaking his head. "I think he's going to catch up to Caty before we know it. I sometimes wonder how that one child can eat so much. The answer is in the inch he seems to gain each day."

Adam groaned again, only this time it was a pained sound, like Adam had hurt himself. "What happened? Did you cut yourself?" Millie was up and on her way to look when Adam answered, his voice as serious as it could be.

"My pie is gone."

She stopped and crossed her arms. "Adam Beale, you are ridiculous."

He looked at her with a solemn face but twinkling eyes. "I take my pie very seriously, Millie."

She shook her head in mock exasperation and sat back down. She couldn't believe he was acting this way over a little pie. And she wished she had made it the first week they'd been married. It would have probably made things easier for them both.

His empty plate put away, Adam sat back down and pulled the headboard to him. He just sat for a few minutes, simply looking. Still.

"Is it not going okay?" she asked.

"Oh no, there's nothing wrong. I'm just listening."

"Um, Adam, how much sun did you get today?"

He smiled in a self-deprecating manner. "I'm perfectly sane. I have an idea of what I want this to look like when I'm done, and I'm checking to make sure it agrees with the plan."

"You'll, uh, let me know if it starts actually talking to you, right?"

"You'll be the first to know."

They both worked quietly for a bit after that. Millie practically basked in the silence. These sounds were now normal. Expected. There weren't any problems that needed to be talked through. Millie didn't feel like she was going to say or do something wrong. They just were…together.

Oh, yes. This was the most perfect Millie's life had ever been. *Thank You, Lord. I'm afraid that this will all fall apart, but I'm trying to focus on the good. And right now in this room is the good. Even if it all ends, I will have the memory of this moment. These last weeks. Thank You, thank You, thank You.*

"I have a question for you."

She looked up, curious instead of terrified. Progress indeed. "What?"

"I thought you would maybe like to come out to the fields with me. See what I do all day. Understand why I love it." A pause. "I'd like to share that with you."

Adam had carefully and patiently shown Millie how all aspects of the house worked. But, the farm and ranch parts were still a mystery to her. "What about the kids?"

"They can come, too. They'll be able to run around and play. I'm sure Genie will find something he can bang together."

"I'd like to go, then. Thank you for asking me." She

smiled, relishing the way she felt free to tease this man. "Although, considering how often you've been looking for ways to come inside this week to get out of the heat, I can't say I'm excited about your timing. Could I learn about farming in the fall?"

Adam didn't respond to her teasing tone. He smiled, but Millie felt her heart constrict at the look on his face. "Sadly, we probably have to go this week or next. I don't think the crops are going to make it much past that point."

Millie didn't know if Adam kept talking after that. Her vision blurred and her ears were ringing. Her body forced her to suck in a deep breath, and spots joined the blur in her eyes. Millie was jerked out of her stupor when the baby moved with such force that Millie thought she might fall out of the chair. Her panic was not making the baby happy.

Millie sat there with both hands on her stomach, trying to soothe the child with a low murmur. "Mama's sorry, darling. It's going to be okay." Millie continued to massage her stomach, thankful it was working to calm the baby down. She looked up from her stomach when Adam's hands joined hers, comforting the child she carried. She just looked at him, crouched there in front of her. Regret on his face.

Millie thought about how perfect the past weeks had been. They had been everything she'd ever wished for as a child. The crops were dying out there and her being upset would not change that. All she could control was how she dealt with the situation, and whether she let her fear tear her happiness in her family apart. So, she could have dead crops and have a family life like she had always dreamed of or she could have dead crops and a dead family life. When she thought about it like that, it was not a hard choice at all.

"I'm sorry. I didn't mean to get so upset. I guess I'd started to get so used to being happy that I didn't remember to worry so much about the drought. I have really enjoyed our time together the past few weeks. I want that to continue. I want that kind of home for our children to grow up in." Millie forced truth to come from her lips. "I want that kind of home for me."

"Me too. I'm sorry I sprung that on you, but I do want you to come and see the crops. See what I do. I'm sad about the crops, but I don't have regrets. I don't. The farm is a form of beauty to me, and I want to share it with you."

Millie didn't want to do it. But, she also didn't want to let Adam down. "Okay. How about tomorrow?"

"Tomorrow? Are you sure?"

"Yes."

Adam nodded. He moved to sit back down in his own chair, and Millie tried not to miss the weight of his hands. He looked down at the wood he'd picked back up. Then at her. "Millie?"

"Yes?"

"Thank you."

Adam sat at the table, watching his children finish eating breakfast and just taking in the general atmosphere of chaos that was present whenever his family gathered together. It was noisy, messy. Really, really noisy. And incredibly messy.

And wonderful. Adam had always loved his family. He'd always loved this house. He'd always loved good food.

But the combination of all three was amazing in a way that he couldn't explain. When Adam had decided to marry Millie, he'd told himself he was doing the best he could for his children and it would be enough. Secretly, Adam had been almost smug. Look what a good thing he was doing.

Adam watched Genie whisper into Millie's ear, getting eggs all over her face where his hands were wrapped around her neck. He had been a fool, believing he was the generous one in the equation. He'd never realized just how much more he'd receive. That vision of the best he could do for his family was a farce. He had congratulated himself on finding a caretaker for his children, but God had seen beyond that. Given them more than they deserved. His children did not have a caretaker. They had a mother.

Adam was pleased to the depths of his gut to be so very, very wrong. Wrong about what life with Millie could be. And wrong about what couldn't be fixed. Adam had spent hours on his knees last night, thinking he had ruined it with his clumsy mouth. Had scoured his Bible this morning for some way to take last night back. To have told Millie about the dying crops in a gentler way. But the solution didn't come from him or his efforts. Millie came out from behind that closed door this morning, eyes red from crying, and she had acted normally. Excited about the day, even though she was probably dreading it. She had fixed it. Not him. Grace and forgiveness tasted like pie this morning.

They finished breakfast, and Adam cleaned up the kitchen while Millie cleaned up Genie. He had the easier task. Done, they left for the fields.

It was early yet, far earlier than the children usually woke. The sun was just rising, and the sky was nothing but pink and blue and promise. This time of day almost felt holy to Adam.

Adam stopped walking, feeling Millie stop next to him. The land was primarily flat, but there were gentle hills. They were on top of one and it offered a fairly good view of bigger fields.

"When I first bought this land, this was all wild ground. Brush and weeds and general mess. Sarah told me I was crazy." Adam saw for a moment the way it had looked back then. "But I was excited, you know? Excited for the chance to take that and turn it into something."

"Sarah didn't want you to be a farmer? Didn't want to move here?"

Oh, that was a question. Adam sighed. "I met her when I lived in the city. She'd never lived on a farm but when I told her my future plans she agreed." How much to tell? How much would be enough for them to stop this seesaw thing they were doing?

"She tried. It took me a few years after her death to understand that, but she did try. Sarah just wasn't happy with this life. I didn't realize how different living out here would be from living in the city."

"Was she afraid the crops would die? That you all would lose the farm?"

That was what Millie was afraid of. That was a logical fear, in Adam's estimation, because the risk was real. It was there. It wasn't enough to stop Adam from continuing to be a farmer, but no one would say Millie was crazy for being afraid.

"No. I don't think so. Funny enough, I'm not sure it ever occurred to her that I might fail."

"She believed in you. I'm… I'm sorry. It must feel like I don't."

Adam turned, wanted to pull Millie into his arms, resisted. "No, Millie. Please." The seesaw was in motion again, and this thing between them was heading back down to the ground. They needed to get off the contraption for good. The kids were screaming and running, chasing each other in the tall grass. Well out of earshot.

"She left me, Millie. Left us."

Millie gasped.

"She was not happy being a farm wife. She did not enjoy being stuck so far away from people. She did not like me coming home covered in dirt. She wasn't worried about the farm or me or even her own children. She was worried about herself."

"She…she left you? Left? As in *left*?"

Millie sounded like she could in no way comprehend the very word. Adam felt shame at ever having thought that Millie would do the same.

"She did. I don't want to really talk about it, but the short version is that I came home and found the kids alone. There was a goodbye note. I went to find her, to bring her back, and I succeeded, eventually. But by the time I caught up with her she was sick. Really sick. She died two days later."

The kids began to run their way, and Adam felt his muscles turn to stone. They veered off again and he forced himself to relax. Swallowed and looked at Millie.

She was watching the kids and a single tear was rolling down her cheek. "She left the children?"

Adam swallowed again. "She did." And him. Sarah had also left him.

"I could never leave the children, Adam. I hope you know that."

Adam was done talking about his greatest failure. This whole idea, this whole yearning to bring her out here and show her the fields was because Adam wanted Millie to see the ground he loved. Wanted to share it with her.

He was so tired of dramatic conversations. Adam was ready for steady. Uneventful. Routine. Farming was all about rhythms and cycles. Predictable repetition.

"It took me months to clear the land," he said, relieved when she didn't interrupt him or question the change in subject. "I started up there, because that seemed to be where the ground was the rockiest. I thought if I did the hardest part first, the rest would seem easy." He pointed as he spoke.

Millie looked out to where he had indicated, shielding her eyes with her hand. "What time of year was it?"

She was willing to move along, too. Adam felt victory in his blood.

"Well, I bought the land in winter. It was covered in

snow and looked just about perfect. The man who sold it to me was honest about what I would find when the snow cover melted, but I didn't exactly believe him."

"You thought he would make his land sound worse than it actually was?" She was teasing him again.

"I know, that sounds ridiculous, but I had this romantic idea in my head. Needless to say, the snow melted and I was faced with reality. And reality was a lot rockier and thornier than I'd imagined."

Millie laughed, lowering her hand to cover her mouth and muffle the sound. "Oh, Adam. I wish I could have seen your face."

"Well, no one could see my face under all the dirt and blood for a good long while after that. Did I mention the thorns?"

Millie didn't even try to muffle her laughter this time. Adam highly suspected the Potters could hear it from their place. It was a beautiful sound, the kind of happy that made others want to come and soak it in. Both children ran up toward her, moving as fast as their little legs would carry them.

"Millie, Millie! What's so funny?" Caty came to a stop right in front of Millie, managing to say one word in between each puff of breath.

Genie didn't stop until he ran full force into Millie. "Mama!"

Adam hustled to get behind Millie and take the brunt of Genie's impact, keeping her from falling to the ground. Even so, she made an *oof* sound that sent Adam's blood racing.

"Eugene Robert Beale."

Everyone's smiles disappeared at Adam's tone. Genie stepped back from Millie, his lower lip wobbling.

Millie tried to reach out for Genie, her tone almost pleading. "I'm okay, Adam. He didn't do it on purpose and he didn't hurt me."

"Eugene, come here right now." Adam moved from behind Millie and pointed to a spot in front of where he was now standing. The boy complied, though that wobble increased and tears were welling up in his eyes. Adam squatted down until he was level with his son. "I know you did not mean to, but you hurt Mama. You could have really hurt her and the new baby."

"Sorrrrrrry!" The word was a wail as the tears began to pour down his face. Adam felt terrible, but his little boy needed to learn to not always be so rough with things. And people. He was only going to get bigger and stronger, and he needed to learn this lesson now.

Adam put his hands on Genie's shoulders but did not pull him for a hug or wipe away the tears. Not yet. "I know you are sorry. But, sorry won't fix it if you hurt someone. Genie, you need to be careful. Be gentle."

"I will." He was nodding his head emphatically as he spoke, every bit of his demeanor relaying his sincerity.

"Okay." Adam pulled the boy into his arms and stood, rubbing his back as Genie's hot breath and hot tears almost seemed to burrow in his neck. Millie came forward, rubbing Genie's back and leaning in to whisper that she loved him.

Genie sat up and looked at her. "Sorry, Mama."

"Oh, honey, it's okay." She smiled and it only looked

a little bit forced. "It's a good thing Daddy is so fast and strong, isn't it? I bet you'll be just like him someday."

Genie nodded and leaned over to give Millie a hug. Millie reached to take Genie completely out of Adam's arms. Adam hesitated, unsure she needed to be holding someone so heavy this far into her pregnancy. He reconsidered in a hurry when he saw the look she was giving him. Millie looked almost ready to fight him for Genie.

Adam let go and Millie walked a few steps away, snuggling Genie and whispering in his ear. Caty wandered after her, not saying anything, just standing a few feet away. Millie set Genie down and moved to her knees. She whispered to both kids, and they giggled. Then, as one, both Caty and Genie turned and ran as fast they could. Millie watched them, smiling, until Caty reached a tree in the distance and started yelling that she won.

They quickly became engrossed in a game of tag, and Millie tried to get up off the ground. Adam came to her side, ready to help her. She ignored his hand, and tried again. Then, she just sat down all the way, leaning back on her hands.

They were at it again, but this time the conflict didn't feel like being stuck on a child's seesaw. This felt like the same kind of mad Adam had witnessed between his mother and father.

"Millie, I can't just let him run into people full force. He needs to learn to think."

Her voice when she replied was cold, even though Adam could see sweat running down her neck. "He's just a little boy. He was excited. He wasn't doing anything wrong."

"He needs to learn to control himself."

"I say he was fine."

Adam looked at her, exasperated. "If I hadn't been there, he would have knocked you completely to the ground, Millie. Not on purpose, I know. But, still. He's old enough to control his body."

"You were mean to him."

"No. I was a father to him."

"Yeah, well, I didn't like it."

She sounded petulant. From the way she forced herself to uncross the arms that had somehow crossed when she was talking, Millie realized it, too.

"Of course you didn't."

The arms recrossed and petulance changed into anger complete with narrowed eyes. "What is that supposed to mean?"

"You'll always be on his side. You're his mother." He left it at that.

Millie stared at him hard for a second. Adam tried to resist smiling as an embarrassed flush seemed to bloom from her neck up to her cheeks. "Yeah, well, don't you forget it."

He wouldn't. But would she remember that she was also his wife? And did he want her to?

Chapter Ten

Things I'm grateful for today:
Genie calling me Mama
Caty asking me to do her hair like I do mine

Millie looked at the list and fought the urge to rip the page out of her notebook. Specifically identifying the good things in her life still felt dangerous. As if by putting all the things that gave her joy down on paper she would somehow lose them all. When she had mumbled her concern to Edith, the woman had completely shocked her by understanding.

"Me, too. It took me a long time to put people on my list. But, God knows what is in your heart. He knows the real list. And He's not a God who takes away the things people care about most for fun. I might not know why things happen the way they do, but I believe He has a reason."

Two weeks had passed since then. Two weeks full of

time with her children. Adam finishing the cradle. Him teaching her how to ride a horse. Two weeks of wonder.

How could Millie list the good things in her life and not list people? The list was a lie without them.

The last two weeks had also been filled with watching the crops droop. Wither. Start to turn from green to a sickly brown. Even though she wasn't an expert, Millie knew the poor plants were all but screaming signs of distress. And yet they still lived. Adam's estimate of them making it only a couple of weeks without rain had been wrong. They were definitely dying, but weren't dead. Yet.

Millie closed her notebook and set it aside when she heard Adam go into the barn. "Caty. Genie. Daddy's home. Clean up your toys and help me set the table for supper, please."

The children did as she asked, and the table was set and ready by the time Adam came inside.

"Hello, Beale Family. How are you all on this fine day?" Adam was obviously trying for a light mood, but he looked tired. And filthy.

"Daddy, you need a bath." Caty's voice was serious as ever as she looked at her father's clothes. Clothes that had been colors other than brown when he'd left the house early this morning.

"A bath? What are you talking about, Caty-girl? I'm clean as a whistle."

"No, Daddy."

Adam's eyes looked big and white in his dirt-caked face. Had he rolled around in mud today? "Well, lucky for me today is not bath day. Saved again."

Caty crossed her arms, looking at her dad with narrowed eyes. And, unlike her brother who had run up for a hug, Caty kept her distance from the dirt and grime. "Mama says you have to take a bath when you're dirty, even if you just had a bath."

This was only a few days old. Though Caty was not calling Millie Mama to her face, she had started referring to Millie as Mama when talking about her to other people. Millie and Adam were trying to not make a big deal out of it. Trying to not draw attention to it or make Caty self-conscious. Millie wanted the girl to do what made her comfortable, even if that meant she never called Millie Mama directly.

But Millie sure loved hearing that word come out of her daughter's mouth.

"Oh, Mama said that, did she? And Mama is the boss?"

"We're supposed to listen to her. You said so."

Adam rubbed a hand over his chin, pretending to think about it. "Well, then. I suppose I'd better go and wash up. Wouldn't want Mama cross with me. But I need a hug and a kiss before I go. I missed you all day long."

Caty began to back up, nervously looking at her father to see if he was serious.

He was.

"Daddy, you're going to get me dirty."

"I have it on good authority that you'll wash clean just fine. Didn't you miss me at all today?"

"I missed you, Daddy. I'll give you lots of hugs and kisses when you are clean."

"Okay," Adam turned and took a step toward his bedroom. Then he quickly lunged and scooped Caty up in his arms. "Oh, look. I found a Caty-girl."

Caty squealed, trying to get away. Adam growled, rubbing his face on Caty. "No, Daddy, no!"

"What was that? My Caty-girl wants me to tickle her? Okay then." Adam proceeded to tickle Caty, and her squeals quickly became gasps as she was laughing almost too hard to breathe. Genie's grin was huge in his face, and he was clapping his hands together in delight.

Adam stopped tickling Caty and looked at Millie. His face was significantly cleaner, but dirt still streaked here and there. "Well? Am I clean enough for supper now?"

Millie shook her head and crossed her arms. "Nope. From where I'm standing, the only people clean enough to eat supper are me and Genie." Genie smiled and nodded his head up and down as fast as he could.

"Mama! He got me dirty!"

Millie told herself to not react to Caty calling her Mama, but she had a hitch in her voice when she replied. "Yes he did, baby. You're right. Okay, how about I help you clean up and then you can eat supper, too? Why don't you go ahead and get started on putting on your nightclothes. I'll come help you in a second."

Caty ran from the room, and Millie looked at Adam, wondering if his heart also felt like it was going to explode. His smile was tender. It spoke to her.

"Well, I better get cleaned up, too, I guess. Genie? Will you please make sure these two don't eat all the supper? Save some for your good old dad?"

Genie's little chest puffed up, and he nodded. He

walked over and stood in front of the pots on the stove, crossing his arms and looking so serious that Millie burst out laughing. Adam was chuckling and shaking his head as he walked into his room to clean up.

Millie found Caty in her nightclothes but with dirt still all over her face. She didn't hate washing up as much as Genie did, but she also wasn't a huge fan of it.

"Good job changing clothes, Caty. Let's get that dirt off your face and we'll be ready for supper."

Caty stood still as Millie washed her face, scrunching up her nose as Millie dipped the cloth and water again and went back for a second pass. "Daddy is silly."

"Yes he is, honey. But don't you worry, we're going to beat him and eat all the supper."

Caty chewed on her lip, another entirely too serious expression crossing over her features. "I don't want Daddy to be hungry. He worked really hard all day long."

Millie set the cloth back in the bowl and leaned down to be eye level with Caty. "I'm just kidding, honey. There is so much food that I doubt we could make ourselves eat it all anyway. And you're right. Daddy works very hard for us."

He did. Fear and panic were still bubbling in Millie's stomach, but her worries had nothing to do with Adam being lazy. Unlike his first wife, her anxiety had nothing to do with her life on the farm either. Millie loved being in this house every day. She loved the children. And, she was getting so much better at looking at her life and seeing all the blessings. At not letting her fear about the future ruin her today.

But Millie still worried. She refused to allow herself to make intentional lists about it. She refused to hold herself back from these children because of it. But the worry didn't go away. If anything, it dug deeper than ever as she realized that her options for protecting herself were limited because she would never consider leaving these kids.

Millie shook her head slightly and bent down to kiss Caty's cheek. "There, all clean. Let's go see what kind of chaos your brother is causing, shall we?"

Millie started to leave the room and felt her heart stutter when Caty reached out and held her hand. The little girl did this frequently. It was still a gift every time.

Genie was spinning in circles when they walked into the room but he quickly resumed his guard position when he saw them. Millie's lips twitched at how he tried to make his face look serious. And how he failed.

"All right, Caty-girl, do I pass inspection now?" Adam was in clean clothes, still rubbing a cloth over his face. His hair was wet and shiny.

Caty nodded and ran to give her father a hug, and Genie joined in. Millie began to dish up food on plates. "Is there any soap left after all you must have used?"

"Oh, a sliver or two. Probably not enough to clean me up tomorrow, sadly."

"I'll put some more out for you after supper." That way, she could hand it to him directly. Millie went into Adam's room as little as possible. Even after months of living here, cleaning and caring for this home, making this home hers, Adam's room felt very much like forbidden territory.

They had never talked about it, but Millie viewed her room as something special just for her. She was not comfortable with Adam being in there, and she actively disliked the thought of him going into her room when she wasn't there, not that he ever had. She felt the same about his room.

Millie couldn't ignore it entirely, though, because it needed to be cleaned. Sheets needed to be changed. The water bowl and pitcher needed to be regularly filled. It was silly, but Millie only went in there when the children were with her. For some reason, it felt safer that way. And there was far less temptation to look around and try to understand the parts of Adam he didn't share with her when she was being watched by a three- and five-year-old.

Millie set the plates of food on the table and took her seat. Adam prayed and the sound of his *Amen* had barely faded from Millie's ears before he took a huge bite of the vegetables she had roasted. He saw her watching him and actually flushed.

"Sorry. I've been dreaming about supper since I finished lunch."

"I didn't send enough food with you?"

Adam took another huge bite, chewing and swallowing so fast that Millie thought he might actually choke. "You did. It was just a long day. Every single animal we own has decided to be stubborn. I think they're plotting against me in unison."

Millie understood better about farming now, but the

ranching was still a bit of a mystery. "I'm not an expert on livestock, but I don't think they actually plot."

Adam swallowed another bite. "They do. There is no other explanation for every single one of them deciding today was the day to stand there and look at me like I'm a fool."

Millie tried to suppress her laugh but failed.

"I saw that, Millie. You better be careful or I'm going to take you with me tomorrow and make you deal with those ornery beasts."

"You have more to do with them tomorrow?" she asked. He nodded as he ate yet another massive bite of food. Adam had stopped coming home in the middle of the day. At first, Millie had thought it was because the cradle was finished. But then Caty had mentioned that she missed seeing him so much, and Adam had said he missed it, too, but that he had some work that needed to get done in the next couple of weeks. After that, he planned to come home as he had been doing.

Millie remembered with shame her thought that he was just making up a story for his daughter. That he was tired of always being in the house with them. But she believed him now. Adam was gone all day, and when he came home he looked like he had fought in a thousand wars.

"What are you doing with the cows, Daddy?" Millie was thankful, again, that Caty asked the question she had been wondering.

"I'm sorting them, Caty-girl."

"For what?"

Adam set down his fork with a serious look on his

face, and Millie's stomach clenched. "I'm going through and deciding which ones to sell."

"Why do you have to sell some?"

Adam glanced at Millie before turning to answer his daughter. Millie put down her fork, too, willing the food she had eaten to stay in her stomach.

"Well, we don't have enough water for them all. It's better to sell some now rather than leave all of them thirsty. But, it's nothing for you to worry about."

"Okay." Caty went back to eating. Genie was humming to himself as he used his fingers to break his biscuit into tiny pieces. Millie and Adam looked at one another across the table, and Millie wished she too were a little girl who could accept with blind faith that her daddy was taking care of things.

Adam waved goodbye at the men taking half his herd to Kansas City. He was so tired he considered a nap right here in the corral. But even with half the herd gone, Adam was still left half to deal with. He needed to get them out to a fresh pasture. Then, he was going to go home.

Home.

He'd had dreams of what would happen inside that wood structure when he'd built it. Dreams of what he had known. A family. Every board he nailed into place was another step toward his ultimate goal.

Then, he had brought his bride there. To live in a place he had literally made for them. Surrounded by the proof that Adam was working toward something. Instead, he ended up watching his wife die there.

And that had been the end of that. Adam would be practical. Settle for the best he could give his children within the circumstances he found himself in. Marry a woman who seemed honest and honorable and hope she would do what she promised.

Adam shook his head as he mounted his horse and signaled the two men waiting that he was ready to start moving the remaining herd. Millie was amazing. The things she had done were amazing. It was a painful truth to admit that she loved his children more than their own mother had. It was a wonderful truth to admit that Millie loved his children like they were her children because in her eyes they really and truly were. She would fight anyone for them. Even him.

It was almost incomprehensible how that had happened. Especially since Millie was carrying her own child. Adam would have thought that she would love the child she was carrying more than the two she married into. But, she didn't. She couldn't. Millie was giving every ounce of love she had to Genie and Caty, and there was no way she was holding back.

He'd been further surprised to discover he felt the same way about her child-to-be. When Millie had first been suggested as a potential second wife, the fact that she was pregnant had given Adam pause. Of course, it explained why she was willing to marry a man she had never met. But Adam recalled wishing she were not pregnant.

And now Adam was excited. He had not made that cradle out of some sense of obligation. He was not trying to placate Millie or win her over. Adam had considered the life growing in her womb. The baby that would be born before the end of the year. A little girl like Caty or a little boy like Genie. A child who would be his.

Adam had looked at the rough wood and seen his child sleeping there. Had looked at the spindles and imagined tiny fingers grasping them. Had made the curved legs so the cradle could rock and saw his child being comforted there.

Adam understood that Millie could love Caty and Genie as her own because he loved this baby as his own. Somehow, in between him avoiding the house and her keeping to herself as much as possible, that had happened.

And then they didn't keep their distance anymore. Adam came home as often as he could during the day to soak up the love that seemed to coat the walls inside. Millie started talking to him without weighing her every word.

Things were good. Inside, at least.

Outside, things were a whole lot harder. Hotter. Drier. But they were going to be okay. He and Mike had spoken after church last week. They were both selling off half their herds. They were both still taking care of the crops in the fields, trying to give the plants the best possible chance of survival. They were both trying to be hopeful for their families, but secretly resigned that most of it would be wasted effort. The crops were not going to make it.

This year. This season. This sense of watching things die would not last. The feeling like a failure was not for forever. They would do the best they could and then they would do it again.

Adam was so thankful for men like Mike in his life. Every week at church, the pews seemed to be a little more empty as family after family called it quits. Moved to the cities. Tried something not dependent on water falling from the sky.

Every week at church, Adam held himself stiff next to Millie. Knowing she saw it, too. Praying she did not suggest they do likewise.

Adam got the cattle settled and wished the ranch hands who had remained a good night. He went home, thankful his horse knew the way. Adam had officially done all that he knew how to do. All that he possibly could do. The money from this sale gave them some security for another year. The crops and the cattle were up to God now.

Adam put his horse away for the night, trying to give the animal the attention it deserved after the difficult weeks they'd had. He walked inside to find Caty, Genie and Millie just standing in the kitchen, smiling at him like they knew a secret he didn't.

"Well, you all look like trouble."

Genie and Caty giggled, and Adam saw Millie's lips twitch. "I'm sure we don't know what you're talking about. We're just waiting on you to get washed up so we can eat supper."

Genie's giggle became a delighted laugh. He opened his mouth, and Caty put a hand over it, muffling whatever he was trying to say. Millie's face twitched again. "You've got to be starving. Why don't you go get clean."

It was the first time she had ever told him to do something. The first time she'd ever ordered him about in the caring, no-nonsense manner she used with the children. He straightened up as though a soldier. "Yes, ma'am."

The water felt blessedly cool against his face as he washed up in his bedroom. Adam tried not to look at the bed, knowing that he would be tempted to lie down, close his eyes and rest for just a minute and that just a minute would turn into sleeping all night long. When Adam walked back into the main room, he saw plates already on the table. Each one was covered with a cloth napkin. His family was definitely plotting something.

Millie whispered to the children, and they all sat, looking at Adam expectantly. He took a second to relish the atmosphere of fun and play that seemed to live in this structure now. Then, he sat down and prayed.

"Dear Lord, we thank You for this day. Thank You for this food and for the energy that went into its preparation. We ask that You continue to bless us as we will continue to praise Your name." Adam looked down at the napkin covering up his plate. "Lord, I also ask that You protect me from whatever trouble these three have concocted. I can tell I'm going to need Your assistance. Amen."

He looked up and saw Millie watching him. "You're something else, Adam Beale."

He winked at her. "Hey, I'm clearly outnumbered here. I need all the help I can get." Adam looked at the napkin. "Am I allowed to take this off?" Both kids nodded their heads furiously, and Adam narrowed his eyes. Looking at their plates. "How about you all go first?"

Millie leaned back in her seat and crossed her arms, resting them on the swell of her stomach. Caty and Genie looked at her and then both of them did the same. Adam decided to play along, and he also leaned back in his seat and crossed his arms.

They all stared at one another until the sound of Adam's stomach growling seemed to echo loudly through the room. He held up his hands in surrender as Caty and Genie laughed so hard they could barely breathe. "Okay, okay. I give up." He pulled the napkin off his plate with a flourish and stared in disbelief. His plate was filled with pie.

A lot of pie.

"Pie for supper!" Genie was actually bouncing up and down in his seat with excitement.

Adam looked at Millie in almost disbelief. "We're seriously having pie for supper?"

She looked embarrassed. "Well, I thought you might like a treat. You've been working so hard for weeks, and I knew you were finishing up today, and the kids and I wanted to do something nice for you to say thank you, and we had a lot of berries left, and I mean, I can make something else real quick if you want, we don't—"

Adam pushed his chair away from the table and hurried over to kneel by where Millie was sitting, still talking nonstop as though she had been caught stealing instead of making him his favorite food for no real reason at all other than she appreciated him and wanted to give him a nice surprise. "Millie, stop." He had a finger over her mouth, but her eyes were still too wide. "I'm sorry. I was just surprised, but in the best possible way. I have never, in all the years I've been alive, had just pie for supper. And I can't remember the last time someone noticed my hard work and wanted to say thank you."

He moved his finger away from her lips and took both of her hands, holding his together around them as if to cradle them. "Thank you, Millie. Thank you."

Her eyes were watery, but she nodded. "I didn't do it alone. Once I convinced Genie and Caty that we should have pie for supper, they were a huge help."

Adam stood up and went back to his seat. He tousled Genie's hair as he walked by and winked at Caty. "Convinced them, huh? I bet Genie said no, didn't he? I bet he cried and begged to not have to have pie for supper." Adam looked at Caty. "You can tell me, Caty-girl. How much of a fit did Genie throw over having to eat pie for supper?"

Caty giggled. "He didn't throw a fit, Daddy."

Adam appeared to be shocked. "What? No fit? You must be joking."

She giggled again and shook her head. Adam saw Millie smiling out of the corner of his eye. She wasn't upset anymore.

That was good. That meant it was time to eat pie. He picked up his fork and took a huge bite, trying to savor the taste as much as possible. It was delicious. Adam thought about all the months that he hadn't known Millie could make pie, and he almost wept. What a waste of delicious pie-eating time.

The kids followed his lead without hesitation, and

Adam smiled as Millie picked up her own fork and began to eat her pie.

Adam was on his third slice, dreaming of how he was going to spend tomorrow sleeping and eating pie and doing only the essential chores, when he heard thunder.

Caty and Genie kept eating, but Millie looked at him with wide eyes. Adam held his breath, trying to stay very still as though that would have some kind of impact on what was happening outside.

Another crash of thunder.

He and Millie put down their forks and raced for the front door. Adam beat her, flinging it open and running down the porch steps to stand in the yard and look up at the sky. It was dark, the moon not visible at all.

The moon should have been visible this time of the month, but it wasn't. It was hidden behind something. Behind clouds.

Millie was a few feet away, also looking at the sky. Caty and Genie came to stand outside, too, staring upward, though Adam wondered if they knew what they were looking for.

A third crack of thunder, and Adam felt it in his bones. Caty jumped and put her hands over her ears. She ran to Millie, who drew her in close. But, Millie never looked down, her face focused on the sheer blackness above as though she could see through it. See what was going to happen next.

Adam blinked when a raindrop almost hit him in the eye. Another on his forehead. The third and fourth came quick, blending with the fifth and sixth and seventh. Adam lost count, drops turning into a stream turning into a downpour.

Caty yelped and ran for the safety of the front porch. Genie clapped and began to spin around in circles, arms held wide. Millie just stood there, getting wet, staring at the sky. Adam went back to doing the same.

Chapter Eleven

Today, I'm thankful for:

Millie looked at her gratitude list with disgust. After going from the pure excitement of seeing rain the night before to the desolate realization that the rain was not going to be enough water to save the crops, she was not feeling very thankful today.

Millie turned the page and looked at the clean sheet, feeling the kind of restlessness in her soul that used to be a constant part of her life. A restlessness that had slowly faded over the past months until it had seemed to disappear altogether. But, obviously not for good, because it was back now, and Millie could barely stand to sit still in her chair.

Millie wanted to yell. She wanted to throw something. Once, in The Home, the matron had discovered a girl had stolen from her. The matron had yelled and ranted and screamed until her face was red and a blood vessel actually burst in her eye. Still, her furor had not been appeased. Then, the matron had begun throwing dishes. Plates. Cups. Bowls. They hit the wall one at a time with a tremendous crash and the tinkling sound of glass scattering across the floor. And, that had somehow worked. The matron had become calmer with each piece thrown. It had worked so well that The Home still had dishes left by the time the matron was done.

The experience had terrified Millie at the time. Her nightmares the following weeks had involved dishes being thrown at her head and with her unable to duck out of the way in time. Today, though, Millie recalled the experience with envy. She looked at the dishes sitting in the cupboard and imagined sending them flying one at a time into the kitchen wall. If the children had not been sleeping in the next room, Millie really thought she would have done it.

The rain had come, and they had danced. Then the rain had stopped. As quickly as it appeared, it was gone. Millie and Adam had stood in the revealed moonlight and looked at the ground.

It wasn't enough. She wasn't a farmer, but she just knew. It wasn't going to be enough.

Millie looked up from where she had been glaring at her notebook when Adam came in the door. He had skipped breakfast this morning, saying he wanted to check the fields. He'd promised to come back with a report, and had said they could eat breakfast then.

Millie stared at his face as he came and sat down at the table, trying to read what he might be thinking as he stayed silent. He had to know she was worried about what was going on with the crops; why wasn't the man talking to her?

Millie started imagining throwing dishes again. Only this time they were not crashing against the kitchen wall. No. Instead, they were hitting her husband in his very hard head. Repeatedly.

Adam exhaled a loud breath that did not quite rise to the level of a sigh.

Millie was done waiting. "Adam?"

"I don't know."

She was supposed to be making breakfast, cracking eggs and melting butter in a skillet. Thinking about what she could make for her husband that he would enjoy. Possibly adding a side of pie. Instead, she was ready to throttle him for his evasive answers and loud breathing.

"What does that mean? You have to know something. You were gone for over an hour."

Adam ran a hand over his face. "The rain didn't last long enough. Didn't go deep enough. But, it was rain. It was water. Not the soaker of my dreams, but maybe just enough of a sip?"

Millie put her hands flat on the table and leaned forward. "What. Does. That. Mean?"

Adam looked at her, his face scrunched in some kind of expression that Millie had never seen before. "I'm not trying to be vague. I promise. Farming is not exact. And it can all change quickly."

"What is your best guess? I won't hold you to it. I just want to know what you think is going to happen."

"I had accepted that the crops were going to die. I'd

done my best and was moving on to minimizing the loss. But that rain did change things. It was enough to keep the crops alive. At least for another couple of weeks. But, I don't know what happens after that. I mean, if it doesn't rain again, the crops will die. And even if we keep getting these little sprinkles, any crop we manage to grow will be small. Probably won't fetch much at market."

Millie sat back, considering his words. She'd asked, and he had answered. Okay then.

Millie stood up and put her skillet on the hot stove. She put a spoonful of butter in there, spreading it to coat the pan. The pies from yesterday were sitting on the side table. They had planned on eating them all day today. Being together all day because Adam was done with his work and waiting was the next step.

They had plans for dead crops and pie, and Millie had been okay with that because she would be with her family. Now there was going to be more work to do. Adam would probably be gone all day today. And tomorrow. The pie would sit uneaten until he staggered in covered in dirt. And the crops might still die. Probably *would* still die if the rain continued as it had for the last months.

Filled with sudden fury, Millie picked up a pie and began to walk without a word to Adam. She strode out the front door, not bothering to close it behind her. She stalked down the porch steps and across the yard toward the barn. Millie managed to open the barn door while still holding the pie, hearing it slam open with a thud that satisfied a grimness in her soul. She was aware of

Adam following her, but Millie did not pause to explain herself. Once inside the barn, safely out of earshot of the two sweet children who were sleeping inside blissfully unaware that life was horrible, Millie used her bare fingers to scoop out a chunk of pie.

And she threw it against the barn wall as hard as she possibly could.

It splattered and began to drip down the wood, chunks falling. The strawberry filling looked a little bit like blood.

It felt good.

Millie scooped out and hurled another handful of pie. Then a third. She was breathing heavily and tears made the mess look like a red blur. Millie was getting ready to launch a fourth throw when strong arms wrapped around her from behind and stopped her.

"Millie. Stop, honey. Stop." He didn't sound angry or horrified that his wife had lost her mind. Instead, he sounded sad. Desperate even.

Millie was gasping, covered in sticky fruit and crust. "It's not fair, Adam. It's not fair." Her voice sounded as raw as her throat felt. Adam managed to turn her around, taking the pan of pie from her hand. She had been gripping it so tightly that her fingers were numb. Adam set the pan down carefully, and the sight of him trying to not make a mess after she had literally coated his barn in pie made her sob even harder.

Hands free, Adam pulled her to him, somehow walking them over to a big pile of straw. He used one hand to kind of shake out a saddle blanket and then he pulled her to sit on the straw next to him. Millie couldn't understand what he was saying over her gasps and the hitches in her crying.

"I don't understand. What is the point? It feels like God is teasing us. If the crops are going to die, why doesn't He just let them die? Why does He keep dragging this out, giving us hope, and then taking it all away? It's mean, and I'm mad." Millie's voice went from despair to fury, and she yelled the last part. Millie wanted to hit someone. She wanted to curl in a ball and never stop crying.

She didn't know what she wanted, she just knew that this needed to end because she could not take any more.

Adam had not cried when his first wife had left him. He hadn't cried when his first wife had died. But he was crying now.

How had he missed this? How had he let Millie reach this level of despair without seeing it? Without helping her? Millie had exploded right in front of his eyes. No. Not exploded. She had disintegrated. Turned herself inside out, losing hope.

Adam's eyes and throat were burning. His skin felt raw where Millie's tears landed. She had quieted down, leaning heavily against him. The only sound was the occasional hiccup in her breathing. Her face was covered in tears, and her hands were covered in pie. She didn't move to wipe away the mess. She didn't move at all.

Adam shifted, moving out from under her. She just leaned against the wall like he had never been there. The concern Adam had felt when she was throwing pie grew in his chest at the sight of her being so still.

He moved quickly, almost running into the house. He walked in to the smell of fire. The pan of butter Millie had left on the stove had burned dry. Adam moved the pan off the heat, thankful that Caty and Genie were still asleep. Leave it to Millie to make sure she broke down in such a way to not alarm her children.

Adam went and got a bowl of water and a clean cloth and walked back to the barn as fast as he could without spilling the water. She was exactly as he had left her.

Adam kneeled down in front of her. "Here, honey, lean forward for me?" She did without a word, and Adam reached around to untie her apron. He took the stained garment off her, leaving her in her shirt and skirt that were thankfully clean underneath. Adam dipped the cloth into the bowl and wrung it out, wishing he had taken the time to warm up the water. He wiped Millie's face, gently moving the cloth over her skin. Once that was clean, he moved on to her hands, holding them one at a time and making sure to get every bit of sticky pie from her skin.

When he was satisfied that she was clean, Adam set the bowl and cloth to the side. She still wasn't moving. Still wasn't talking. "I'll be right back, honey." He murmured the reassurance, realizing he'd left the first time without a word. Had she noticed? Cared?

Adam went to the well and filled the cup with water. He drank it, trying to appease the fire in his throat so he could better help Millie. Then, he filled the cup again and took the water back in the barn to Millie. She was still sitting. Still quiet and motionless. Still sad. Being around her, Adam felt like sadness permeated the air.

He sat back down, moving Millie to lean back against him. She didn't protest. Adam moved the cup up against Millie's lips. "Please take a drink for me, Millie. Please?"

She did. He set the cup down and just held her. Adam rubbed her back and breathed in her hair. It smelled of the flowers in her soap and pie. Adam would never think about pie the same way again.

All Adam knew to do was to hold Millie. Murmur in her ear that she was okay, that everything would be okay. So, he did.

Finally, Millie spoke, her voice rough. "I'm so sorry. That was unforgivable."

He moved slightly, using his hand on her chin to have her face him. "No. You don't have to apologize. You didn't do anything wrong."

She made a distressed noise and moved her face away from him. He let her go. "I stormed out and threw pie all over your barn. I yelled. I—I—I—"

"You got mad at God. You can say it. You still don't have anything to apologize for."

"I threw a giant fit and acted like a child."

Adam considered his words, wanting to give validation to how Millie felt, but also wanting to comfort her. "God understands. He can take you being angry at Him. He loves you no matter what."

She didn't answer.

"And, to be honest, I'm a little angry, too. This drought feels personal. It feels like we are being punished for something, and it is bitterly unfair."

Still no answer, but she was looking at him now and

that was progress. "I've yelled at God before, Millie. I've doubted. I've thought He was mean. That's okay. It's allowed. Faith doesn't mean you have to like whatever happens in your life. It doesn't even mean you have to accept every hardship without strong emotions. Faith is feeling angry and scared and disappointed and believing anyway."

Millie turned to lean against him, her head against his chest. He missed being able to see her face, but this felt almost like she was cuddling against him. And he found that he really liked the thought of Millie leaning against him for comfort.

"Adam, why are we doing this to ourselves?"

"What, Millie? What are we doing?"

"Farming. I know you said you feel called to it, but it hurts. Have you ever tried to do something else? How do you know you wouldn't like something safer if you don't try it?"

If Millie had said those words to him a few months ago, he would have been insulted. Furious. Adam would have thought that Millie was exactly like his first wife. That he had married yet another woman who cared about herself more than anything else.

Thankfully, they were not in the same place they had been a few months ago. Her words left him feeling raw and vulnerable. But they weren't a betrayal. Millie was struggling, and she was asking her husband to help her.

He would.

Adam increased the pressure of his arms wrapped around her, using one hand to hold her head firmly against his chest. Her cheek was resting over his heart, and Adam hoped that she could hear it. That it might soothe her.

"I want to talk for a bit, and I want you to just listen. Can you do that for me, please?"

She gave him the barest nod, pushing against him as though she wanted to burrow into his chest. Adam kissed the top of her head.

"Nothing is safe in life. I'll admit, farming is hard. We can't control the weather or insects or disease."

She didn't say anything, but Adam felt like she was listening. Her breathing had slowed down, and Adam felt it against his body in a steady rhythm.

"But nothing is completely safe. No matter what I chose to do, something bad could happen to take it all away. The job could go wrong. Or one of us could get sick or hurt. Something bad could happen to one of the children. Life is nothing but one really, really scary risk."

Millie moved her hands to grip his shirt, fisting the fabric.

"So that is the world we live in. And, we have to figure out how to cope. I don't know for sure what the answer is, but I think we should find as much joy as we can while still honoring God. And, as long as we keep our faith that there is a plan, even if we can't possibly fathom what it is, then we will be okay."

Millie's voice was soft, her words a vibration against him. "You're right."

"It's not a matter of being right. It's a matter of us both being happy and doing the best we can. If you told me you were bitterly unhappy living on the farm,

I would listen. If you truly thought you could only find happiness somewhere else, I would listen." That was a lesson he had finally learned in the months after his first wife had died. "But I don't hear you saying that. I hear you saying you want to be somewhere that is perfectly safe. Millie, that place simply does not exist."

Millie didn't speak again, and Adam told himself to be patient. To let her process what he'd said. Think about it. Decide how she felt about it.

What would he do if she spoke up and said that she really did not want to be a farmer's wife because it made her bitterly unhappy?

He would listen. Or, at least, he would try. Adam had tasted life with he and Millie as a team—more than two strangers trying to live in the same house. That was the life Adam wanted for his children. That was the life Adam wanted for himself.

He felt Millie take a deep breath and knew she was getting ready to speak.

Please, God, open my ears so I can listen.

Chapter Twelve

Millie wanted to ask for another drink of water, but that would have felt too much like stalling. Her husband had spoken to her so honestly—he deserved her honesty in return.

"I don't want to agree with what you said. I want to argue the point with you. But I can't. Not right now."

Millie felt Adam relax underneath her. "I'm not saying that I would worry the same amount if you were a banker," she continued. "I really think I would worry less, but I don't know." She thought about it for another second, trying to give Adam's opinions the same consideration she had given her own. "Maybe not. Maybe I would worry about bank robbers. Or the bank closing. I'm pretty good at finding things to worry about, in case you hadn't noticed." She smiled as she felt Adam laugh underneath her cheek.

"But you asked me what was motivating my desire for you not to farm. And you were right. My sole motivation is fear that the crops will fail and all your work will have been for nothing. If there wasn't that risk, I would not ever want to move. I love our farm. I love working in the garden and having so much room for the kids to play. I even like the chickens and cows and riding the horses, but don't tell them that. I'm just scared."

Adam's hand was rubbing her back, and Millie closed her eyes. She was done for now. Millie had seen Genie collapse into deep sleep after throwing a fit. She'd laugh and shake her head and say the child had worn himself out. Millie now understood how he felt. She wanted to sleep, right here where she was warm and comfortable and protected.

"Thank you for telling me that. I know you don't see it, but we *are* going to be okay. I really hope the crops live, and I'm going to work hard to make that happen, but even if they die we are still going to be okay."

Millie didn't really know what to say. She was going to be here, with him and the children, no matter what. So, she would hang on and hope he was right.

"Mama?" Caty's voice came from outside the barn, and she sounded panicked.

Millie scrambled to her feet, grateful when Adam helped her. He nodded toward the barn door. "Go on. I'll clean up in here and be there shortly."

She wanted to argue with him. Millie had made the mess; it wasn't fair that Adam had to clean it up.

"Mama? Daddy?" Caty's voice was closer.

Millie ran out the barn door. "We're here, Caty." The girl ran to her and squeezed her tight around her stomach, laying her head down on the bump. "Oh, Caty, it's okay. It's okay." She sounded like Adam now. Caty let go and looked up at her, tears coming down her cheek.

"Where were you? I woke up and the house smelled bad and you weren't there."

Millie leaned down. "Jump on three, all right?" Caty nodded and did just as Millie asked. Even at five, Caty was a small girl. It was a bit awkward for Millie to pick her up and hold her, but Millie did it anyway. Caty put her head down on Millie's shoulder and started to shake with the tears that escaped. Millie made her way to one of the rocking chairs on the front porch. She sat down, Caty in her lap.

Millie just rocked for a while, not in any hurry to make this sweet child get up. Millie rubbed Caty's back and whispered how much she loved Caty into the girl's ear. It seemed to be a day for the Beale women to get upset and need to be consoled.

When she was ready, Caty sat up and looked at Millie. "I got scared."

Millie nodded, the solemnity she felt in her heart keeping her face somber. "I know. I'm sorry. I'd guess that not being able to find me was really, really scary."

Caty bit her lower lip. "I thought maybe you lefted me."

Millie could not stop her gasp. "Caty, no. Never. Look at me. Are you looking?"

Caty nodded.

"I will never leave you. Never, ever."

Caty's eyes were thoughtful again. "What about if you die?"

Millie jumped as Adam sat down in the rocking chair

next to hers. She hadn't realized Caty had cried long enough for Adam to clean up Millie's mess and join them. Hadn't realized Adam could hear what Caty was saying.

But she was grateful.

"Why are you thinking about Millie dying, Caty-girl?" Adam was leaning forward in his chair, one large hand stroking down Caty's wild unbrushed hair.

Caty shrugged, not making eye contact with either one of them. "Sometimes mamas die."

Millie's eyes met Adam's.

Adam continued smoothing her hair. "Yes, Caty. Sometimes mamas die."

"What if Mama dies?"

Before Adam could answer, Millie held up a hand, silently asking him to let her answer this question.

"Caty, will you look at me again, please? I want you to see my face, so you know I'm telling you the truth."

Caty looked.

"I get scared a lot, Caty. I get scared about things I can't control. And I worry and worry and worry even though worry doesn't make it better." Caty was still watching her with solemn eyes. "But those worries are just bad thoughts. They're not real. I am here, and I will never, ever leave you on purpose. And if I die, you can be sad. That's okay, too. But then I will be in heaven and I will be watching you and loving you and I will always be there for you. All that matters is that I love you and you love me. That's it."

Caty looked at Millie and Millie looked right back. She hoped that whatever the girl saw, that it would reassure her that Millie meant every word. Millie knew the heartache that came with worrying about things you couldn't control. She didn't want that for her sweet girl.

"I love you, Mama." Caty leaned forward for one last, fierce hug.

"I love you, too, baby. Why don't you go wake up your brother. It's late, and we all need to eat breakfast. Do eggs sound good?"

"And pie?" Caty almost sounded like Genie.

Millie wasn't sure she ever wanted to eat pie again, but there was no way she was denying Caty anything today. "Yes, and pie."

Caty went inside, and Millie let out a long shaky breath. Adam reached over and held her hand, melting back into his own chair. They sat there for a while, rocking and holding hands. Millie tried not to notice how warm his hand was. How the callouses made it feel strong. How sturdy it was.

This was just because of their rough morning. That was all. A child they both loved had been upset. They were both worried about the crops. Things had been emotional and draining and they were just two adults who were seeking a bit of comfort. It didn't mean anything.

"I really, really, really wish I didn't need to head out to the fields today."

Millie groaned, feeling like she had been awake for twenty hours instead of two. "Do you have to go right now? I mean, does it have to be today?"

Adam was quiet, and Millie found herself almost wanting to cry again at the thought of him leaving.

What in the world was wrong with her today? She needed to stop all of this emotional mess.

"I don't have to go out right away, and I won't be gone all day. I mean, there's not a whole lot for me to do. Most of it is up to the water and crops now."

Millie nodded. That was something, at least. The door flew open, and Millie and Adam dropped hands like they were about to be caught doing something wrong. Genie came running out on the porch, still in his nightclothes.

As always, he had a huge smile on his face. Millie held out her arms and he came and sat in her lap. Caty was behind him, and Millie was glad the distressed look was gone from her eyes. Adam reached out, and the girl curled up in his lap.

They were hours behind schedule. There were things that needed to be done. And the four of them just sat in those chairs and rocked. Not talking, just being. Together.

The omelets were delicious, as always. The kids chattered and rambled and laughed. He ate pie, and enjoyed its sweetness—though the laughter and chatter of his children was even sweeter. All in all, the day had recovered in a spectacular fashion.

And all Adam could think about was leaving. He needed to get out of this room, out of this house. As soon as he felt he could do so without alarming Millie and the kids, Adam said goodbye, grabbed his hat and walked out the front door.

He saddled his horse and gathered his tools without

even realizing he was doing it. The next thing Adam knew, he was riding out across his land, surrounded only by the blue sky and silence.

He still felt trapped. Felt like he needed to urge the horse into a gallop and keep going until they both collapsed from exhaustion. Adam got off the horse and walked through the fields, noticing how much better the plants already looked. He pulled any weeds he saw, trying to make sure the water and nutrients went to the crops and not the nuisance plants.

That done, Adam could have gone home. Gone back to Millie and the kids like he'd said he would.

He didn't.

Adam rode out to the small cemetery where his first wife was buried. It was a surprisingly peaceful spot, shaded with several large trees. Adam sat down underneath one of those trees, leaning back against its trunk. Birds were singing, filling the air with announcements that life did, indeed, go on.

But to what end?

Adam bent his knees and rested his forearms on them, just staring at the place where Sarah had been put into the ground. He'd been furious with her. Almost relieved she had died.

Adam had actually thought that her dying solved a lot of problems. No one would ever have to know she had been determined to leave him. No one would ever have to know that she had actually done it. He would not have to spend the rest of his life legally tied to a woman who had fled. He would not have to spend the rest of his life being whispered about. Pitied.

Adam had been happy that a woman died. Not just a woman, but the mother of his children.

What kind of man was he? Adam wasn't sure he knew.

It had taken a long time for Adam to understand that Sarah was just human. Someone who was probably doing her best. Someone who had tried to tell him how unhappy she was.

It had taken a really long time for Adam to think of his first wife and remember the good times. The children they had made. It had taken...Millie.

Adam had been so clear on what he wanted when he'd begun the search for a mail-order bride. So very clear in his mind and in his communication with Millie. He did not want love. He did not want that kind of relationship. He was looking for a mother for the children, not a wife for the man.

Adam was all kinds of a fool. Every kind.

When Millie had been distraught this morning, Adam had not been thinking that he needed to comfort her because she was the mother of his children. He had not been thinking at all. None of it was deliberate. His Millie was upset, and he needed to help her. It had been as simple and as mixed-up as that.

When had she become his Millie? And what was he going to do about it? Adam had held her this morning, had called her honey. When she had fallen apart in his arms, all Adam wanted to do was tell her how much she meant to him. How much he liked her. Loved her.

Did he love Millie? Adam didn't want to. Romantic emotions were messy. They didn't make sense. Didn't last. He wanted to build a life for his children with a firm foundation, and love felt squishy, unstable. Love ended. It turned to hate.

Friendship was better. Safer.

Safer.

Adam was a hypocrite. All his lecturing Millie on being brave and taking chances and going after happiness, and here he was hiding under a tree ready to run away because he might love his wife.

He did not need to figure this out today. There was nothing to be afraid of. For all Adam knew, Millie wanted nothing to do with love either. She hadn't exactly had an ideal first marriage herself. Sure, she had not objected to his comforting or his terms of endearment this morning, but she had also been very, very upset.

Adam sat there under the tree for over an hour. When he finally stood up, his muscles were stiff and he was no closer to a solution. But he kind of thought he maybe wanted to try for a romantic relationship with Millie and maybe see where it went. He also kind of thought he was making a huge mistake.

Adam found Millie hanging laundry in the yard. The kids were playing, the air filled as ever with squeals and giggles. Adam wondered, not for the first time, how Genie could spend all day making noise and never lose his voice. That child was something else.

Caty was right there with him, smiling and running. But she still had that air of seriousness about her. Always had it. Adam had just thought her personality was just naturally more serious, but now he wondered.

She wanted safety, too. Like he did. Like Millie did. But the thought of his daughter living in constant fear and worry that her safety would be taken away made him want to cry. He didn't want mere safety for his little girl. He wanted her to have a full, joyous life. Not a cautious, safe life.

And, Adam was quickly finding that he wanted the same for himself.

He walked up to Millie, reaching down to grab the next piece of clothing out of her basket. He draped it over the line, smiling as Millie handed him a couple of clothespins. They worked together in silence for several long minutes.

When the basket was empty, he turned to Millie. "How are you doing?"

She looked at the barn, red covering her cheeks again. "I don't know. I mean, I'm definitely mortified. And tired. But the rest is just... I don't know." She breathed out a small huff. "How are the crops looking?"

"I can already tell a difference. That rain wasn't much, but it was enough for today."

"Enough for today." Millie repeated his words softly. Her eyes found his. "I'm sorry, again, for this morning."

"I'm not."

"I...what?"

"I'm not sorry at all. I think you had all those emotions and thoughts inside of you and they were almost like a poison. I'm glad you got them out, and I'm really thankful that I got to be there for it."

"You're thankful that I threw a giant fit and then cried all over you?"

"Yes, the same way I'm thankful that Caty told us her fears. I'm thankful she said it aloud and it wasn't some kind of secret for her to keep inside anymore. I'm thankful that I was able to comfort her after."

Millie watched Caty, now sitting in the yard braiding long grass. Adam decided to listen to his own advice and get his feelings out in the open.

"Millie, I'm also glad I was able to comfort you."

Her eyes were wide when she turned back to him.

"I know what I said about us being just partners and friends. But I'm finding that I maybe want more."

Her eyes widened even further. They looked almost too exaggerated in her face.

"I don't know where it would go. And I want to be careful because I don't want to destroy our friendship, destroy what we've created for the kids. But I keep thinking that we can have more. And I want to follow my own advice and try to not let worry about tomorrow ruin my today."

Millie wasn't blinking and she was standing entirely too still. Adam felt his heart start to pound, but he made himself go on.

"If you say no, you're not interested, I will completely respect that. But I think you *are* interested, even though you're scared like I am. But, I'm asking it anyway. Millie Beale, may I please court you?"

Millie blinked, and Adam saw her throat move as she swallowed. She licked her lips and cleared her throat. Adam braced himself.

"Yes."

What? "Yes?"

She took in another long, deep breath. "Yes. I'm terrified beyond belief. But I don't want to be seventy years old, looking at the good life I'm sure we will have had, and regret never trying to make it a wonderful life. I want Caty to have more than two adults who like each other as her parents. I want her to see two people who love each other. I want to try, Adam." She looked at the barn again, an incomprehensible look crossing her face. "You are a safe place, Adam. If I'm going to fail at this, I trust you to catch me. I don't know where this will go, and you know that scares me spitless. But, yes."

Adam had spent hours tormenting himself with this idea, and she said yes in five minutes. Okay then.

He nodded. "Then, Mrs. Beale, will you go for a walk with me later today? Enjoy the countryside?"

Millie's grin was huge. "What about our children?"

"We'll sneak out during their nap time. We won't go far, I promise."

"Then, yes. Again. I would love to go for a walk with you."

Chapter Thirteen

To Do:
Finish knitting Adam's socks
Put up the rest of the vegetables from the garden

Millie stared at her list, unable to think of anything else to write down. She was having a hard time focusing, and it was all that man's fault. She remembered seeing other women go all daft whenever a man showed them attention. She remembered thinking those women were foolish. Silly. And now, here she was. A grown woman, married with children, and she just wanted to sit and stare at space because Adam had taken her for a walk yesterday. Had asked to do the same today.

Yes, Millie had turned into one of those witless women. And it was most certainly all that man's fault.

Things had seemed to change so fast, and yet nothing had really changed at all. True, they said they were courting. But their conversations were the same as they'd been before. Their physical interaction was unchanged. The only difference was that the air was filled with the possibility and promise of more. It did not sound like much of a difference at all, but everything felt radically new.

Exciting. Terrifying.

Millie went from being eager and giddy to being absolutely panicked. This was the biggest risk she had ever taken. They were both committed to remaining friends and good parents for their children even if they decided they were not suited romantically. But Millie knew from a lifetime of experience that being committed to something and having it work out were two very different things. After all, they had been committed to keeping their relationship not romantic at all and look at how that had worked out.

Millie's brain knew that a life spent avoiding risks was a life wasted. Millie's heart knew that Adam was a good man. Millie's wary instincts, though, knew this could go wrong. Given the history of her life, it probably *would* go wrong. She was going to mess this up and he was going to make her leave. Millie's instincts were screaming at her to run before that could happen.

She turned the page, feeling like if she could just get the worst possible scenario down on the page and out of her body then the fear would go away. Her writing was harsh, the lead dark and ragged on the clean white.

Leaving Adam
I have savings from my knitting
I can get a job
I could take the children with me?

Millie dropped the pencil in horror. What was she doing? This was what her instincts said to do? It was unfathomable.

Millie pushed away from the table, almost running to her room. She made it to where her Bible was on her bedside table and dropped to her knees, ignoring the pain in her joints and the protest from the baby inside. Those words that had come out on paper? Those words were not from God. They were not truth.

Tears bled down her face as she clutched the Bible and begged God for forgiveness. She had cried more in the last weeks than she ever had in her life. It hurt. It cleansed. Millie was helpless to stop it.

She stayed there, asking God to fill her heart. To come in and push out the evil that threatened to destroy her. To cut out the despair and let the wound of her insecurities finally begin to heal.

Millie was still there thirty minutes later, forehead on the quilt that Adam had given her when she was nothing more than a stranger to him. She felt drained, not a foreign feeling after the last weeks. But this draining was almost welcome. Like maybe the crazy thoughts that tormented her were gone.

It wasn't going to be that simple. Millie knew that. But she also knew that she was done thinking about them. Feeding them. Millie struggled to her feet, and walked back into the family room.

She closed her notebook, put it off to the side. She didn't want to spend any more time in those pages. Not right now.

The morning passed quickly with the routine that

was quickly becoming Millie's bedrock. She cared for her family. Played with her children. Enjoyed every second, even when the work was hard. It felt good to live purposefully. Instead of making plans, Millie was living them.

Millie watched the clock and put the children down for their nap just as soon as possible. Genie, as always, didn't want to take a nap.

"Not tired, Mama. Play." He made the same argument every single day. Millie leaned over from where she was sitting on the side of the bed and stroked her palm down his cheek.

"I know, baby. But I'm sure if you close your eyes, you'll fall right asleep anyway." He would. He always did. Once his body realized it was actually going to be allowed to rest, it had no problems falling asleep.

Caty usually curled up, hands under her cheek, and closed her eyes without complaint. She wasn't fond of naps, but she never argued. Until today. She was still sitting up, looking at Millie suspiciously.

"Are you going somewhere, Mama?"

Millie sat up a little straighter. Leave it to her smart girl to figure out something different was going on. "Why do you ask, Caty-girl?"

"Yesterday you were cleaner after we woke up. You had on a nicer apron. And your hair was different."

Yes. It had been. Millie had run out of time before she could fully dress for her walk with Adam, but she'd managed to clean up some.

"I went for a walk with Daddy yesterday."

Caty's eyes narrowed. "Are you walking again today?"

Millie nodded.

"I come!" Genie sounded outraged that Millie would go on a walk without him, and Millie grinned.

"No, Genie. This is adult time. For adults to talk."

He looked dubious.

"Are you going to put on nice clothes again for Daddy?" Caty didn't sound upset. She sounded like she was plotting something.

"If I have time, baby. Is that okay?"

Caty nodded and abruptly laid down in the bed. She rolled toward Genie and spoke in a furious whisper. "Shh. Be quiet, Genie. We have to sleep so Mama can walk with Daddy." Caty then closed her eyes and did the best impression of a sleeping child that Millie had ever seen.

Millie's heart felt like a bucket overflowing. She managed to stay there, thinking about how much she loved these children, until both of them were truly asleep. Then she rushed to change. Millie almost always wore an apron over her clothes, but she didn't want to for her walk. She pulled out the dress she normally saved for Sunday, feeling the need to go beyond a serviceable skirt and blouse. She was just repinning her hair when Millie heard Adam come home.

She looked in the mirror, running her hands over her clothes as though to brush away wrinkles that weren't there. Adam knocked on her door, and Millie felt her heart race.

She opened the door and couldn't stop her smile as Adam's eyes widened when he looked at her. When Adam didn't say anything, she giggled, sounding and feeling very much like a schoolgirl with a crush on the boy in the next desk. "Hi."

Adam cleared his throat. "Um, hi." He cleared his throat again. "You look lovely."

Pleasure at his words rose from her toes all the way to the top of her head. "Thank you. It's the same dress I wear every Sunday. Nothing too special."

Adam shook his head. "No. It *is* special. I feel bad now, I'm still in my work clothes. If you'll give me a few minutes, I can go change."

This time it was Millie's turn to shake her head no. "You're fine the way you are. I like your work clothes." He looked doubtful. "Really. Besides, the kids won't nap all day, and I want to have as much time as possible to walk with you."

That seemed to do the trick. Adam stepped back and turned to offer Millie his arm as though they were in some fancy ballroom. It was a gesture she had seen men in tuxedos perform for women in fancy gowns in Saint Louis as they walked to or from their carriages. No man had ever extended his arm for her that way, though.

Until today. Now.

She took his arm and let him lead her out the door. Millie had made sure both kids knew where she would be if they woke up early. She really hoped they wouldn't wake up early.

They walked a few minutes, stopping on a small hill that offered an unobstructed view of the land for miles. Millie's hand dropped away from Adam's arm as she turned in a small circle, taking it all in. This part of the country was flat. And big. It didn't make sense, but the world felt physically bigger here.

It was a hot day, full of bright blue sky and a huge sun without a single cloud. Nothing to suggest rain. The prairie that had gleamed gold and green when she first saw this land was now the faded yellow of vegetation barely holding on. But it still looked like an ocean rippling with waves. It was still wide and open and free.

"What are you thinking?"

She stopped and gestured to the land surrounding them. "I was thinking about the city."

"The city?"

"I was, about how crowded it would probably feel to me now. How noisy." She closed her eyes and just felt the open space. "Sometimes going into town is nearly too much. Like everything is too close. I can't even imagine what the city would feel like now."

Adam nodded his head. "I took the cattle to Kansas City last year. Went with the men. Even though we were surrounded by livestock and ranchers, I still felt like I was being pressed in between two pieces of glass. I couldn't see what was closing in all around me, but I felt it. That's part of the reason why I didn't go this year."

Millie started walking again, Adam matching her slow pace right at her side. "I'm glad you didn't go," she said. "I'm not sure I would like being here without you. I think the house would feel a little too far from town then." And she would miss his company. Hearing about his day. Knowing he was just there. But Millie left those thoughts unspoken.

"Well, I shouldn't have much cause to go to a city

any time soon. And if I did, I would probably bring you and the kids anyway. They've never seen a city."

"Could we do that? All leave the farm? What about the chores?"

"Of course we can. And we will. Once things calm down a bit here, I'd like for us to go somewhere. A small, fun trip. One of the neighbors would gladly help out."

Millie thought about all the work it took to keep the farm going, even when doing the bare minimum. Doing it for two farms seemed like a huge favor to ask. "Wouldn't they mind? Doing extra work so we could go have fun?"

"That's what neighbors do, Millie. We'd do the same for them. Actually, I'm sure we will. Edith and Mike usually go back and visit their family a couple of times each year. We'll cover their chores then."

"What is there to do with children in Kansas City?"

"Actually, I was thinking we could go to Saint Louis. If you want."

"Saint Louis?"

"I kind of want to see where you grew up."

Millie stopped walking, the tightness in her chest making her feel out of breath.

Adam stopped, too. "We don't have to if you think it will bring back bad memories. Honestly, it was just an idea."

Millie forced in several deep breaths. She sometimes missed her city. She was also thankful beyond belief that she'd left it.

"I shouldn't have said anything. I know you had a horrible time growing up."

Millie nodded her head, focusing her gaze on the wide-open country around them. "I did. But I do miss it sometimes. It was the only home I'd known before this place."

"Well, you can think about it. We won't have any time for a trip for several months."

Millie exhaled a deep breath and started walking again. Adam joined her.

"It's a greater distance to travel than Kansas City. I'm not sure it would be worth it."

"Like I said, you can decide. No rush. But for what it is worth, I would like to see the place that made you who you are."

"Why would you want that?"

Adam's voice was gentle but sure. "So I can thank it."

Adam had been thinking about reaching out and taking Millie's hand ever since she had let go of his arm. His fingers twitched as he glanced at her hand, noticing how empty it was. How close.

He was courting his wife. They were admiring their land. But he was afraid to hold her hand?

No. Adam reached out, slowly, and interlaced his fingers with hers. He kept his touch as light as possible, giving Millie every chance to pull away. If he felt hesitance or resistance, Adam would withdraw.

But instead, Millie's fingers squeezed his, tightening the grasp. *Thank You, God.*

"Was it a better day today? Did Genie give you any trouble?"

Millie's smile was tender. "He wasn't trouble yesterday. He was just a little boy who didn't want to take a nap. But he fell asleep quickly today."

"I hope you know you've had a really good run. I love him but that child can be an absolute beast. I've seen him throw fits that would put an entire contingent of toddlers to shame."

Millie rolled her eyes, not looking like she believed him in the least. She also didn't sound particularly sorry for him. "He's a perfectly normal child. You just got spoiled by Caty. She's probably the best behaved child I've ever met." She squeezed his hand once, a brief pulse that Adam savored. "In fact, when I first met them, Caty was the one I worried about."

Adam understood that. He'd done his fair share of worrying about her, too. There was something sad about a little girl who was too good. "She's been so much better since you arrived. More like a child." Adam wasn't trying to compliment Millie and get in her good graces. His words were the absolute truth.

"They are so completely different. Genie is loud. He seems to have too much emotion, like he just can't keep it inside. It's usually good cheer and humor, thankfully, but it just seems to erupt from him."

Adam chuckled. Millie wasn't wrong. Not at all. If Genie's disposition was the least bit unpleasant, he would be a terribly difficult child. Instead, he was a boy whose good cheer seemed to infect everyone around him.

Millie's hand pulsed against his again. "Now, Caty

is a completely different child. When I first met her, I thought she disliked me. But she's not like that. She's every single bit as loving and good-natured as Genie. She just hides it a little. Makes you look for it. But, once you know what you're looking for, she practically drowns you in love and affection."

"That's a perfect way to describe them. They were like that even as babies. You're right that we were spoiled by Caty. She would just look at you with those eyes. Never fussy, never difficult. Just quiet and cuddly. All she wanted was to be held close and she was happy. And quiet. Did I mention quiet? I never realized how quiet until Genie came along. He was also a good baby, but oh my, how he wanted attention. He would wake up grinning and babbling and it seemed like he didn't stop. I swear he even made noises in his sleep."

Caty laughed, and Adam gave her his most aggrieved look. "I'm serious. That child didn't want to be quietly held. No, he wanted to be entertained. To have you pay attention to all of his nonstop noise. My ears are still ringing."

"I wish I had seen it." Millie's voice was wistful, and Adam stopped walking for a second. He turned to face her, trying to figure out a way to give her that experience.

He couldn't.

Instead, he lifted his free hand up to cup her face. "I know. I'm sorry I can't give that to you." His lips quirked. "If you like, I can recreate Genie's earliest years. I'll just follow you around all day banging two pots together as close to your ears as I can while smiling."

Millie burst out laughing. "Um, no, thank you. I'll settle for all the years to come that I'll get to enjoy."

"You're sure? Well, if you ever change your mind, just let me know." They resumed walking, a slight breeze blowing strands of Millie's hair loose. "What do you think the new baby will be like?" Adam's first two had been so radically different. Maybe this one would be somewhere in the middle?

"I don't know. I kind of can't imagine it as a real baby. I mean, I feel him or her in there. But, the thought that this thing inside of me will be a real baby in a few months just kind of shocks me. I just don't know how that is possible."

"When Caty was born, I remember wondering where she came from like she had just been left on the front steps in a basket or something. Even though I knew she was coming, had prepared, it was still a surprise."

"Well, that makes me feel better." Millie looked away, her voice softer. "Were you there when Sarah had Caty and Genie? I mean, close by?"

Adam swallowed hard, his heart beating faster just in the remembering. "I actually delivered Caty."

Millie stopped, looking at him with her mouth open. "You what?"

"Yeah. Sarah went into labor in the middle of a snow-storm. I couldn't get out. Even if I could, I was terri-fied that I would get stuck and not be able to get back with the doctor."

"So you delivered the baby yourself? Just like that?"

"Not *just like that*. I had no clue what I was doing. Sarah and Caty did all the work—I just kind of kneeled there feeling useless. I had nightmares about it for months after."

"I can't imagine."

"Yeah, well, don't you go getting any ideas. I learned my lesson. When I realized Genie was going to be born in the winter, I made sure to have ten plans in place to make sure we'd have help." He smiled, thinking of all the time Millie spent planning things out in that notebook of hers. "I made you look like someone who never planned anything at all. I had every woman in a thirty-mile radius on standby to come help. I had every man ready to go get help. They mocked me for months after, but it was worth it. I did not have to deliver Genie, thank the Lord."

"I don't know. I was really nervous about someone I've never met helping me. I think I'd like it if you delivered this child."

What? What? "What?"

"I don't really know anyone here. But I know you. And you've done it before. You're going to be this baby's father. You *are* its father. I really think it would be better if you delivered the baby."

Millie's face was blank, but her eyes were twitching…with humor. Adam realized he could add her to the list of people who would probably make fun of him. "That's the meanest thing anyone has ever done to me, Millie Beale."

The twitches broke free and she burst into laughter. Loud, long shouts of glee, with gasping breaths in between. She let go of his hand and put her hands over the place where her cruel heart was beating. He crossed his arms and glared at her. Or tried to.

"Your face, Adam. Oh my word, your face. Oh, I wish someone else had been here. I need witnesses."

He tried to increase the severity of his look, but his lips weren't cooperating. She looked so happy. So very happy. "I'm glad I could amuse you."

She reached out, put a hand on his forearm. Her voice was breathless mirth. "I'm sorry."

"No, you're not."

More laughter. "Okay, okay. You're right. I'm not. That was the funniest thing I've ever seen."

"You're a cruel woman."

"You have to admit, it was funny. A little bit?"

"No."

"You're right. It was a lot funny. I'll never top it. Fifty years from now, this will still be the funniest thing I ever did to you."

Adam decided to just enjoy her glee—and the way she talked about them being together fifty years from now, looking back over their life together. He looked at the sky, noting the sun's position. "We should probably head back."

Millie didn't answer. She just took his hand, firm and natural without any hesitation like this was the only way they walked now, and started in the direction of home.

Chapter Fourteen

"Millie? Are you about ready?" From his tone of voice, Adam was beyond ready. And very nearly out of patience. Millie chuckled to herself. They were still courting. He hadn't even kissed her yet. But he sure sounded like a truly aggravated husband right now. The kind who had been waiting on his wife for years instead of a few months.

True to that thought, Adam appeared in her bedroom doorway. "You set?"

Millie tried to smother her smile and look apologetic. She didn't think she succeeded. "Yes. I just need my list."

"Where is it? I'll grab it."

Millie shook her head. Men were so funny sometimes. "It's in my notebook on the table. I'll be out in just a second."

He disappeared, muttering something that was probably best not repeated to her ears. Millie took one last look at the mirror, trying to reassure herself that she did not look as clunky and massively pregnant as she currently felt.

She walked into the family room and froze. Something was wrong. Adam was standing there, looking at her open notebook. He had one palm flat on the table. The other was clutched into a fist at his side. He raised his head up and looked at her, and Millie stepped back. She had never seen such fury before. Such raw anger and hurt.

"Adam?"

"What is this?" His voice was low.

She took a small step forward, spoke cautiously. The question felt dangerous somehow. "What is what? The list for town?"

"You're making lists about leaving me? About taking my children with you?"

What? Taking his children? He never referred to them as just *his* children. They were always *their* children. The both of theirs. What was he looking at that would make him think she would take the children and leave him? Then, she remembered. *Oh, no.* Why had she left that page in there? "Adam, I—"

"No." His voice was harder than she had ever heard it.

"But I—"

"No." It was a roar. A yell.

Millie heard both kids run up the front steps. Pound across the porch. They appeared in the doorway, eyes wide. Genie was behind Caty, and Millie noticed that the girl was almost shielding her brother. From them.

Adam moved his head, still leaning over the table and that notebook. His voice was no less harsh when he spoke to his children. "Caty, Genie. Go back outside and play. Now."

Adam turned his head back, once again focusing his rage on Millie. She felt like she couldn't move. Couldn't breathe around the weight on her chest.

Caty looked at Millie. Looked at her father. "But Daddy, I—"

"Catherine Susan. You go outside with your brother and play right this instant. Do not make me tell you again." He kept his gaze on Millie, but Caty flinched as though she had been struck. She turned stiffly and walked out, pushing Genie in front of her. Millie heard Genie protesting. Caty's voice high and sharp in reply. Then silence. The door swung back and forth where she hadn't shut it.

Millie felt her anger rising, competing with her panic for space in her brain and heart. "You didn't have to talk to her that way. Caty didn't do anything wrong."

Adam stood up straight, his gaze feeling like a bullet heading toward her heart. "I am well aware of who did something wrong here. And don't tell me how to talk to my daughter."

Oh, she shouldn't have made that list, but he was going too far. After months of sharing those children with her, waiting for her to love and claim them, he had no right to try to take them away. No. "You mean *our* daughter?"

"No. I mean *my* daughter."

"Adam, you are—"

"No. Millie, I don't know what you're thinking." He looked at her notebook with a disgusted sneer. "What you're planning. But if you think you can take my children away from me, you better sit down and reconsider. That is not happening. Ever."

Adam's anger distorted his features. This man was completely unrecognizable to Millie.

"Adam, I. Am. Not. Taking. Our. Children. From. You." She emphasized each word, as though he were slow. If that insulted him, it was too bad, because right now he was acting more dense than a pile of bricks. "I would never do that. Even if I decided to leave, I wouldn't take the children. What kind of person do you think I am?"

Millie closed her eyes in frustration. Why had she said that? Implied that she might leave, just without the kids? She wasn't leaving, period—even if he was an angry fool.

Adam crossed his arms, somehow lowering his voice to an even deeper tone.

"You are not leaving me. You are not leaving my children. And, I swear, if you try to take my children from me, I will hunt you down. I will spend the rest of my life making you sorry."

Millie took another step back. She didn't know this man. Didn't know how to talk to him.

"It's not what you think. You're overreacting, ruining things for no reason."

"Then explain it to me. I can't wait."

"I wasn't ever going to do it. Never."

"And this, this was just…what? Why did you write those words down on paper, in your beloved notebook, the one full of ideas you intend to see through?" His voice was the sharp edge of a knife, cutting her.

"I just wanted to write those thoughts down. Get them out of my head so I could stop obsessing on them."

"You were obsessing about leaving me and taking my children?" The last was a roar. Adam's voice was a wounded animal, a hurt so primal it made Millie's eyes water. He wasn't listening. He wasn't understanding.

"No! They were just horrible thoughts. I knew they were horrible. Wrong. But Adam, I swear to you, I was just writing down words. I never, ever intended to do it. Never. I swear it. I've never lied to you—you have to believe me now. I was just writing down the thoughts to get them out of my head."

He was breathing heavy, still in a fighting stance. Millie didn't dare try to touch him. Not like this.

"If you didn't mean it, why did you keep it? I've seen you rip out pages before when you changed your mind about whatever you had written down."

He wasn't wrong. "I don't know. I wrote that list. Then I cried and prayed. Asked God for forgiveness. Then I guess I forgot."

"This list upset you so much that you broke down over it, but then you forgot all about its existence?"

"I guess." It sounded like a lie, but it was the truth. "I just don't know, Adam."

"There seem to be a lot of things you don't know. But that's okay, because there are things I don't know either, so I guess we're even."

"Adam." Tears were rolling down her face, and Millie angrily wiped them away. Adam looked at her and snorted.

"Save the tears, Millie. They're not going to work."

The hysteria Millie felt rolling in her body made its way to her voice. "They're not supposed to work! Why are you making this such a big deal? Why can't you understand that I didn't mean it? I was never going to leave."

"You wrote it down. I'm not making this up—it's right here." He picked up her notebook and shook it, then threw it back on the table like he was too disgusted to even touch the bound paper.

"Yes. It's right there. In my private notebook. You had no business reading through it. Opening it at all. I was just scared, Adam! I didn't mean it. I swear I didn't."

He stilled and that was the scariest thing Millie had seen yet. "You're telling me that you never thought about leaving me. About leaving us?" His voice had a desperate hopeful undertone that made Millie feel sick to her stomach.

Millie looked at the ground, but Adam saw the shame in her eyes before she lowered them. Not just shame. A confession. She looked as though she had been caught in the actual act.

She was going to leave him. How had he been this wrong? Had she been faking about everything? Adam remembered all the times he thought she was falling in love with him. Like he already was with her. He was going to be sick.

"How far did you get?" His voice sounded dead, but that was better than letting her see him cry.

"Wh-What?" Oh, she was good.

"How. Far. Did. You. Get? When you were going to leave me."

"I wasn't going to leave you."

"No. Your face gave you away. How far did you get?"

"Adam, I—"

"Did you pack a bag?"

She averted her eyes. Another look of shame. She had. She had actually packed a bag to leave him. The thought was so horrifying that Adam knew he couldn't be here anymore. He didn't know if he wanted to punch a wall or sob like a baby. Or both. Right now he just wanted to get away from her.

This wasn't like when Sarah left. Wasn't like when she died. This was so much worse. Millie had contemplated leaving him and taking his children with her.

His children.

Even if he believed her about not meaning that part, she had packed a bag to leave. To leave them all.

His children were too young to remember their mother. Caty had a few vague impressions, but overall Sarah was nonexistent in their world. That was a sad fact, but in a way, it was also a blessing. They would never know that their mother had been willing to leave them, had put her own happiness above theirs. Had abandoned them completely.

But his children knew Millie. They loved her.

They called her Mama.

Caty and Genie would absolutely remember Millie. Would know that she was supposed to be their mother until she died. When she walked out that door, there would be no way Adam could protect them from the knowledge that Millie left them right along with him.

What had he done?

Adam took a step toward the door. He needed to find his children.

"Adam, wait." Millie moved quickly, reached out and held on to his arm as though she could physically make him stay. Adam felt a bit like a wild animal. A beast caught in a trap that could not see anything beyond getting free. But, he didn't yank his arm away from Millie. He didn't allow his anger to take physical form. Perhaps he was still human after all.

"Please take your hand off me." He was afraid to move for fear he would lose all control.

She did, finger sliding down until he could not feel her touch anymore. "I'm begging you to listen to me. If you care about our family at all, even a little bit, please listen to me." She had a hand over the stomach where his child rested.

Except it wasn't his child. That was a fairy tale he'd told himself when he had thought they could all pretend to be one big happy family.

Except, it was his child. That was the reality he had created when he had married this woman.

He did not try to walk away. After a second, Millie began to speak. She had been furious earlier. Upset with him as though he had done something wrong. She'd even tried to chastise him.

She wasn't angry now. Her voice was full of despair. Regret.

Another act?

He simply did not know. He didn't know if he even cared. But he stood still.

"Adam, do you remember what our marriage was like months ago? I'm talking about the day you came home early to get your tools to help the family that was moving. The day I realized all the crops could die because of the drought. Do you remember that?"

He didn't look at her. Didn't respond. Adam just focused on standing still and trying to listen to her words beyond the thundering of blood in his ears.

"That was when I packed a suitcase. I did not even realize I was doing it, to be honest. I was thinking about the crops dying and being homeless again. I completely panicked. I looked up and I had my suitcase out and clothes in it. I swear I stopped the second I realized what I was doing."

He just stared at the door.

"I couldn't do it. Even then, I realized there was no way I could leave you all. Leave the children. I thought about what it meant to leave Caty and Genie, and I absolutely could not do it. So, I unpacked. I never made a move to leave again. Never, Adam. Not when you told

me the crops were going to die. Not when you had to
sell off half the herd. Even now, if you ask me to leave,
I'm going to refuse. I am Caty and Genie's mama, and
I will be here for them for the rest of my life."

That last sentence was true. She was their mother.
Adam had no intention of watching his children lose
another mother. That meant that he would never tell her
to leave. Millie was going to be here. As his wife. But
it didn't mean anything beyond that.

"Please." Her voice broke. He ignored it.

"When did you make the last list? The one about
taking my children? The one that was just thoughts in
your head that you were obsessing on so you had to
get them out?"

Millie's words were a sob. "The morning of the day
we went for a walk and you told me about delivering
Caty."

Adam swayed on his feet. He pulled out a chair and
sank into it. That had been a wonderful day. The day
that Adam associated with their courtship being real.
Their marriage being real.

That was the day she wrote down a plan to take his
children?

Millie sank to her knees in front of him. Begging.
On her knees. He could feel the swell of her stomach
against his shins. She reached for his hands, but he
pulled them away. Up high where she could not touch
them. She lowered her arms.

"I am sorry. It doesn't matter I guess whether I meant
it or not because it hurt you no matter what. But I didn't
mean it. I was torturing myself by trying to figure out

just how bad things could get—so I could figure out what to do in the absolute worst case. But as soon as I wrote it down, I knew how wrong it was. You were never supposed to see that list, because it was not a real list. I just use my notebook to ramble sometimes. To write down the worst thing so I can see them in black and white. How can you understand my breaking down in the barn but not understand this?"

Because the barn was about God. This is about me.

He didn't say that, though. He didn't say anything. Adam pushed the chair back so he could stand up without touching Millie. Then he walked out. He made sure to close the door behind him.

Adam found Caty and Genie on the other side of the barn. Genie was using a stick to draw in the dirt. Caty was on her back, staring at the sky. Adam saw tracks where tears had dried on her cheeks. He laid down next to her, pulling her into his arms. She curled into him, using him as a cushion, her cheek flat against his chest. "I'm sorry, baby. I shouldn't have yelled at you." Adam rubbed her back, making firm circles and hoping the repetitive pressure would comfort her.

"Where's Mama?"

Adam was glad she couldn't see his face. He kept his voice gentle. For his daughter. "She's inside the house."

"Is she okay?"

Adam increased the pressure of his hands, though he didn't know whether that was for Caty or for himself.

"Yes, honey." He wasn't about to say anything else. Besides, he was the one who had been hurt here. Not Millie. His words were the truth.

"You yelled at her." Caty didn't sound angry. Just sad. And confused.

Adam sighed, continued to rub her back. He saw Genie watching them, stiller than he had been in months. Adam reached out his free arm. "Come here, Genie."

Both children settled against him, Adam chose his words carefully. "Mama and Daddy had a fight. I'm sorry you all saw that. I'm sure it was scary." Adam felt Genie nod his head against his chest. Caty was just motionless. "Sometimes mamas and daddies have fights. It just happens. Like how sometimes you two fight with each other. It's okay, though. I promise you, everything is okay."

Caty raised her head and looked at Adam. "Did you two say sorry and make up?"

"Yes, Caty-girl." This time Adam did lie to his daughter.

Chapter Fifteen

Millie's notebook was still on the table. She hadn't touched it in the last four days. Had not even acknowledged its existence. Adam had not touched it, either. The book was in the exact spot it had landed when Adam had thrown it down during the fight. The Fight.

As far as Millie was concerned, the book could stay there until it disintegrated. Maybe Adam would get sick enough of it to throw it in the fireplace. Millie simply did not care.

"Mama, are the biscuits done?" Caty looked up at her, excitement in her eyes. She had made this batch of biscuits all by herself and was almost hopping up and down in excitement.

Millie relished the child's happiness as a touch of warmth in her heart. The only things she seemed to feel anymore were emotions associated with the kids. Everything else was cold. Dead.

"I don't know. We'd better open the door and check." Caty actually did hop then. Millie opened the door and they both peeked in at the balls of dough that had risen and turned a golden brown. "Well. What do you think?"

Caty clapped her hands. "Yes."

Millie used a thick towel to pull the pan out of the oven. She set it on a table to cool. "Caty, these are the best looking biscuits I have ever seen. Do you think we should eat one just to make sure it tastes okay?"

Genie was on his feet, blocks forgotten as soon as Millie mentioned eating biscuits. "Yes!"

Millie took a biscuit and split it in half, using a knife to spread butter on each piece. She gave Caty one half. "It's hot, honey."

Millie blew on Genie's. No matter how much she warned him, he would just shove the whole piece in his mouth, no matter how hot. When it was cool enough to not hurt him, she gave Genie his half of biscuit.

"Fank you, Mama." His words were muffled by the biscuit. As expected, he shoved the entire piece in his mouth, cheeks bulging with dough and butter. There was no way to be sad around this little boy.

"Well, what do you think, Caty-girl? Are you our new official biscuit maker?"

Caty nodded and offered Millie a piece of her half. Millie took it and popped it in her mouth. Millie felt pride bloom in her chest at how good it tasted. Her daughter had done an excellent job. "Yep. You're the biscuit maker now, Caty. These are great."

Caty ate another bite. "I think Daddy will like them, too."

Millie forced herself to smile. "Yes. I know he will.

In fact, he will probably try to eat them all if we don't watch him."

Caty smiled and finished eating her biscuit.

"Okay, you both need to clean up your toys and wash up for supper. Then you can help me set the table. Daddy should be home soon."

Millie was proud of how calm she sounded. Caty was too smart of a girl to not notice the tension between Millie and Adam. They had both gone out of their way to act normal in front of the children. As normal as possible anyway. Caty still gave them both looks in the evening, like she was trying to see beyond their words and read their true feelings. But otherwise both kids seemed oblivious to the change in Millie and Adam's relationship. Their days continued as they had since Millie arrived.

Millie wished for some of that innocence. No matter how much she pretended things were okay, she knew, felt in her bones, that they were very much not okay. Not at all.

And Adam was the same—visibly disappointed not just with their relationship, but with the weather, too. He hadn't told her, but Millie wasn't stupid. It had not rained again. The crops that had perked up with that small bit of moisture were back to dying. Adam was gone all day, but he was not working in the fields. There was nothing to do. The fields were about as vibrant as her marriage.

He was avoiding the house. Avoiding her. Millie would have been angered, but she was too busy being thankful that she did not have to deal with him.

The door opened and Adam walked in. He was filthy and soaked with sweat. Whatever he was doing, it was physical work. Millie wondered if wearing out his muscles helped wear out his mind. Maybe she should try it.

"Daddy, I made biscuits! All by myself! Mama said I am the official biscuit maker now."

Adam picked Caty up, ignoring her squeals as she felt how dirty he was. "She did, did she? Well then, I guess you're the official biscuit maker. It's a good thing I like biscuits."

Still trying to push away from his chest, Caty giggled. "And you like Mama's biscuits the best of all, and I make them like she does, so you'll like my biscuits best of all."

Adam never even looked in her direction. "Yes, I believe I will. Hey, why do you keep pushing away, Caty-girl? Don't you want to hug your daddy who loves you so much?"

Another giggle. "You always get me dirty, Daddy. And wet. Yucky!" Caty looked at Millie. "Mama! Help me!"

Millie froze, remembering how this would have played out before it all went wrong. Adam put Caty down, smacking a kiss on her forehead. "Okay, okay. You win. I better go get cleaned up so I can eat some of those delicious biscuits."

He still never looked in Millie's direction. She ordered herself not to notice. Or to care.

Adam held his hand out toward Genie. "Will you come with your poor daddy? Keep me company while I clean up?"

Genie took his hand and they went inside his room. Millie heard Genie chattering through the closed door.

"Caty? Will you please go make sure Daddy closed the barn door? Make sure the chickens are put up, too?" Millie knew both of those things were done, but she desperately needed some time alone. Just a couple minutes. Just to pull herself together enough to make it through supper without breaking down.

Caty ran out the front door and Millie sat down, resting her forehead on her folded arms on the table. Things were so bad. Four days had done nothing to fix anything between Millie and Adam. How long could they go on like this?

Millie had known better than to dream of more. She should have stayed with the essentials. Shelter. Food. A safe future. Instead, she had tried for more. Had begun to hope that she and her husband could build a real love together. And that dream had failed.

Millie sat up when she heard Caty's feet on the steps.

They made it through supper.

Afterward, Millie sat at the table and watched the children play. She didn't spend the time writing in her notebook like she had when she first came here. She didn't spend it knitting in the rocking chair next to Adam like she had in the weeks before The Fight. It was getting too hard to get up from the floor, so she did not sit down there to play either.

Millie just sat at the table. Adam played with the kids, talked to them about their days. Having not seen him all day, the kids soaked up his attention, and Adam gave them lots of it. Millie used to watch this scene and feel blessed that Adam was such a good father. Now she just felt lonely.

Growing up, Millie had spent a lot of time watching families. In restaurants. In church. On the street. Children with parents who seemed to just adore them. Millie had watched, gone back to The Home and remembered. And felt alone.

Millie felt that now.

She made it through, though. Through the time between supper and bedtime. Through watching Adam say prayers with the kids and tucking them in.

Adam left, and Millie sat on the edge of the children's bed, trying to find a comfortable position around the stomach that seemed to grow more and more each day. A reminder that even more change was coming. She and Adam were about to be further bound.

"Good night, my darlings. I love you." Millie kissed their sweet cheeks one last time, pulled up the covers another inch and left the room, being as quiet as possible. She did not even look in the direction of the family room as she headed the few short feet to her bedroom door.

"Millie? Will you please stay out here for a few minutes? We need to talk."

Adam's nightmares had little to do with the scary things of this world. Instead, they were this—Millie trying to escape to her bedroom and him asking her to stay. Him trying to think of how to be unstuck out of this moment and her sitting there, unreadable and not talking. They had played this out over and over in the months they had been married. They seemed destined to keep doing so.

Nightmares were bad enough. Living them was worse. Living them over and over again was too much.

Millie came and sat down at the table, and Adam braced himself. He had spent all week doing the maintenance projects he'd avoided for months. The ones that were nothing but hard work. He'd built a fence. Repaired a wall. Cleared brush from where the creek flowed when water was actually plentiful. He'd worked until his muscles ached. Until it felt like punishment instead of accomplishment. Until it was time to go home and pretend for his children.

Adam sighed. He had done a lot of thinking while working. He didn't want to, but he had. He'd replayed their fight. Imagined this conversation. Played through scenarios as he wiped the never-ending stream of sweat out of his eyes.

And, in a twist of things that had threatened to bring him to his knees, Adam realized he was exactly where he'd started before Millie had even arrived. That he wanted what he'd had at the beginning. Until he had tried to change it and blown the whole thing up.

"Millie." She looked at him, but he couldn't read her expression. That was probably for the best, all things considered. "Thank you for sitting down and talking to me. For listening to me. I want to say I'm sorry."

Millie's eyebrows moved, but that was all.

"I was, and am, still very upset about what I read in your notebook. The fact that you actually packed a suitcase hurts, especially when I think about what that would have done to the children. Then, you spent months with thoughts of leaving in your head. Thoughts of taking the children with you."

She started to open her mouth, but Adam held up his hand. "Please. Let me finish. Then I will give you all the time you want to respond. I'll listen to whatever you have to say."

She closed her mouth and nodded.

"I thought about what you said. And I believe you that you would never leave, because of the children." He did. "I have seen how much you love them. Of course you are not going to leave them." The next part was harder. But necessary. "I also believe you when you say you are not going to try to take my children from me."

He didn't bother to tell her that it would not work, even if she tried it. That he would not let his children be taken from him. Making that point would not serve any purpose other than fueling his anger. "I believe you, because I can't take the children from you, either."

She gasped and tears filled her eyes. Adam pushed down the urge to comfort her. "The children love you, and I love them. I still want what I have always wanted. I want them to have two parents who adore them. Who give them the family they deserve. You are their mother. You are. Just like I am their father. You could no more hurt those kids by taking them away from their father than I could by taking them from their mother."

Millie blinked rapidly, but her eyes were still shiny.

"So. You are not leaving. I am not leaving. We both want the children to be loved. Happy. I think we are right back where we started. We need to be friends. A team." Adam swallowed hard, pushing aside the dreams he'd had when he'd asked to court her. "But, nothing more. Our original plan was the right one."

Millie looked like she wanted to say something, but she didn't. She was letting him finish, just like he'd asked. He only had a couple more things to say.

"I don't think this whole fight was your fault. I think it was bound to happen. We were both burned badly by our first marriages. Neither of us trusts very well. I just don't see how we can ever move past all that. This was going to happen, and it's probably better that it happened sooner rather than later. Easier to go back to what we had before, which was pretty great."

It was. Adam just needed to keep reminding himself of that fact.

"I only have one more thing to say, and then I'll be quiet. I'll listen." He was almost done with this conversation that felt more like the live flaying of dreams. "I want to tell you that I love the baby you are carrying. That has not changed. I was wrong to tell you that Caty and Genie are my children. They're not. They are ours—every bit as much yours as mine. And that is what I want. I want you to love them as though you gave birth to them. That is how I feel about the baby you're carrying. Still feel. It is mine—ours."

Adam looked to where the cradle waited in the corner. The thing he had made to comfort and protect this baby. His baby. "It's important to me that you know that. I meant what I said. I want us to be friends. I do not want to hurt you anymore."

Adam drained the rest of his water from his cup. "Okay, I'm done. You can talk now."

Millie looked at where her fingers were clasped in her lap. She was quiet for several minutes, and Adam steeled himself to give her the same latitude she'd given him.

Finally, she raised her eyes and looked at him. "Okay."

"Um…okay?"

She nodded. "Yes. Okay."

She was quiet for several more long seconds. Adam thought perhaps she was done talking about the subject, but she made no move to go to her room.

"I think you're right. This fight was because you don't trust me." She swallowed, a hard motion that rippled in her throat. "And I don't trust you. I could have come to you with my fears, instead of writing them down. But I didn't. I was afraid of your reaction. And I was right to be afraid."

Even though she was agreeing with him, her words hurt. But he didn't argue against them. He just nodded. He stood when Millie did, waiting to see what she was going to do next.

"I'm done talking for tonight. I think we're both done. I'm going to take a walk. Think about things. But I'd like to start building our friendship tomorrow. See if we can get back to where we were before everything went wrong."

"I'd like that."

Adam was heading to his room, unable to watch Millie walk out the door, go for a walk without him, when she yelled his name. Loudly.

She was leaning against the doorjamb, one hand braced as though it was holding her up. Adam ran through the room to get to her. "Millie! Is it the baby? Are you okay?"

Her voice was thick, but not with pain. With terror. "Fire."

Adam looked in the direction Millie was pointing.

The entire horizon looked like it was burning down.

Chapter Sixteen

Millie had never seen so much smoke before. It looked like the entire county was going up in flames. Maybe the entire country.

Caty and Genie came into the family room, peering through the door at the wall of black. Millie's scream must have been loud. And scary.

Genie started to cry, and Adam picked him up. Caty leaned against her father. Millie looked at Adam, trying to stay calm for the children. "That's a really big fire."

Adam was similarly frozen, staring in the distance at the black billows that never ended. He slowly turned and handed Genie to Millie. She took him, thankful for the warm body to hold close and try to heat up the blood that had frozen in her veins.

"Adam?"

He just walked forward a few steps and stared. Millie's breath stuttered. Then his shoulders slumped and he bowed his head. Millie stopped breathing altogether. She reached out and took Caty's hand, pulled the girl close. Millie didn't know if she was comforting the kids or leaching comfort from them. Hopefully both. Definitely the latter.

Adam raised his head and looked her way. "Sorry, Millie. I needed a second."

"That's got to be a huge fire."

"Yes. Bigger than any other prairie fire I've ever seen."

Prairie fire. So that's what this was. The too-dry grass was on fire. Millie swallowed. Hard. She took a couple of breaths slowly through her mouth, focusing on the feel of Genie's weight in her arms and Caty's heat at her side. "Okay. What are we going to do?"

Adam wiped a hand across his brow. Then he finally faced them. "I don't know."

Millie had to put Genie down before she dropped him. Her entire body was shaking. Adam always knew what to do. Or, at least, he always thought he knew. While his confidence that things would be okay was usually annoying, Millie found his lack of it made dots appear in her vision.

"Daddy, is that a bad fire?" Caty was still gripping Millie's skirt, but her eyes were focused entirely on her father.

Millie breathed out hard. *Please, Lord, help me. I need Your strength right now. My children need it.* She squatted down in front of the frightened children. Adam followed suit, kneeling on the ground and pulling his daughter into his arms.

"It's not a good fire, Caty-girl."

"Are we going to die?" The words were whispered

but they exploded in Millie's heart and tore it apart. Millie moved from a squat to flat-out sitting on her bottom and reached out for Genie. She wanted to pull Caty in, too, and shelter all her children as much as she could. Including the one still growing inside.

But Adam's fingers were white where he held on to Caty, and Millie guessed that he would not let the girl go easily. That question must have been equally as painful for him to hear.

"No, Caty. No."

Adam scooted over to sit on the ground across from Millie. He pulled Caty into his lap, mirroring the way Genie was sitting in her own. Then he leaned forward and held out his hands. Millie didn't hesitate. The second her hands were in his, she felt things settle.

The ground was beneath her. Her husband's hands joined her to him. Their children were safe in the shelter they created with their bodies. All was solid. Warm. Real. And blessedly steady.

Adam's hands squeezed hers tight for a few seconds, and Millie squeezed right back. Things had felt so fractured between them just ten minutes ago. But they were still a family. They still loved their children. They were bound for forever, even if they never spoke to one another again.

Adam squeezed one last time. "It's going to be okay."

Even if that wasn't true, the words were still a balm to the fear that felt like raw, burned skin covering her body. "What are we going to do, Adam?"

"First, we're going to pray." Yes. Yes, they needed to pray.

"Then, I'm going to try to get some information. If we see that smoke, then others do, too. Someone might have already gotten a group together to go investigate. If not, I'll go rally some people to do that. We need to find out how far away the fire is and how fast it's moving."

Millie nodded. That not only seemed logical, it sounded wonderful. Information was good. Knowing what they were dealing with, even if it was bad, had to be better than watching that smoke and not knowing.

Millie pictured what she had seen of the prairie. Flat and filled with tall grass. And so dry right now. Not much would stop a fire from getting to them. Maybe the tilled soil in the fields would be a small obstacle to the flames, but Millie doubted it. The only other thing in the fire's path would be homes.

Homes.

"Adam, people are going to need help. Wherever that fire is, it's someone's land. Someone's home."

His eyes were solemn, almost midnight black, as they looked at her. He nodded. She was not telling him anything he didn't know.

Millie lowered her eyes in shame. She had spent the last few minutes worrying about her own family and something that might happen to them. That fire wasn't a potential threat to others, though. It was a nightmare happening to those people right now.

"How can we help them?"

"We need information first. But, in general, there's not much we can do to stop the fire. We'll go there and try, of course. They will need help moving livestock. Moving what possessions they can get out of their homes. Getting to safety."

Millie pressed her tongue against the back side of her front teeth. This was not going to be good. But sitting here upset wouldn't accomplish anything. She needed to be calm for the children and then do what she could to help. And pray that they would not need help themselves.

They prayed, and Millie pictured Adam's words as a blanket that could surround them. Comfort them. Adam finished and just held her hand quietly for a few moments. Millie used that time to say her own silent prayer.

Then Adam lifted Caty and set her on her feet. He reached over and did the same with Genie. Millie immediately missed the feel of his small heart against her chest. Adam stood and leaned down. He easily helped Millie to her feet, and she was thankful for his assistance.

Once they were all standing, Adam placed one hand on Millie's shoulder and the other on her stomach where her—their—child was still growing. His eyes were no less intense than when the family had been seated on the ground.

He leaned forward and kissed Millie's forehead. No force of will could have stopped the tears that slid hotly down her cheeks. She wanted to tell him to be careful. She didn't want to tell him goodbye. She couldn't manage to say anything at all.

"I'm going to head out. I'll be back."

"What should I do? Will the women be gathered somewhere? Will there be people hurt by the fire who need help? Should I pack?" Millie's mouth seemed to spew out a list of options as though she was writing in her notebook.

"Get together anything that might help if people are hurt. Clean sheets. Bandages. Honey for the burns. Anything else you think might be useful. I'll send word back to you with what to do next."

Millie nodded. She wanted a more specific answer, but knew that Adam lacked just as much information as she did. Millie needed to let him go find out more about the situation. Send word.

It only took Adam a few minutes to gather what he thought he might need and saddle his horse. Millie stood in their front yard and watched him ride away. Then she looked at the smoke and tried to determine if it had really moved closer to them or if her fears were just distorting her perception.

"Mama?" Caty was standing a few feet behind Millie, holding Genie's hand.

Millie turned and smiled at her daughter. "It's okay, Caty. Daddy will come back."

Caty nodded, but her entire demeanor shouted her doubts.

Millie walked over to the children. She took a child's hand in each one of her own and led them up the front steps and inside the house. Once there, she shut the front door. They didn't need to watch that smoke any more right now. Their focus was required elsewhere.

She led the children over to the table, pulled out a chair and sat down, and pulled the kids in close. She kissed each one on the cheek and ruffled Genie's hair.

Smoothed a hand down Caty's braid. Looked into their eyes and gave them a real, reassuring smile.

These were her children, and she tried to comfort them as much as possible. That was something she could do. Something she *would* do.

"Okay, my darlings, let's talk real quick. There's a big fire out there."

Caty nodded, her eyes so much like Adam's.

"Fire." Genie repeated the word and nodded his head.

"Daddy went to go help, but we need to help, too. Can you do that with me? Can we help Daddy?"

Both kids immediately nodded, even though Millie doubted Genie truly understood what she was saying.

"Great. I knew you would both be my big helpers. I'm so proud of you both."

Caty's smile was small, but genuine. Millie stood up, ready to be moving.

"Genie, can you get your blocks and play for me on the rug? That would help me so much."

Genie's face lit up, and he did exactly what Millie asked. Not having him underfoot or worrying about what he was doing would make Millie's next tasks much easier. "Thank you, Genie-bug. You're such a good boy."

"I know." Genie's tone was so confident that Millie actually laughed.

Caty was still standing, waiting for Millie to tell her what to do to help. Millie wanted to ask her to play with her dolls, but that wouldn't be fair. Caty would obey, but she would not be lost in fun play like Genie currently was. Instead, she would worry. Just like Millie.

"Okay, baby, Daddy said we need sheets. And honey. And anything else we think will be useful. Can you help me with all that?"

Caty nodded quickly.

"How about you go and get a couple of the large burlap bags we have? We can pack things in them." The words were barely out of her mouth before Caty moved to the cabinet where the bags were held.

Millie looked at her notebook, still on the table. Her hands were itching to sit down. Open it. Write out all the ways this fire could go and what they would do in each circumstance.

No.

Millie was still angry that Adam had violated her privacy. Had read what had always been hers alone. But, she had to admit she was also at fault. She had spent so much time and energy on working out the what-ifs instead of working on the right now. Adam had a responsibility to her, but she also had a responsibility to him. And how in the world was he supposed to know what she wanted, what she feared, if she never told him? That was beyond unfair.

"Got them!" Caty set the bags on the table, right on top of the notebook. It was time to act. She could figure out her notebook and her marriage later.

"Okay, Caty-girl, let's get the extra sheets."

Adam was familiar with how fast things could change. His life had shattered in the time it took him to pick up and read the note his first wife had written when she left him. Everything had changed again when she died. His world had changed in the time it took him to say his vows to Millie. It had changed when he read her notebook and saw all those contemplations of his failure. And now, with a glance in the sky, it was changing yet again.

That fire had to be massive. Unstoppable. The grass was dry and the wind was blowing. Toward them. Yes, things were about to change yet again.

Normally, Adam would head to town. That was the most likely place for men to gather. But, his house was between town and the fire, and Adam doubted that men would be moving away from the blaze to gather. Unsure of where else to go, he headed to Mike's place.

He saw Mike and Edith as he approached their house. It was almost dark now, but the moon was ironically bright. Cheerful. Mike's horse was saddled, and Mike was hugging Edith. From a distance, they looked like one person. Adam suppressed his sudden jealousy. He didn't want that. Or at least, he was resigned to not having it.

Mike broke away from Edith and waved at Adam. "I'm glad to see you. Neil Cott came by and said the men are all meeting at the Coltridge place. That's probably the next area the fire will take."

The Coltridge farm wasn't that far away, in rural terms. About two hours. That was much too close in the case of a prairie fire.

"Okay. Let's go." Adam wanted to get out there and see what was going on. Do something to cool the acid boiling in his gut.

Mike nodded, mounted his horse and waved goodbye to Edith. Adam nodded his own goodbye, trying to ignore how similar the panicked look in Edith's eyes was to Millie's when he'd left.

They made the ride to the Coltridge farm in silence, both men pushing their horses. There wasn't anything they could say that they both didn't already know. That smoke had not been there this afternoon. It was there now. The fire was big. It was moving. In their direction. And there was a serious shortage of water and resources to stop it.

The air was hazy when they made it to the Coltridge house. Adam dismounted and squinted, trying to lessen the sting of smoke in his eyes. Adam saw the same grim look on Mike's face that he felt on his own. The boiling acid in his stomach had shifted into a solid piece of lead.

Adam quickly joined the line of men passing buckets of water in a long chain. The end of that chain was a line of ground the group was trying to saturate. The hope was that the fire would not be able to cross the damp ground. That it would be contained and eventually burn out. That it would stop.

Five hours later, Adam's arms were one solid ache. His shirt was drenched and his eyes burned as fiercely as the fire they were trying to fight. And it felt like it was all for nothing.

It wasn't working. Word quickly came down the chain of men that the fire was crossing the line of water. The wind was simply blowing lit grass over the line. And not just over but several feet past the line. This fire wasn't just moving, it was actually jumping.

The men closest to the fire came back to the creek

they had been using as a water source. Adam recognized most of them, even though they were filthy from head to toe. Seth Coltridge spoke, his voice hoarse from either the smoke or emotion. Probably both.

"It's no use. The fire is coming this way. It's already eating my fields." His voice broke, though none of the men drew attention to that. "It'll be at the barn and house soon. We're just wasting time and energy trying to fight it at this point." Tears fell down the man's face as his wife ran up to him and threw herself at his chest. "Thank you all for your help. But you need to worry about your own places and families now."

Adam wanted to argue. To suggest trying it for just a little bit longer. Maybe a wider water line would help. Maybe they could get extra water to where the fire was crossing over and use the water to put out new fires started by blowing grass. Maybe they could dig a trench—too large for the fire to pass. Maybe the winds would die down or change.

Maybe.

Maybe.

Maybe.

Adam looked from where he had been focused on the wall of smoke in the not so distance. The men were seemingly all talking at once, throwing out the ideas Adam had thought of along with several other options. Good men, who were hot and tired and scared. Men who had effectively just been told that they needed to stand by and watch their dreams literally go up in smoke.

"Excuse me, men! Excuse me!" Pastor Willis was almost yelling, trying to be heard over all the voices.

The pastor was every bit as hot and tired as the rest of them, having come to help his congregants even though his own home in town was likely safe. The fire was heading in its direction, yes, but it would have to cross a large river to actually get there.

The group quieted down and the men turned to the pastor. Adam could hear the sound of Mrs. Coltridge crying, but he tried not to focus on the sound. Or imagine similar noises coming from Millie before the day was through.

"Okay. We need to stay calm. And organized." Though he looked as grimy as the rest of them, the pastor's voice carried clearly and with that hint of authority that came from addressing groups of people on a weekly basis. "If we can't fight this fire, we need to make sure we do as much damage control as possible."

Adam found himself nodding with the rest of the men. He wanted to fight the fire, too. But at the end of the day, there were forces that were actually beyond their control. And if the fire was going to come either way, they might as well be prepared to the extent possible.

Pastor Willis continued, "We can't save crops or houses. But we can save livestock and people. And some possessions." Though he was a pastor, Eric Willis had grown up the son of farmers. He knew about the reality of living out here beyond the town limits.

"We should gather the livestock and get them on the other side of the river, into town," Mr. Sinclair spoke up, his comment met with general murmurs of approval.

The water line had been ineffective. The small creeks

and ponds dotting the landscape had similarly had no real impact. But the river dividing the fire from town was quite large. Worst-case scenario, they might have to destroy the bridge that spanned it to keep it from carrying the fire across. That would leave people stranded on the town side, but would also keep the fire away.

A few of the older men conferred quickly, and Adam was content to let them come up with a plan. His entire body was starting to feel tingly, a sense of unreality about this entire situation seeming to grow up from his feet and bloom at his head.

Lord, this isn't fair. It just isn't fair. Why?

There wasn't an answer. Not even the sense of one.

Finally, all the plans were made. Pastor Willis prayed, and men started moving out in groups. Mike and Adam mounted their horses and headed back home. Mike's ranch hands would move their livestock toward town. Adam's house was on the way to town, so they would meet up with Adam's remaining hands there and take Adam's livestock, too. All the livestock should easily make it to the property on the other side of the river that others had agreed could be used to shelter the animals so long as necessary.

Mike would go home. He and Edith would pack a wagon full of as much stuff as they could. Then Mike would send Edith toward town, stopping first at Adam's house. Adam would go home and help Millie pack. Then, he would send Millie and the kids with Edith, all heading to safety in town with as much stuff as they could bring.

Adam and Mike would stay at their homes, each with

a horse. They would fight as long as possible to protect their homes from the fire. Maybe lessen the damage somehow. Then when the flames were closing in, they would go to town and join the others.

It was a plan. One that filled Adam with dread, but a plan nonetheless. And moving surely felt better than waiting. Or staring at the ever approaching wall of smoke.

Chapter Seventeen

To Do:
Wait
Wait some more
Worry
Lose my mind
Wait
Worry
Oh, and wait

Millie couldn't do it. She couldn't just wait for Adam to come home anymore. She was absolutely going to lose her mind.

Millie had filled two hours preparing supplies. Waiting for word of where to go and how to be of use. Waiting for some kind of update about the smoke that seemed to cover every bit of sky, covering the pale blue of dawn with deathly black.

A rider had come hours before and told her that Adam was fighting the fire. But it was okay, because so far there had not been any injuries so her supplies and help were not needed.

It was okay. Because Adam was *fighting a fire*. The thought of her husband being close to the blaze was anything but okay. Of course, the man left before Millie could correct him of his misperception.

Eventually, Millie had put the children to bed. They had protested. Resisted. But once Millie got them to actually stay still for a few minutes, they had both fallen asleep. That left Millie free to sit at the table and brood. Stare at the notebook. The one that had brought her so much comfort. The one that had brought her so much pain.

Millie was alone. Her husband just wanted to be her friend. And the world was on fire. She reached for the notebook and opened it. Ripped out the page that had caused The Fight. Tore it up into tiny little pieces. Turned to a clean page.

It didn't take her long to make a brooding list. Petty as it was, the list made her feel better. Millie was resisting the urge to start crossing off some of the listed ways to worry to show that they had been accomplished when she heard a rider come up to the house.

Millie didn't even make it the door before it opened, and Adam walked in. Him not properly brushing down or stabling his horse was not a good sign. He looked so tired. Wet with sweat, covered in dirt and soot. She wanted to ask a million questions. Yell at him for making her stay here and wait for answers. Instead, she just stood there like a fool and waited for him to speak.

Clenched her hand to keep from brushing his hair back where it was almost matted against his forehead.

"Daddy!" Caty's voice made Millie jump. She and Genie seemed to almost jump straight into Adam's arms. She hadn't even realized they were awake. Just as quickly as they appeared, Adam seemed to sink from standing to sitting on the floor, still clutching both kids.

"You smell like smoke, Daddy," Caty's voice was muffled as she pressed her face into his neck, but Millie still heard the words and smiled.

Genie leaned back and put a little hand on each of Adam's cheeks. "Dirty!" His grin covered his entire face, and he looked like he had discovered a stash of candy.

Adam's chuckle was warm. "I know. I am smelly and dirty. I definitely need a bath."

"No bath!" Genie looked horrified by the thought, and Millie smiled again. Two smiles in less than a minute. She wasn't angry anymore. Just tired. Weary, actually. Millie had never understood the difference in those words until this very minute. Now, she felt it in her bones.

"No," Adam agreed. "No bath. Not right now anyway." He looked up at Millie, and she sat back down in her chair. It felt too awkward standing over the rest of her family.

Her family. These three people sitting on the ground had become her family. She loved them. And they were in danger. Adam looked at her and the children grew quiet, probably picking up on the air that suddenly seemed as thick as the smoke outside.

"We tried to stop the fire, but couldn't."

Millie nodded, unsure of what else to do in response.

"It's coming this way. We can just be grateful, all things considered, that no one has been hurt. And we all have enough time to prepare, so that's another blessing."

Millie nodded again, dumbly. Numbly.

Adam leaned down to kiss both kids on the head, then stood and joined Millie at the table. He leaned across and took hold of both her hands. His hands felt too warm, and Millie turned them over to look at the palms. He had blisters in hot red rows across each one. She looked at him with wide eyes.

"It's okay, Millie. It's from all the buckets of water I passed trying to put out the fire. I had gloves, but they didn't exactly hold up to the task."

Millie abruptly let go of his hands and went to get the salve and bandages she had placed in the burlap bags with the other supplies.

"My hands can wait. I need to tell you what's going on and then I have to get going. Our time is limited by the fire right now."

Millie felt irritation bubble over out of nowhere as she got a bowl of water and some clean toweling cloth. Yes, she was scared. She had no idea what they were going to do. But, she wasn't helpless. And she could certainly take care of her husband when he was hurt. "So talk, Adam. I can do this and listen at the same time."

Both kids looked at her with open mouths. They'd never heard her use that tone of voice before, not even on their most unruly days. Adam also looked at her like he was in shock. Well, good. At least she wasn't alone.

Millie sat back down at the table and began to clean the blisters, being as gentle as possible despite her irritation. She felt Adam's fingers jerk and looked at him before speaking, her voice much softer this time. "I'm sorry, Adam. I'll try to be quick. Please tell me what's going on." By the time she had his hands bandaged, he'd fully explained everything to her. Dawn had turned to day, and Millie refused to look out the window where the wall of black was still coming for them.

She wanted to argue that there had to be another way, but did not. Her husband would not have made this decision lightly. If Adam believed they needed to leave this house that he'd built with his own two hands, then that was what they needed to do. And her job was to make it as easy as possible on him.

Adam went to hitch the wagon, and Millie looked around the house considering what would count as items important enough to bring. Millie picked up her notebook and began sorting the possessions in her sight into two columns. One for items to bring and one for items to leave behind. Her hand shook as she wrote, but she managed to fill both columns.

The door opened as Adam came back inside. "Okay, the wagon is ready."

His look darkened when he saw her holding the notebook. Feeling self-conscious and defensive, Millie set the notebook down on the table and busied her hands in her apron. "Okay. What do you want to load first?" She didn't dare mention the list she had been making.

Adam surveyed the room. "We'll do the large pieces first and then fit the smaller pieces in around them."

"Will everything fit?" Millie had zero experience with wagons and moving entire households.

"No. But we can take the most important stuff. We'll leave behind things that can be easily replaced. Things that take up more space than they are worth, comparatively."

Time moved quickly after that, which was almost a relief after an entire night of time feeling like it had stopped. They loaded her bed, dresser and rocking chair. The kids' bed and dresser. The kitchen pots, pans and dishes.

Adam managed to fit all the of kids' bedroom items into the wagon. That was good. Both children were sitting on the grass out front, watching the loading process without saying a word. Their eyes were wide, and they were unusually quiet and still. Even Genie. If the fire destroyed the only home they had ever known, the children would be devastated. Hopefully, having familiar items with them, wherever they were, would help lessen the pain.

Millie wiped her hands off on her apron and surveyed how much room they had left in the wagon, trying to picture how much else they had left inside the house. They hadn't even touched Adam's room or the family room yet. Her bedroom still had all the smaller items. There was no way, to Millie's eye, that it would all fit.

Adam was looking at the smoke and frowning. Millie looked, too. It was still there. Still black. Still coming at them.

"Adam?" Millie was conscious of the children listening, so she tried to keep her tone light and calm.

Adam turned and brushed his hands off on his pants. "Just checking. It's still coming at us, but we still have time."

"What's next?"

"Your room."

"My room? We already have the big pieces. We don't have anything from your room, yet."

"I know. That's okay. Why don't you rest for a minute? This has to be hard on the baby."

Adam started to walk back inside the house and Millie hurried to follow. "Adam, wait."

He stopped and looked at her, but his face did not betray any impatience.

"We can't take all of my things and none of yours."

"Millie, I don't care about my stuff. I understand why you want me to take it. But I don't need it. I just need you and the children to be safe and happy. That's it. That is what I want most in this world right now."

"But that's not fair. I didn't even have most of the stuff in that room a few months ago. I'm not attached to it. You've had your things for years. You can't just leave it all behind."

Adam walked to Millie. He looked at her for so long that she felt the urge to squirm. Adam lowered his head until his forehead was leaning against hers. "I'm sorry, Millie." He raised his head, reaching out and caressing her cheek, resting his warm hand where it stopped cupping her chin.

She didn't have breath left to speak. His touch took it all.

His other hand joined the first, and Millie found her

face being cradled. His heat came through the bandages on his palms, and Millie closed her eyes, focused on the softness touching her skin.

"For our fight—I'm sorry. I took something that wasn't mine to take when I read your notebook. You should be allowed to write down your private thoughts without having to worry about my reaction. No matter what they are. And I jumped to conclusions instead of talking it out with you. Even when I said that I was listening, and that I believed you, I didn't. I used my love as punishment. I withdrew it at the first sign of trouble. That wasn't me being practical, Millie. That was me being a coward."

Millie's eyes began to water, and breathing became even more of a struggle.

"In a way, this fire is a blessing. If it had been a fast disaster, I could have lost you and the kids without even the chance to say goodbye. That's all I could think about on the way home. What if it had moved too fast for anyone to warn us? What if we had not seen the fire until it was too late? I would have so much regret, Millie. Regret that I treated you so harshly. Please, forgive me."

Adam stood there waiting, still holding her face as through she was something precious and beloved. Millie stood there waiting, trying to come up with enough air to answer him. "I understand, Adam. And I'm sorry, too. We have a lot to talk about."

He smiled and leaned down to kiss her forehead. It was a gesture Millie was coming to associate with this man. "Yes. But not now. We need to finish and get to town."

Millie stood up straight, proud of her steady voice. "Adam, you still don't have to leave all your things behind to make room for mine. I don't want that kind of sacrifice. I don't want to spend the rest of my life knowing you lost everything to prove a point to me."

Adam's own voice was solid. Unmovable. "It's not just to make a point. It *is* the point. I will be happy if you and the kids have your things. All the kids. We're getting the rest of the items from your room. Then we're getting the cradle and baby clothes you've been working on. That should all fit nicely with the space we have left."

Millie looked at him. He looked at her. Then he smiled, winked and walked away. *Winked.* The man was preparing for his house to burn down and he winked and trotted off like he was having the time of his life. Millie suppressed a snort. *Lord, I think my husband might be officially crazy. Thank You?*

Preparing to leave when they had both missed a night of sleep was hard, but it was about to get a whole lot harder. The wagon was loaded. The kids were still sitting like frozen deer, breaking Adam's heart. But, the best thing he could do for them was get them into town. Get them safe, surrounded by friends. Away from this ever-thickening smoke.

Adam felt some of the tension leave his body when he heard a wagon approaching the house. That would be Edith in her own wagon. The livestock had left an hour ago. It was finally time to get his family on the road.

He waved to Edith. She wasn't alone. Adam recognized the man driving the wagon as one of Mike's hands. "Hi. Did you all manage to get most of it packed?"

She nodded, and Adam noticed her eyes were rimmed in red. Whether it was from the smoke or tears, he couldn't tell.

"We're set here, too. Millie's inside—I just need to get her."

Adam spoke to the kids as he walked up the front steps. "Okay, guys. You all are going with Edith and Mama. Make sure you have everything and get ready to load up." Adam saw Edith climb down from the wagon and kneel in front of the kids as he walked inside the house. He was thankful yet again for good neighbors.

Millie was standing in the middle of the family room, looking at the furniture they couldn't fit into the wagon. "I feel like we're leaving all of the furniture here."

Adam nodded slowly. "It looks that way, I know. But it will be much easier to replace a table and chairs than it will be to replace most of the small stuff. I packed my tools on the wagon. I can easily remake everything here. It'll be okay."

Millie nodded, but she was biting her lower lip. There wasn't really going to be a way to reassure her. He and Millie had gotten over their fight, but the base issues remained. She didn't trust him to provide. To keep her safe. And she had been right about him not fully trusting her either—fear causing him to lash out at any hint that she might be considering leaving him. But he was learning to trust her. He was sending his children with her. Away from him. And he knew she would care for them with all she had. In his heart, he did trust her. Like her, he'd just been scared.

But there wasn't time to deal with this right now. For now, they were together. Working as a unit. And in danger. Adam would do what needed to be done in this moment and have faith that there would be time to work the rest out later.

"Edith is outside. It's time for you and the kids to head to town."

"Me and the kids? What about you?"

"I'm not coming right away."

Some of the color left Millie's face and she leaned forward to grip the back of one of the chairs. "What do you mean?"

Adam walked over and gently pushed Millie down into the nearest chair. He squatted down in front and took her hands. "I want you and the kids to go to town with Edith. You all will be safe together, and you won't be alone. I'm going to stay here and try to fight the fire. Stash things in the root cellar and collapse the roof. If there's a thick enough layer of dirt as a barrier, it may protect them from the fire."

"But what about the fire? What are you going to do when it gets here?"

"I'm keeping my horse. I'm going to keep working as long as it's safe and then I'll ride to town. I'll be with you before nightfall."

"Then we'll stay and help you. If it's safe for you, then it's safe for us. And the work will go quicker with me to help."

"No, Millie. The wagon can't move near as fast as

a single horse. Plus, that fire could turn unpredictable. Could start moving faster than we guess. Jump. I'm not taking that kind of chance with my family."

"But *you're* my family. You're willing to take that kind of chance with yourself?"

He was her family? Adam gripped the arms of Millie's rocking chair tighter, trying to steady himself. Her words were the truth. They had become a family the day they'd married. No one could doubt that she loved and claimed his children, but hearing Millie include him in the group she called her family shook him—and filled him with joy. He wanted to tell her how much her words meant to him, but he didn't have time for it right now. That fire was coming.

Adam tried to soften his tone, but he wasn't going to give in on this. "Yes, Millie. I'm your family. That's why I'm going to do what I need to for all of us. I'm not going to do anything stupid, but I'm staying."

Millie nodded and stood. She walked out the door without saying anything to him. Adam sighed and watched the door close behind her. *God, I need help. We both do.* He saw her notebook on the table and opened it up to where her list of scenarios had been. Ways that he could fail.

She never considered the ways that he might succeed. That they might succeed. That made a lot of sense, actually. Millie's life so far had not exactly been an exercise in faithful hoping leading to positive outcomes. Instead, she had survived because she had prepared for the worst. Because she had adapted to every calamity she faced.

Every minute of her life must have seemed like an exercise in being self-sufficient. A deterrent to ever hoping for the best or relying on others.

And yet, Millie still tried. She truly did. She hadn't been raised with loving parents who always provided like Adam had. She had not grown up going to church, hearing that the Lord loved her and was there for her. Adam had.

No, his Millie had absolutely no reason to even try to have faith. But, she did. And as her doubts arose, she dealt with them in the best way she knew how. The only way that had ever worked for her before in her life. She wrote it out. Looked the worst in the face.

Was that really any different from Adam praying about his doubts? No. It wasn't. Acknowledging a doubt wasn't the problem. Letting the doubt rule was where things went wrong. Running and hiding instead of staying and doing the hard work was the problem. Refusing to see things through, that was the problem.

But Millie wasn't doing any of those things. She was right here, loving his children. She was here, supporting Adam. Making his life better. Letting him be a part of the life growing inside her womb.

Millie was just scared. Adam was scared, too. Instead of accusing her, he really needed to try to just be there with her and her fear. Not leave her alone with it.

Adam picked up the pencil and opened the notebook to the next clean page.

Option 1: The fire does not make it to our land.
We are safe. We have our faith in the Lord

and each other· We help others rebuild and live happily-ever-after· We praise God for all He has given us·

Option 2: The fire destroys everything, but we are safe· We're together· We have our faith in the Lord and each other· We rebuild and help others rebuild and live happily-ever-after· We praise God for all He has given us·

Millie,

I lied when I said the reason I could never leave you was because I couldn't take the children's mother away from them· I could never leave you because I can't take you away from me· The children are not the only ones who need you· I do, too·

Forgive me·

I love you·

Adam closed the notebook and took it out front. He saw Millie and Edith talking, the children sitting in the front of Edith's wagon.

In Edith's wagon?

"Millie?"

She turned and looked at him, hands on her hips. Wisps of hair had fallen out of her braid hours ago. The heat and sweat from loading the wagon had curled the strands, and they fell against her face and neck. While her pregnancy had not been visible when they married, it most definitely was now. Millie's apron was dirty, and Adam saw a small tear in the sleeve of her shirt. Making his way back to her face, Adam noticed her lips were firmed in a stubborn warning.

She was beautiful. Not just beautiful. Millie was the fulfillment of a dream. She was the dark rich soil he turned by hand. The brown eyes of his cattle as they lumbered in the corral. This woman was a house full of laughter. Warm stew and hearty bread and pie. Children who were loved beyond being.

"Are you listening to me, Adam Beale? Because I meant every single word I said."

Adam still stood there, awestruck. Millie wasn't some resource he needed to make his dreams come true. She was his dream.

"Adam!"

He shook his head, a subtle movement that in no way reflected the jangling in his brain and heart. "Sorry, Millie. What did you say?"

Edith actually laughed out loud, but Millie never cracked a smile.

"I said that I am staying with you. Edith will take the kids to town, so they will be safe. But I'm not leaving this place without you."

"Millie—"

"No. The only way you are going to get me to town is for you to take me. That's just the way it is."

Both children were looking at Millie like she had lost her mind. Genie's eyes were huge and Caty's mouth was actually dropped open. Edith looked like she wanted to sit back and just enjoy Millie telling Adam how it was going to be.

And the smoke was just getting closer and closer.

"Millie, be reasonable. You're wasting time. I need you to go to town with the children." Adam's voice went husky, but he didn't care. "Please."

"I'm not leaving you, Adam. I'm not."

Adam walked over to her, crossing his arms over his chest. Hers remained at her hips and from the way her skirt was bouncing, Adam would bet she was tapping her foot in frustration. Her face was set, almost like a mask. Except for her eyes. Millie's eyes were shiny with tears. They were terrified. Desperate.

Adam breathed in, slow and deep through his nose. Then he released the breath. *Give me the right words, Lord. Please.* He uncrossed his arms and held out the hand not still holding her notebook. He smiled gently as Millie's face went from blank mask, to shock, to wariness. Yet, despite her obvious confusion and hesitancy, she still put her hand in his.

Chapter Eighteen

Adam's hand was firm as he led her to sit on the front steps. Firm, but not angry, even though she had clearly pushed her husband past the limits of his temper. *Please, God. Please, he has to understand. He just has to.*

They watched as Edith took the kids and led them out to look at something in the barn. She was a good friend. Millie hoped that she would have children of her own to care for soon. Edith and Mike wanted that, and they would be such good parents.

Adam didn't let go of her hand once they were both sitting. Millie saw him set her notebook down with his other hand. What was he doing with her notebook?

"Millie, tell me why you want to stay. Help me understand." Adam's voice wasn't the least bit accusing. He genuinely wanted to understand.

"I just want to help you. And I don't like leaving you here alone. What would we do if something happened to you?"

"I have plans in place. There is money in the bank,

set aside for you in case something happens to me, and I know you saw the box with extra cash from under my floorboards that I put into the wagon. Plus, you'll own this land. Even if a fire destroys the buildings and the crops, you'll be able to get a decent price for the place. And our friends would help you. They would. I'm not saying it would be easy, but you and the kids won't be homeless. Won't be broke. I promise."

Millie felt frustration well up inside. It made sitting still next to him difficult. "I don't care about losing the man who provides for me. I care about losing you— Adam." Millie reached over and picked up her notebook. "I was out there with Edith. I put the kids in the front of our wagon and I climbed up, picked up those reins, and it just hit me." Millie's words were falling out fast and almost slurred, her fingers white where she gripped the notebook in her lap. Her chest was heaving, her breaths audible and ragged.

Adam placed a hand on her back and began to rub in soft circles. "What, Millie? What hit you?"

Millie swallowed hard. She gestured with her notebook. "This. I thought I wanted financial security. To leave this farm. To do something safe. But that's not what I want. When it came time for me to take my belongings and leave for safety, I felt like…like…well, I don't even know what."

Millie's skin got tight just remembering. "My parents were teachers. My first husband was a shopkeeper. No crops, no drought, no fire. But disaster found them— took them from me. Both times. Even though I keep trying," Millie raised her notebook again, "to control the future, to make myself safe, it's just a lie. I'm not in control, and I never will be."

She opened her notebook to that jagged edge that had held the page he'd read. "See this? I listed all the ways my world could be torn apart."

"I know."

"Well, I never listed prairie fire. In fact, I didn't list hundreds of ways bad things could happen." Millie put the notebook, still open, back on her lap. "I also didn't list all the ways things could go right."

Adam's hand stopped rubbing in circles and just stayed still on her back.

"I can't get on that wagon and go to town because I can't leave you. I'm not just worried about my husband dying, I'm worried about the man that I love dying. The father of my children."

Adam's hand fell from her back. It felt like a rejection, but Millie made herself keep going. She was doing the exact opposite of what they agreed on just the night before—only moments before she saw the smoke in the distance—but she didn't care. Millie was done trying to bend the world to her will. She was going where God led her, and He'd led her heart to Adam.

"I want to help try to save this place. I love it here, too. This land, it doesn't just call to you. I want to be in this house, the first place where I ever felt like I belonged. I want my garden, the vegetables that are growing because I tended them. The food I'm growing to feed my family. I want to watch Caty and Genie run wild in the only place they've ever called home. I want this. And you."

Millie picked up her notebook, started ripping out pages. "I don't need this, Adam. I don't need a fake life on paper. I need a real life. Here with you."

Millie went to rip out the next page in her notebook when Adam's hands came firmly down on her own to stop her. He pulled the notebook out of her grasp and held both of her hands in his own. "No, Millie. Stop."

Millie was going to throw up. And since he was holding her hands and keeping her from getting away, she was probably going to end up throwing up all over herself and Adam. He didn't want her like that. He wanted her to stop.

"I love you, too."

Wait. What?

Adam let go of her hands and picked up the partly destroyed notebook. He flipped a couple of pages and put it back in her lap.

That wasn't her handwriting. The two options were definitely written by a man. She ran her fingers over the words as she read them.

"You did this?" She knew he had. He was the only man with access to her notebook. The only one who would rewrite the topic of their fight in such a manner.

His hands came back up to her face, making her wish he would never stop cupping her cheeks like this. "While you were outside realizing you love me, I was inside realizing I love you. I understand why you write your lists. I actually think it's adorable. Your notebook isn't the problem."

Millie was trying to listen, trying to focus on his words, but she also wanted to replay his declaration of love over and over again in her mind. Later. She would do it later.

"*We're* the problem. Or, we were. The fact that we both used our past experiences with other people to predict what we would do—or what others would do to us—in the future. It doesn't work that way, honey. You're right about not being able to predict every bad thing that could happen. It's a waste of time to even try. We're not in control."

Millie nodded within the safety of his hands. "God is." Her voice was a whisper. A confirmation. Adam leaned forward and kissed her on the forehead. Then he kissed her on the lips. Millie was ready to melt right into him when he pulled away.

"Okay, Millie. The fire is still coming at us."

"Please don't make me leave you. Let me stay?"

Adam let go of her face and stood. He looked where the horses were patiently waiting with the wagons. "I don't want you to hurt yourself. Or the baby."

Millie stood and put a hand on his arm. "Agreed. I won't do anything crazy. I'll just help as much as I can and be with you."

"Okay. We can send the kids with Edith. Mike's hand who came along can take our wagon."

"Really?"

"I don't know if it's the right thing to do, but I want you to stay with me. I'm scared senseless that you'll end up getting hurt, or the baby will, and that I will regret this decision for the rest of my life. But it's true that this is your home and you have every right to try to save it. And there's no one I would rather have with me."

"Thank you, Adam."

Adam and Millie said goodbye to Edith and the children. Watched both wagons leave. Then, they were left alone. The smoke was no longer in the distance. It now was close enough that it had the appearance of fog, a fine mist that stung Millie's nose when she breathed in too deep. Millie looked at the sky, foolishly hoping for rain. The parts she could see above the haze were a clear, brilliant blue.

Adam wet two bandanas in the well, and they each tied one over their mouth and nose. That helped keep most of the smoke out. He was probably a horrible husband for letting Millie stay, but he couldn't regret it. They had tried being married as two separate entities. Now, he wanted to do it the right way. Two parts of one whole, together.

They filled the root cellar with as much stuff from the house as they could fit. Then, they covered it with several sheets and blankets. Millie watched as Adam filled in the last two feet with dirt. It seemed too much like filling in a grave, and Adam had to focus on the thought of coming back and pulling these things out of the ground unharmed.

By the time he was done, the smoke in the air had gone from a thin fog to a much thicker haze. There was an orange glow in the distance that made his nerves prickle. The land was flat here with visibility stretching out to a considerable distance, so he knew that the fire was still several miles away. But if they could see it, it was time to leave.

"We need to go, Millie."

She stood from where she'd been leaning against a tree. "We're done? I thought you wanted to wet the house and barn down."

"I can see the fire. That means we need to leave now. We've done the best we can—the rest is in God's hands."

Millie turned to look in the direction he had pointed. She gasped and held her hands to her mouth. Adam walked up behind her, wrapping his arms around and resting his hands on the swell of her stomach. "It's okay. It's still far away. But we're not taking any chances."

Millie lowered her hands from her face and leaned back into him. "Okay. Let's go to town and be with our children."

Adam had just helped Millie climb up into the saddle when Mike rode up to the house. He'd been riding his horse hard, and his voice was alarmed. "Adam! Millie! We need to go. The fire jumped over by my place. It's right behind me."

Adam's stomach dropped. That orange glow he'd seen in the distance wasn't the fire line. Or, at least it wasn't the only part of the fire line. The flames were much closer, and now Millie was in danger. All because he had let her stay. He mounted his own horse, hoping the riding lessons he'd given Millie would see her through this new ordeal.

As they reached the main road, Adam could hear the fire. *Please, God. Please. Take care of Millie and the baby.* They were riding as fast as they could, taking Millie's pregnancy into consideration.

They rounded a curve, and the smoke visibly thinned. Adam looked at Mike and saw his own relief mirrored there. They still needed to hurry, but Adam no longer felt like they were running for their lives.

The passed the rest of the ride in silence. Every once in a while, one of the three of them would turn around and look as though the fire were a wild animal chasing them. Even though they were clear of it at the moment, they all knew it was a matter of being clear for now. Adam was acutely aware of the wind that seemed to be pushing them, and the fire, forward.

Finally, they were in the last stretch before reaching town. The smoke was thicker here. The fire was close. Adam felt his lips tighten in annoyance that fires couldn't travel in a nice straight line.

"Is that the fire I hear?" Millie sounded frightened, and Adam wished he could touch her. He listened for a second, trying to hear whatever was scaring Millie. There was a roar in front of them, soft but getting louder as they progressed down the road. Were they riding right into the fire?

Mike looked at Adam and grinned wide. "It's not the fire. It's the river."

The last time Adam had seen the river, it had been low. The drought was affecting everything. It sounded like it was full now, though. Things must have gotten better in the area upstream that fed these waters. That was good for someone, at least. And right now, it was good for them, too. The bigger and more robust the river, the bigger and more robust the defense for the town against the fire.

Adam's gratitude crashed and broke into a million tiny pieces when the river came into view. It was large and wet and just what they needed. But the bridge was gone. The people in town must have been as worried about the fast-moving fire as they were.

They were going to have to go into the water to get to the other side. The cold, rushing water. The river that was supposed to protect them suddenly looked as dangerous as the fire they were fleeing.

They stopped at the river and dismounted. Millie leaned into Adam's left side, and he used his left arm to pull her close and squeeze her tight. "What do you think, Mike? You take the horses across, and I'll take Millie?"

"That water is going really fast, Adam. I think I should go with you to help Millie."

"I'm not helpless. I'm sure I can get across without both of you." Millie's voice was indignant, but she didn't try to pull away.

Before they could argue it out, Adam saw several people come out of the church and run over to the river. The pastor. Edith and the kids. Several men from the area.

"Stay there. We'll come to you." The pastor's voice was nearly drowned out by the running water, but Adam understood him.

The men quickly tied a rope to the remains of the bridge on their side. Then, several of them crossed the river, slowly battling the current. Adam and Mike waded into the river on their side to meet the men and help them emerge.

The rope was tied to the remains of the bridge on their side. Then, Adam and Mike each took one of Millie's arms. They entered the water where the rope ran across. Another man followed them, ready to help in case they needed it. Two more men followed with the horses.

Adam leaned close, wanting to make sure Millie heard him. "Just hold on to the rope. This will be over in no time." Together, the group crossed the river. It was cold from the beginning, but the current didn't become punishingly strong until they were about a third of the way across. Millie faltered at one point, and Adam increased the pressure on her arm, trying to hold her up. His muscles were shaky by the time they walked out of the water on the other side.

They had made it.

Edith passed a blanket to Adam and then threw herself into Mike's arms, making him stumble back a few steps. "Michael Potter, you scared me to death! Everyone else made it to town already. I thought something had happened to you." Edith's voice became muffled where she was pressing her face into Mike's neck.

Adam put the blanket around Millie, who was holding both Caty and Genie. Adam hadn't seen them run to her. He turned and thanked the men who had crossed to help them. Then Adam squatted down and opened his arms. "Hey there, darlings. Do I get a hug, too, or is that just for Mama?" Adam laughed as the two little bodies rushed him.

"I was scared, Daddy. I didn't like it."

Adam pulled Caty closer and kissed her on the head.

"I know, Caty-girl. I'm sorry you were scared, but we're all okay. And we're together again."

It didn't take long for them to change into dry clothes and gather with the others inside the church. The sun had set, and the sanctuary was lit by multiple candles and lamps.

Genie was asleep, lying down on the pew with his head in Millie's lap. Caty was sleeping in Adam's arms, her head a welcome weight on his shoulder. Adam reached out and held Millie's hand, scooting to close the gap between them on the pew.

"You can lean on me to sleep, Millie." His voice was low, one of many soft tones filling the space.

"I don't think I can fall asleep. My body is exhausted, but my mind keeps racing."

"Are you hungry? There's a table of food over there with just about everything you can think of on it."

Millie smiled faintly, running her fingers through Genie's hair. "No. I just want to sit here, feel you all around me and try to clear my mind."

Adam managed to reach inside his borrowed coat and find the notebook and pencil he'd retrieved from their wagon earlier while Millie was changing clothes. He pulled them out and passed them to her, feeling his heart squeeze at the look on Millie's face. "Here. This might help you clear your mind."

Millie took the notebook and set it on her lap, clear of Genie's head. "How did you manage to do this?"

Adam let his smugness saturate his tone. "I have my ways. I told you I would make sure you have everything you needed."

Millie sniffled and her voice was thick with tears. "I already had everything I needed right here. But, thank you for the notebook. I love you, Adam Beale."

Adam leaned over and tipped Millie's face up to his. He brushed the tears from her cheeks and then kissed her mouth. It felt like home. Adam had done everything he could to avoid having this with Millie, and yet there they were. And it was perfect.

A noise came from outside the church, men talking rapidly. Loudly. Adam set Caty down on the pew next to Millie, covered the girl with his borrowed coat and went outside to see what was happening.

The problem was obvious once he went through the church door outside. The other side of the river was an orange glow. The fire had caught up to them.

Chapter Nineteen

To Do:
Thank God.
Love my family.

It certainly wasn't the most specific to-do list that Millie had ever written, but it was all that needed to be done today. All that was important. She closed her notebook and set it to the side as Adam walked up to her. He looked tired, and Millie could only imagine what she looked like. She wasn't entirely sure she was going to be able to get up off this pew without his assistance.

"It's still smoldering out there, but the fire is almost dead."

Millie nodded. "When do you think we'll be able to go back home?"

Adam's face was solemn. "There probably isn't a house to go back to, Millie. You need to prepare yourself for that. I'd guess that fire destroyed everything in its path."

Millie reached with her hand, silently asking Adam to help her stand up. He did, pulling her into a hug and rubbing firm circles on her back. Both the standing and the pressure from his hands felt amazing. "It's still our home, Adam. Our land. So, when can we go back and start to rebuild?" Her words were quiet in his ear, just for the two of them as though they weren't standing in a crowded church full of families who had lost everything.

Adam hugged her hard and then stepped back. He held her face in his hands and kissed her forehead. Then he held out a hand and smiled almost impishly. "Walk with me?"

Stretching her stiff muscles sounded like the best idea Millie had ever heard. She looked at Genie and Caty, sleeping the deep, boneless sleep of children, on the pew. They would be fine. Millie took Adam's hand and let him lead her down the church steps into this new day.

The sky was somehow blue. How could that be? The air was filled with the smell of stale smoke. Millie stopped walking, thankful that Adam also stopped without questioning her. She closed her eyes and focused on the things around her that were good and solid. Adam's warm hand. The ground under her feet. The sound of the river. A hundred little noises as people comforted one another and got on with the business of living.

Overcome with the beauty of this world and the fact that she truly was okay, Millie opened her eyes and took her first look across the river. It wasn't near as bad as she had feared. From the noise and orange glow last night, Millie had imagined the entirety of the country being swallowed up. Destroyed beyond recognition. But, it wasn't quite that bad.

Yes, the land had obviously been ravaged by heat and flame. But, it was still recognizable. Millie could still make out the road. She saw trees, blackened but still standing. The land had not given up without a fight.

"Are you okay?"

Millie nodded. "It's not nearly as bad as I thought, which probably sounds crazy. But all I saw last night was that orange glow. I kind of assumed everything recognizable would be gone." Millie looked at the smoldering fire and thought about all that Adam had truly lost. "Are you okay? All your hard work. It's gone."

"I think I'm grateful. We went into this fire as two people. We came out as husband and wife. Truly. I don't care what we find at home and I don't care what we could have done differently. This fire made us both wake up. Fifty years from now, I will think about this fire with gratitude and fondness. I will."

Millie was just watching him with wide eyes at this point. He was thankful for the fire. Because it brought them together. Adam wasn't crazy. He was a wonderful, faithful man who understood what was truly important in life.

And Millie was doing it again. She was trying to be in control. In charge. She was acting like her actions alone had created today. When would she learn that the Lord was in charge? When would she cede her sense of control to Him, trust Him and His ways even when it felt like everything was falling apart?

Millie looked at Adam, hoping to not scare him. "I'm sorry, Adam. I need a minute. I'm not mad at you, I promise. I just need a minute to think." No, not think. Her trying to think her way out of situations was a large part of the problem. "To pray. Would you give me a few minutes to pray? Please?"

Despite her attempt at assurances Adam still looked scared. But he immediately nodded. Millie quickly walked, somehow finding an area without any people in it. She was breathing hard and fell to her knees, closing her eyes tight to squeeze back the tears that were burning their own path of destruction on her soul.

I'm sorry, God. I'm so sorry. I keep thinking I understand, and then I mess it up. Again and again and again. You are in control. Instead of trying to rule my world, I need to put my trust in You. My hope in You. Even when Your ways make no sense to me, You are still here. You still love me. I'm not good at trusting people, Lord, but I am going to try. To trust You. To trust Adam. I'll probably mess it up. On a daily basis. But, I'll keep trying. The tears were still coming, but they no longer felt like fire. They felt like a cool washing. *Forgive me, Lord. Thank You for all You have done in my life.*

Millie felt herself calming down and spent several minutes just sitting with God. Finally, she felt…at peace. Now she needed to go find Adam. He must be beyond worried right now. She had just left him there.

Millie was trying to get to her feet when Adam appeared out of nowhere to help her up. Millie smiled, grateful for the words that came to her from nowhere. And everywhere. "Hey, Adam?"

"Yes?"

"I love you."

Adam's answering laugh was so joyful that several people turned to look and Millie thought they were probably wondering what could possibly be that wonderful on this particular day.

"So, everything will be gone, Daddy? Burned up?"

He and Millie had decided to prepare the children before taking them back home, but Caty's questions were ripping Adam's heart out of his chest. "I don't know, honey. We won't know until we get there and see."

Genie was sitting on Millie's lap on the bench of the buggy. He had a block in each hand, but wasn't banging them together in his normal fashion. In fact, he was being incredibly quiet. He might not understand what was going on, but he knew that something bad had happened.

They had spent four days in town, waiting for the fire to completely smolder out. Mr. and Mrs. Sinclair had graciously given them, and other people waiting to go home, rooms at the boardinghouse. It had been a tight fit with the four of them in one room, but Adam had been nothing but grateful.

They'd spent the days resting. The fire had taken a huge emotional and physical toll on all of them, Adam included. The town had also met for daily worship services. The current situation seemed much less scary when gathered with friends and praising the Lord.

Finally, the fire had died out. The ground had cooled. And now, it was time to go. They needed to see what they were dealing with. Then, he and Millie could go through their list of needs and available resources. Together. They would decide how to handle the future. Together.

"It's not that bad." Millie's voice was hesitant, and Adam appreciated what she was trying to do. The fire had been thorough in its ravaging. But it had not taken everything. They saw evidence that not all was lost. Trees standing, limbs still stretched out in defiance. Random patches of green here and there, screaming loudly that they had survived.

When they approached the turnoff from the main road that would lead to their farm, Adam almost suggested going alone at first, maybe so he could find a way to make it look less bad. But he knew Millie would never agree. And, she'd proven rather good at getting her way when it came to them staying together.

When they finally arrived at the turnoff, Adam stopped the wagon. This used to be the part of the journey from town when Adam would feel his heart fill with pride. This was the beginning of his land. Of what he had created.

But it wasn't his land. And whatever came from it was not his creation. He'd known that, but the point was far more salient today. He was a steward of what God gave him. Turning to look at his wife and children, Adam smiled. God had given him a lot.

As they rode toward the house it became obvious that none of the crops had survived. The fields were a solid blanket of thick black char.

"Oh, Adam. Is there any chance the plants are alive under that? That they will come back?"

He wanted to say yes. "Probably not. I'll go out and look later, but I just can't see how any of them would have survived."

"All your hard work. I can't believe it is gone."

Neither could he. "On the bright side, I'm not going to be in the fields from sunup to sundown for a while. And harvest won't be time-consuming at all this year."

Millie laughed. And sobbed. "That's not funny, Adam."

He kept a straight face. "I'm also a lot less worried about drought right now."

Millie's laugh won out right along with Adam's smile.

Things became more somber when they approached the house and outbuildings. The barn and bunkhouse were gone, nothing left but a few charred timbers scattered on the ground. Adam couldn't tell about the root cellar yet, but he hoped the things he'd put inside had survived.

The house was still standing. Kind of. The rock chimney was still there. That counted for something.

Both children burst into tears when they saw what was left of the house. Genie began to sob loudly. Caty was crying quietly, but the tears were nonstop down her little face. Millie was trying to comfort them both as best she could.

Adam stopped the wagon in front of the house, got out and reached out for Caty. She practically leaped into him, squeezing her little arms around his neck as hard as she could. Adam could feel her body shuddering. He looked over Caty's shoulder and saw tears running down Millie's face, too.

It suddenly all felt like too much. All Adam could do was hold his daughter and let her grieve. Watch his wife do the same while comforting their son.

After a few minutes of Adam murmuring reassurances in her ear, Caty calmed down. Adam set her down and took Genie from Millie. Then he helped Millie down from the wagon.

"Our house is gone." Genie's voice was full of nothing but sadness.

"Hey, look at me, kiddos." Adam squatted down and moved both children to stand in front of him. Millie came to stand at his side, resting a hand on his shoulder. "The fire was bad. But it's going to be okay."

"You always say that, Daddy." Millie snorted at Caty's accusation. It was true.

"Yep. And it is. We've had sad times before. But we always are okay, aren't we?" Both kids nodded, though Adam suspected Genie was merely copying his sister. It would have to be good enough for now.

"And we are going to be okay this time, too. We are together. We love each other and God loves us."

Caty looked between Millie and Adam with a skeptical look on her sweet little face. "We *all* love each other?"

That questions actually startled Adam, and he felt Millie's hand tighten on his shoulder. "Yes, baby. Of course we do."

"Everyone?"

"Yes, baby. Everyone."

"So you and Mama love me? And Genie?"

"Of course we do, Caty. We both love you so much." Millie's voice was adamant. Adam was about to confirm her words when Caty spoke again.

"And you and Mama love each other?"

Millie's hand left his shoulder as it came to rest over her mouth, eyes wide. Millie looked at him and he stood to be at her side. He felt like an errant teenager who had been caught doing something wrong. By a five-year-old with big brown eyes.

Adam started to speak and was embarrassed to find he needed to clear his throat. He did so and tried to ignore the smirk Millie was hiding under her hand. Fine lot of help she was. "Yes, Caty. Mama and I love each other. So much. Just like we love you and Genie and the new baby. For forever."

"Okay." Caty smiled and all the tension left the air. "Okay?"

"Yes, okay. Hey, Genie, do you wanna play tag? I'm it!"

With that, Caty began to chase a shrieking Genie around the yard, using a lot of the fallen and burned debris as obstacles that only added to their fun. Millie lowered her hand, and Adam saw the smirk morph into a giant smile. That smile further morphed into a laugh, loud and long. It was a glorious sound.

"What's so funny, Mrs. Beale?"

"You…" Her words were broken up by deep breaths and more laughs. "You looked so scared to tell a little girl that you love your wife. I'll never forget that look. Ever."

Adam crossed his arms over his chest, pretending to be irritated. Millie didn't seem to be concerned about his wrath, however. "If you'll excuse me, I'm going to go see what survived in the root cellar. Are you coming?"

Still smiling, Millie reached out and took his hand. "With you? Always."

Epilogue

To Do:
Love

This wasn't a church, but it felt more holy than their first wedding. God had certainly been at her first wedding to Adam. He had been here through their marriage so far. And He was here now. Oh, yes. She was renewing her vows to Adam in front of their children. Their friends. And the Lord. He was in every single part of this day and all the events leading up to it.

Millie closed her eyes and breathed in deep, feeling the life that seemed to fill the air. Fill her lungs. Fill her heart.

She opened them and saw Adam smiling at her. He reached out and took her free hand, even though the pastor had not yet reached the part of the ceremony requiring it.

It didn't matter. This day wasn't about doing things

in a certain order. It was about them. The family they had created. The family they had become.

Millie looked around, trying to keep her breath. Her husband was in front of her. Their son was standing right next to him, one fist clutching Adam's pant leg. Caty was next to Millie, grinning wide to reveal the gap where teeth had recently fallen out. And baby Hannah was held securely in Millie's arms. Millie still couldn't believe that she was a part of such a perfect family.

But she was. And, it had nothing to do with making lists. With carefully crafted plans.

When it was time for Millie to say her vows, she felt like her heart was trying to leave her chest right along with her words. She felt the tears rolling down her face but refused to take her hand from Adam's to wipe them away. Let them stay, they were a testimony to the sincerity of her feelings.

Adam used his free hand to wipe them instead. Then he used that same hand to wipe his own. They kissed and turned to face the crowd who had joined them out in this field. The crowd that was currently clapping and whooping, likely scaring every living creature in a five-mile radius.

The pastor had looked at them like they were crazy when they'd said they wanted to renew their vows here in the dirt. But, after they'd explained their reasons, he'd grinned and declared it a perfect idea.

They were standing right in the middle of the field that Millie had tried to control. The one that had made Adam so defensive. The place that had burned. Been destroyed.

The place that had come back with new life.

The group made its way to the rebuilt house, carefully navigating the rows of green sprouts that covered the landscape. Millie had made several pies yesterday. Once she told Edith what she had planned, Edith wasted no time in organizing the women. Each had also brought a pie to share. Only Adam and Millie would understand that the simple reception of pie actually held a much deeper meaning.

Still holding her hand, Millie saw Adam shake his head at something.

"What is it?"

Adam looked at her, his grin as deep as ever. "Nothing. Absolutely nothing. I just can't believe how good these crops look already. Those are the strongest-looking plants I've ever seen."

Mike, who was also holding Edith's hand as they walked, snorted. "It's not a mystery. It was the fire. The soil is so rich now you'd almost have to try to kill your crops to make that happen."

Millie stopped and looked at the fields, seeing the fire in her mind. Remembering the heat of the flames. The day they had finally returned home to view the devastation. God surely worked in His own way.

Adam reached out and took Hannah, reclasped his free hand with Millie's and they started walking again. "It's going to be a bountiful harvest."

And it would be, no matter what came next.

* * * * *

If you loved this story, don't miss these other sweet mail-order bride romances

MAIL ORDER MOMMY
by Christine Johnson

HIS SUBSTITUTE WIFE
by Dorothy Clark

PONY EXPRESS MAIL-ORDER BRIDE
by Rhonda Gibson

Find more great reads at www.LoveInspired.com

Dear Reader,

This is my first published book and my first Dear Reader letter. If you're reading this, thank you. You're part of a dream come true.

I've always loved historical stories set on the prairie land I call home. My mother could tell you how I used to wander through my grandpa's fields in a long calico skirt and ankle boots, pretending to be a pioneer fresh off a covered wagon. But she won't. Mainly because I'm not going to let her.

This story, especially Millie's need for control, is dear to my heart. It's my prayer that I, and you if you need, do not let fear control our lives. Instead, may we find peace and comfort in faith.

I would love to hear from you. You can find my email address and social media links on my website at www.victoriawaustin.com.

Victoria

THE NANNY'S TEMPORARY TRIPLETS
Lone Star Cowboy League: Multiple Blessings
by Noelle Marchand

After being jilted at the altar, Caroline Murray becomes the temporary nanny for David McKay's daughter and the orphaned triplet babies he's fostering. But when she starts to fall for the handsome widower, can she trust her heart?

HER CHEROKEE GROOM
by Valerie Hansen

When lovely Annabelle Lang is wrongly accused of murder after rescuing him, Cherokee diplomat Charles McDonald must do something! To save their lives—and their reputations—Charles proposes a marriage of convenience. But will this business proposition turn to one of true love?

AN UNLIKELY MOTHER
by Danica Favorite

When George Baxter, who is working undercover at his family's mine, finds a young boy who's lost his father, he's determined to reunite them. Caring for the boy with the help of Flora Montgomery, his former childhood nemesis, he instead discovers hope for a family of his own.

THE MARSHAL'S MISSION
by Anna Zogg

Hunting a gang of bank robbers, US Marshal Jesse Cole goes undercover as a ranch hand working for Lenora Pritchard. But when he discovers the widowed single mother he's slowly falling for may know something about the crime, can he convince her to tell him her secret?
